Just have sex with me, *Jessie thought,* aching to say the words to Joshua

Keep it impersonal. Please. Ha, fat chance. Jessie was getting more than she'd bargained for when she'd taunted the devil into making love to her.

"Finish it," Jessie whispered. He had already devoured every inch of her body with his mouth, teeth and tongue. She was wet with need.

"Patience." Joshua smoothed her hair back from her damp brow, his eyes softer than she had ever seen them. "I want to look at you. You're so beautiful and damned responsive. The perfect mistress."

Yes, Jessie thought, an odd twinge pinching her heart. *That's what I am, a mistress. A business arrangement. Give me what I want, and I'll give you what you want. A fair trade...*

Jessie tugged at his shoulders until his heavy, welcoming weight covered hers. She reached down, her fingers closing around his hard length. It felt thick and long, silky and...alive. "I want you deep inside me," she begged, not at all sure her body could accommodate him now that she felt the size of him.

"It'll fit just fine, sweetheart. Trust me," Joshua murmured, and Jessie realized she must have spoken her thought aloud.

Then with a hoarse cry he slid into her slick heat... and Jessie was lost.

Blaze.

Dear Reader,

What fun I had writing my first Blaze novel! I've been reading, and loving, these sexy, sensual books since they first hit the stands. And longed to try my hand...um...imagination at one of my own.

Joshua Falcon is The Glacier. Who could love a man as cold as ice? He doesn't believe anyone can. Consequently, emotion has no place in Joshua's life. But sex does! He's a busy man, so his affairs are brief, expedient, torrid and mutually pleasurable.

Jessie Adams wants more from Joshua than his body. And she's prepared to risk anything to get it. Once she has her heart's desire, she'll be on her way, thank you very much. Neither of them will be hurt, because both will have gotten exactly what they want from their affair.... Or will they?

Through sexual indulgence, Joshua and Jessie find the one thing they were missing in their lives. Love.

I hope you enjoy reading Jessie and Joshua's story as much as I enjoyed writing it. I'd love to hear from you. Come visit my Web site at cherryadair.com or e-mail me at cherryadair@qwest.net. Happy reading.

Smooches,

Cherry Adair

P.S. Don't forget to check out tryblaze.com!

Books by Cherry Adair

HARLEQUIN TEMPTATION
492—THE MERCENARY
833—SEDUCING MR. RIGHT

TAKE ME

Cherry Adair

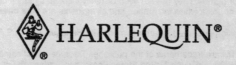

TORONTO • NEW YORK • LONDON
AMSTERDAM • PARIS • SYDNEY • HAMBURG
STOCKHOLM • ATHENS • TOKYO • MILAN • MADRID
PRAGUE • WARSAW • BUDAPEST • AUCKLAND

To my friends at Delphi TDD with love.
You make me laugh.
And I treasure you all.
CBD

ISBN 0-373-79055-4

TAKE ME

Visit us at www.eHarlequin.com

Printed in U.S.A.

Prologue

"MARRY ME."

"*Excuse* me?" Jessie Adams narrowed her eyes at the stranger sitting in the back booth of the diner. He hadn't finished his first cup of coffee before he'd beckoned her back to his table.

And she thought she'd heard it all. *Marry me? Oh, brother!*

Outside, rain slashed in sheets across the midnight-dark parking lot, empty save for his low-slung silver sports car. Diamond drops of rain peppered his dark hair and the broad shoulders of his black wool coat. The neon café sign in the fogged window sputtered, illuminating his face.

Lord, he's a hunk. And a welcome diversion tonight. It had been a lousy day. Week. *Month.* Jessie sighed. *This too shall pass.* She'd read that somewhere and hoped like hell it was true.

Briefly she fantasized that Prince Charming had come in for the singular purpose of sweeping her off her feet. That his proposal was for real. Unfortunately the way her luck had been running lately he was a mugger after her last twenty bucks and the take in the cash register.

She gave him another surreptitious once-over. In truth, she was like the cartoon dog chasing the car. What would she do with him if she actually caught him? The thought made her smile.

"Well?" he demanded.

"Well, what?" Jessie tried not to drool. He smelled so good she wanted to snuggle up to him, close her eyes and just inhale.

"Will you marry me?"

Be still my heart. "Is it Thursday?"

"Friday."

"Sorry, I only marry total strangers on Thursdays." She topped up his coffee. "You'll have to wait 'til next week."

"Next week is too late." His pale gaze sharpened on her face, slid lower to her flat chest, skinny legs, then shot upward. "What the hell happened to your hair?"

Jessie's hand rose self-consciously to the over-processed orange-yellow blotched clump. "I dyed it." In the hope blondes had more fun. Ha!

"Whatever you were aiming for—"

Didn't work. "I like it," Jessie snapped. Her chest felt hard, heavy and tight. He was a stranger. Why did she care what he thought of her hair? "Drink up. We close in twenty minutes." Thoughts of midnight reminded her of more pressing problems. The two-week notice to vacate her studio apartment had four days left. So far, she hadn't found anything else affordable. She'd move to Sacramento or Tahoe. *If* she had more than twenty-seven dollars to her name. *If* her mother's boyfriend hadn't shown up and swiped her car. And *if* she—

"You're perfect." The man's sexy drawl stopped her from turning away. "I have a proposition for you."

I just bet you do. "Listen, pal, my feet hurt, I have to finish my shift, and as much as I'd like to sit and schmooze, I have to clean the kitchen before I go, so if you don't mind..."

"Hear me out—"

Jessie wrote his ticket and slapped it on the table. "If you want more coffee, help yourself."

There wasn't much to do in the spotless kitchen. Other than a couple of truckers at dinner, she'd been alone all night, which meant zilch in tips. Jessie finished loading the dishwasher, then turned to see the guy, hands in the pockets of his coat, standing in the kitchen watching her.

She knew exactly what this sophisticated man saw. She was no beauty. She was too thin, and if she was ever going to get boobs, she hoped it was before she was old enough for them to sag. Her mutilated hair was scraped away from her face and piled untidily on top of her head like orange and yellow straw. All she had going for her were her eyes. Some trucker had once told her they looked like cow eyes. She wasn't so sure it was a compliment, but at least he'd been sincere.

"How old are you?"

"Boy, you're persistent. Has anyone ever told you no?"

"One too many times. How old?"

Jessie tilted her head and eyed him with undisguised curiosity. He appeared rich, spoiled and used to getting his own way. He had beautiful hands. Long, strong, tanned fingers with clean, shiny nails. Jessie always noticed hands.

She automatically hid her bitten nails behind her back. "Twenty…five."

He laughed. It sounded rusty. "Nice try, honey."

"Twenty-one."

"Legal."

Jessie backed up against the refrigerator as he strolled toward her. There wasn't a snowball's chance of anyone coming in at this hour of the night. He could do anything to her, and no one would know. She flinched when he touched her face. She really shouldn't have been sarcastic last week when the car had been stolen and she'd asked God, "What else can happen?" God didn't like sarcasm. It was Jessie's curse. She sighed. She supposed this guy was better than being struck by lightning.

"Perfect." He turned her chin this way and that, his hand warm on her skin. He smelled even better close up. Jessie's mouth actually watered. Instinctively, she understood he had no sexual interest in her, no need to control or dominate. Her heart wasn't pounding because she was afraid of him...not very anyway.

"How about this, pal? I give you ten seconds to take your hands off me, or I call the cops?" His hand dropped, but the ghost of his light, warm touch lingered on her skin. "What do you want from me?" Jessie asked hoarsely.

"I want you to marry me. Now. Tonight. We'll drive into Tahoe, get married and I'll have you back in time for your next shift."

"You're crazy!"

"I'm desperate," he countered, voice grim.

Who isn't, pal? "Why me?" Jessie slid out of his reach and walked back into the brightly lit diner. He was right behind her. He grabbed a mug off the stack behind the counter and followed her back to his table by the window.

What on earth was a guy like this doing here? The diner wasn't his kind of place. The only reason people stopped here at all was that it was right on the California border into Nevada. The small coffee shop mirrored a million others across the country. Red vinyl seats, worn down by a million butts, beige Formica tables scarred by cigarette burns, tacky Christmas decorations. The invasive smell of grease and food had permeated the plastic plants hanging in dusty profusion from toggle hooks in the yellowed ceiling.

Jessie tried to ignore the décor. Sometimes she physically ached for beauty. For stability. For some damn thing that couldn't be conned, stolen or sweet-talked from her.

She wasn't opposed to working, but it would be nice to get a break for a change. Unfortunately she wasn't delusional enough to believe a total stranger would stroll into the diner two days before Christmas and sweep her off her worn tennies and lay all that at her feet.

"I'll make this short and sweet." The stranger took the carafe out of her hand and motioned her to the opposite seat, then filled both cups and placed the coffeepot in the neutral territory between them. Intrigued in spite of herself, Jessie flopped down on the scarred vinyl seat.

"This is purely a business proposition." He raked his fingers through his dark hair. It fell neatly back in place. *Figures.* "Here's the situation. My father and his brother owned a development company. My father died ten years ago, he left the company to my uncle Simon with the understanding his half would in turn go to me. I've worked my ass off while my cousin Paul gallivants around the world doing God knows what. That company is fifty percent mine. I've earned it, damn it. Now Simon wants to retire, but he insists Paul and I settle down before he gives his company to a couple of 'playboys'— *his* quote. My uncle, in his infinite wisdom, has decided Paul and I should settle down and get married."

Jessie's eyed him skeptically. "For real?"

He nodded curtly. "Unfortunately, yes. To top it all off, the first one to marry gets controlling shares. Simon is obsessed with this ludicrous notion."

"So, what's the problem? A good-looking, rich guy like you must have a gazillion women to choose from."

"I asked someone," he said tightly and with obvious reluctance. "She said yes—to my cousin."

Jessie cradled her forgotten mug between her hands. "Ouch. There must be someone else you cou—"

"They're getting married in San Francisco tomorrow at noon. Our meeting up tonight is going to work out to both our advantages. I'm sure you'd like financial freedom. Do whatever you like? Go anywhere? Sure you do. And all *I* want is a contract marriage. I'm not interested in emotional entanglements. I don't want a real wife, I want a wife on paper. Now. Tonight."

He glanced down at her 34A chest and her name tag. "Marry me, Vera. I'll give you a monthly allowance for as long as you live. Hell. I'll buy this damn diner for you if you want it."

Jessie stifled an hysterical laugh. Her name tag had been left over from the last waitress, and she hadn't cared what people called her. "I don't want the diner." Just looking at him made her silly heart do summersaults.

"Listen, having control of this company means *everything* to me." His eyes glowed pale and determined. "Surely you've wanted something this badly in your life?" He leaned forward. "Do this for me, and when the time comes, if there's something you want more than your next breath, I'll make it happen. You have my word on it."

"Anything, huh?"

"Anything."

Lust at first sight. The attraction she felt for this man was undeniable. But then what was not to attract? He was unbearably handsome, strong, powerful, wealthy and, most dangerous of all, he *needed* her. The attraction was obviously not reciprocated in the least. However, Cinderella hadn't complained when her prince whipped her out of the kitchen.

"How do I know you're on the level?" *Oh, please, be serious.*

He pulled a business card from his wafer-thin leather wallet and a cell phone from his overcoat pocket. "Here's my lawyer's card. Call him, confirm who I am, ask about my uncle's ultimatum."

Jessie took the card. She was nuts, she was crazy, she was out of her mind for even considering his proposition.... What did she have to lose?

She reached for the phone and began punching in the numbers before she thought to ask, "What's your name?"

"Joshua Falcon."

The man on the other end of the phone was not happy to be woken by a lunatic stranger at midnight. Jessie stumbled through enough questions to confirm that Joshua Falcon was who he said he was, and was richer than Croesus.

The lawyer wanted to talk to Mr. Falcon. *Right now.* Jessie handed him the phone and slumped back, openly eavesdropping.

Watching her, he spoke into the phone. "You're damn right I'm serious." He listened for a while. "In a diner on the California-Nevada border." He looked over at her, his pale eyes narrowing. "Why *wouldn't* she? She's probably getting minimum wage and living in a cramped apartment with her cat. I'll fax a copy of the marriage license and bring the original to your office later." There was a short pause. His laugh made Jessie shiver. "No honeymoon. I'll have her call you back to make arrangements for the settlement.''

Joshua listened. "No need for sarcasm. She's worth more than her weight in gold. Oh, and Felix? Call Simon as soon as you get my fax." There was a long pause as he listened. "All right," he agreed with some reluctance. "Take the Lear and meet us at the courthouse in Reno at nine. You can hand deliver the marriage certificate to my uncle.''

He folded the compact phone and stuffed it into his pocket.

"I don't have a cat."

"I beg your pardon?"

"I said I don't—"

"That was rhetorical. Get your coat," he said, impatiently buttoning his own. He tossed a twenty on the table.

"I don't have a coat, either."

"You don't have a coat?"

"Gee, is there an echo in here?"

Scowling, he removed his coat and tossed it to her. "Put this on and let's get this over with."

"Wow, you certainly know how to bowl a girl over with sweet talk." The wool coat smelled of him. It was thick and dark, and held the scent of potent male and fresh citrusy cologne. Jessie's insides turned to mush. She had that standing-on-the-highest-diving-board feeling. Exhilarating, thrilling terror.

"Christ." He watched as she turned off lights. "I must be more tired and desperate than I thought."

Jessie froze with the keys in her hand. "Listen, bub, I didn't come in here on *my* knees begging you, did I? Make up your mind." The keys dug into her soft palm.

"Well?" She glared at him. "Do you want to marry me or not?"

He looked down at her. "God help me. Yes."

At 9:45, Joshua slapped the marriage certificate into the hands of his lawyer, Felix Montgomery.

At 9:46, he walked out of the courthouse.

He did not look at Jessie once.

Prince Charming didn't even kiss the bride.

1

December
Seven Years Later

PARTY GUESTS, dressed in holiday finery, ebbed and flowed through Simon Falcon's home. From a safe distance, Jessie watched her husband scan the festive throng with pale, bored eyes. Born to wear the stark black tux and crisp pleated shirt, every immaculate inch of him screamed wealth and bone-deep self-confidence. With his aristocratic features and go-to-hell eyes, he was like a king surveying his kingdom. And the dangerous edge of his sex appeal was universal enough to make every female head turn.

Seven years hadn't changed him. But *she'd* changed considerably. No way would Joshua recognize the woman he only knew as his absentee waitress-wife, Vera. And only she knew her sophistication was nothing more than a thin patina. Her standards were now extremely, and friends told her, unreasonably, high. So be it. She was perfectly content with her life just the way it was, thank you very much. There was only one thing she wanted from Joshua Falcon.

Their marriage had given him control of Falcon International. Now it was her turn to get something she desperately wanted from their marriage.

More than anything on earth, Jessie wanted a child.

And Joshua was going to make that dream come true. He'd promised to give her whatever she wanted more than anything else in the world.

Now she was collecting.

A couple of months ago Jessie had instructed her lawyer to inform her husband she was ready to make her request. Joshua had complied immediately. He'd offered to pay for the insemination process at the in-vitro fertilization clinic of Vera's choosing.

Jessie wasn't sure what she'd expected him to do. But sending her off to a clinic to accept some stranger's donation wasn't it! The whole point here was that she wanted her *husband's* baby.

The good news was he obviously had no interest in children, nor did he want anything to do with any progeny. Which was fine and dandy with Jessie. What he didn't want, he wouldn't take away.

She squared her shoulders and took a fortifying sip of wine. Exhilaration made her heart pump harder. She resisted the urge to run her hands over her hips to make sure the silk jersey wasn't bunched anywhere, then righted the circlet of holly she'd woven into a wreath for her hair. Feeling like a gunslinger checking his holster, she choked back a laugh.

The smile died on her lips as she caught Joshua's gaze, holding it, although it took every ounce of her newfound sophistication to do so. Her chin lifted a notch and she saw his lips twitch. Their eyes locked as he started across the room toward her. Blood pounded in her ears. Forty feet…thirty feet…*don't talk to him, lady!*…eighteen feet…

Joshua was taller, fitter, better looking than any other man in the room. Her heart pounded so hard she barely felt the individual beats. Everything about him assaulted her senses as he moved inexorably toward her. Adrenaline raced in effervescent bubbles through her bloodstream. The wine was tasteless as she took a gulp then held the cool glass against her hot cheek. Sixteen feet...

Simon almost gave her heart failure as he came up beside her and circled his arms around her waist. She hadn't noticed his approach. He kissed her cheek. "You look like a Christmas angel in that red dress, honey. What are you staring at so intently— Oh, Joshua's here."

"Stay, Simon." Jessie held on to his arm like a lifeline. "Just long enough to introduce us, okay?"

"Are you sure you know what you're doing, Jessie?"

She'd fibbed to Joshua's uncle, only telling him half her plan. Her laugh sounded strained even to her own ears. "No."

For seven years she'd imagined making love with Joshua. She'd dreamed about it. Longed for it. Ached for it. Every time she read about him, either in the business section of the newspaper or a sleazy tabloid, Jessie had wished she were the woman on Joshua's arm. In his bed.

She'd tried unsuccessfully to banish her husband from her mind and heart while putting her nose to the grindstone in the intervening years. She'd finished high school, gone to college, all the while carefully managing to avoid him. Until tonight.

Now there was method to her madness.

The physical attraction she was experiencing was as powerful, as terrifying now as it had been all those years ago in the diner. Lust made her mission easier. And if the feelings were reciprocated...

It had taken forever, yet, in a second, he was right there within touching distance. His cologne was more subtle, more sophisticated, than she remembered, but the base scent, the essence of the man, remained. She'd never felt more *female* in her life as Joshua's hot gaze burned through the thin silk of her dress to the pulsing skin beneath.

"Simon." Joshua greeted his uncle, his voice low and husky, his eyes on Jessie.

"Joshua." Simon sounded atypically jovial as he clasped his nephew's hand. "How're you doing, son?"

"Introduce me to the lady." Joshua watched the sunrise of a blush paint her cheeks as he allowed the heat of his gaze to travel slowly from her lush mouth to her eyes and back to her mouth. A cloud of dark, Raphaelite curls framed her face and drifted about her shoulders as she looked up at him. Her brows, dark and silky, formed a gentle arch above eyes of sparkling chocolate brown.

Joshua had reluctantly accepted Simon's heavy-handed invitation to the Christmas party. He didn't do Christmas. For a second when he'd spotted the dark-haired beauty beside his uncle, he'd imagined *she* was Simon's surprise. Considering every surprise he'd ever had at this time of year was a bad one, and familiar with his uncle's wily manipulations, he'd almost turned around and driven up to his cabin in Tahoe as he did every year during the holidays.

He felt sufficiently mellow to wait his uncle out. With her supple, slender body, she was enough of an inducement to make him stay. For now. Her subtle fragrance teased him. A holly wreath nestled in her dark hair. Her skin looked smooth and pale against the flame-red floor-length gown. The matte fabric covered her from throat to ankle in a sensuous sweep, without showing so much as a panty line.

He felt a rush of heat as her small breasts shifted with

her breathing. She was doing her damnedest to appear unaffected, but the lady was as aware of him as he was of her.

Joshua felt the familiar adrenaline rush for the start of the chase and wondered if she, too, was thinking of tangled sheets and sweat-dampened skin.

"Jessica Adams, my nephew, Joshua Falcon."

Her name was familiar. "You're the interior decorator my uncle's always talking about. You do good work."

A grin tugged at the corner of her mouth. "Thanks. Simon and Patti are always a pleasure to work with."

And she'd be a pleasure to have in his bed. "Go away, Simon," he told his uncle without looking at him. Jessie's mouth curved slightly as she observed him maneuvering his uncle. Joshua couldn't remember reacting so explosively to a woman in his life. The shiny strings of the tiny Christmas balls in her ears tangled in the darkness of her hair. She rubbed her wineglass against the pulse pounding at her throat.

He used every vestige of control to keep from tossing her over his shoulder caveman style and dragging her to his lair.

The very thought startled him. He was not an impulsive man, nor was he given to flights of fancy. He stuffed his hand in his pocket. He was almost tempted to cut his losses and walk away. Sex was one thing, an excess of emotion another.

Hell. Christmas always brought out the worst in him.

He knew he was looking at Jessie with unabashed hunger. His blood pressure shot up another ten points as he heard her stifle a moan. "Are you here alone?" he asked.

She either was or wasn't available. He'd never competed for a woman in his life. Although, Joshua thought, surprised by his reaction, he might be tempted in her case.

She smiled. "Just me and 299 party guests." She had an extraordinary mouth, generous, her lips pouty without being petulant. Joshua needed a taste. Just one. He almost leaned over to take it but managed to remain fixed in place, his libido jumping. She was available, he wanted her and she appeared interested. It was turning out to be a good party, after all.

He smiled. "Can I take you home?"

"Actually, I just got here," she drawled, eyes bright. "But thanks for offering. Simon," she turned to his uncle with a smile that made Joshua's skin tingle, "I'd love another glass of this excellent Chateau Whatever."

Simon gave them both a pointed glance before he snatched her glass and went off to the kitchen.

Jessie tilted her head a little to look up at him. Brown eyes twinkled as bronze lights of laughter danced in the sparkling depth. She was all sass and flirty eyes. And damn well irresistible. Joshua wanted to bury his hands up to his elbows in her hair, assure himself that it was as soft as it looked. He wanted to run his fingers along her slender curves. He wanted to lay her on cool sheets in a candlelit room and make love to her until she melted like warm honey.

But first things first.

"Before we leave," he said flatly. "I need to make something perfectly clear. I'm married."

Obviously taken aback she gave him a startled look. "Goodness, a philanderer with integrity. How refreshing."

He realized he'd tensed for her response. There was something about her that led him to believe she was nothing like his female companions to date. He hadn't

paused to wonder why he'd told her the truth when he'd
never bothered to tell anyone else before. She'd be just
as capable as any other woman to run directly to the
tabloids with the news flash.

His marriage wasn't a marriage at all. It was a piece
of paper, nothing more. He knew it, the girl knew it. But
this woman, with her glowing eyes and ripe mouth,
might not understand.

For the first time since he was a boy, Joshua felt a
flush ride his cheekbones. "It's purely a business arrangement. She doesn't give a damn what I do. We've
been separated for seven years."

"Poor her."

"The arrangement was mutually agreed on," he said
flatly.

"Why bother telling me?"

"Because I don't want any misunderstandings. I'm
powerfully attracted to you. Hell, flat-out, I *want* you,
Jessie Adams. But I'm not interested in a long-term en-
tanglement, and marriage will never be on the table."

"Because you're already married."

"Because I never have, nor will I ever have, any interest in the state of holy matrimony. I married to facil-
itate a business deal, she married me for money. If this
is a problem, tell me now."

"The *problem*," Jessie said sweetly, "is I don't care
one way or the other. And I think it's a bit presumptuous
of you to think I *would* since we've known each other
all of two minutes. Your marital status has no effect on
me at all one way or the other."

"Good." Joshua only now realized how damned boring life had been lately. It had been a long time since
he'd felt the roar of his blood and the thrill of the chase.

"Let me guess. Your wife's a petite, blue-eyed blonde?"

Joshua stared at her blankly. He vaguely remembered Vera as a tall, skinny...blonde? Redhead? Whatever. Somehow he'd lost control of the conversation. He wasn't sure where or why, but it mildly annoyed him. "What's that got to do with anything?"

Brown eyes gleamed devilishly. "I'm trying to point out that I'm not your type."

"How do you know what my type is?"

Jessie fluttered her long eyelashes at him. "Small, blond and busty. Would you like me to name them for you?"

"I think I can remember," Joshua said dryly, narrowing his eyes in mild annoyance. CEOs had quailed at that look. She—damn her sassy hide—had the nerve to grin.

"And why would you be so interested in my lady friends?" he asked silkily, suddenly finding tall, slender dark-haired women extremely appealing. The air about her seemed to crackle with electricity.

"What?" Little Miss Sass was distracted for a moment watching *his* mouth. "It's hard to miss your exploits when every tabloid and newspaper finds the subject absolutely fascinating."

A point to the lady for her swift recovery.

Joshua glanced down. Her nipples were clearly delineated by the fabric of her dress. As he watched, the small buds peaked. He stifled a groan and shifted his stance.

"Lord," she said, voice thick, "you are direct, aren't you?"

"If I was any more direct, I'd come right out and tell you I want to take you to bed."

She smiled. "I believe you just did."

"I'm hardly the first man who's wanted to sleep with you."

"You're the first man who's said it straight out within moments of meeting me, with about three hundred witnesses." She didn't move away as he rested his hand on the small of her back. He could almost feel her skin vibrate beneath his fingers.

"I want to see you."

"You *are* seeing me."

"Without all these people around."

"If you're staying with Simon for the weekend, we should bump into each other sometime."

"That's a little too vague for me." He scanned her animated face. Her eyes still danced as she crossed her arms over her chest. At the view of her plumped breasts on the shelf of her arms, his mouth went dry.

He wanted her. He planned to have her. Soon.

"Several of us are going parachuting tomorrow, and since it's too far to drive home, then back again so early in the morning, I'm spending the night here. You're welcome to join us, Joshua."

Her husky voice saying his name made him want to yank her into his arms. He craved her mouth under his. He wanted to back her against the wall and have her, right there in Simon's sunken living room, in front of hundreds of guests. Lord. He couldn't remember ever being this hot, this fast.

Jessie glanced at him under her lashes. She took a small step back. "I've heard people should live life as if their personal diary would be published in the newspaper every day." She looked up at him with those big brown eyes. "I've read *your* personal diary in the tabloids for years. Just standing here talking to you is going to give me notoriety I've never had before. I'm not sure I'm ready for prime time."

More than likely their first meeting would be splashed across every tabloid by tomorrow morning. He didn't give a damn—unless she cashed in on his weak moment of honesty concerning his marriage. Then every snoop reporter in the country would be on the hunt for Vera.

Despite the risk, pursuing Jessie held an indefinable, underlying attraction that had nothing to do with her slender body. Something about her made his heart go from zero to a hundred in seconds and he'd be damned if he knew why.

"Do you realize," he asked, his voice thick, "that we're standing right under the mistletoe?"

Her long lashes fluttered as she glanced up, then directly into his eyes. Yes, her eyes told him. Of course she knew where they stood.

"Lord, woman, don't look at me like that." He didn't recognize the roughness in his own voice. "What do I have to give you for just one kiss?"

"Here?" Jessie scanned the room.

"Yes, damn it."

"Chloroform?"

"Oh," he mocked, "I think I can find something that works just as well and is far more accessible." He hailed a waiter, and handed her two brimming glasses of pale wine. "Here."

Jessie automatically clutched both glasses as she looked up at him. "What am I supposed to d—"

He touched her cheek, just the barest of touches, and she closed her eyes, tilting her face up. He kissed her softly on the mouth. Christ, it was as bad as eating one damn peanut. She tasted of Simon's excellent Chateau

Coutet, laughter and something he couldn't quite put a name to.

His fingers tightened briefly in the springy silk of her hair as her tongue shyly touched his. His lips moved with expertise over hers, Jessie's lashes fluttered then drifted closed. He felt her small breasts brand his chest as she leaned into him. He swallowed her ragged moan as he deepened the contact and lost himself in her response.

And then she was gone.

One moment he was standing with an armful of pliant willing woman, the next *he* was holding two dripping glasses and *she* was several feet away.

"Give me a call sometime." Jessie fluttered her fingers and melted into the crowd, disappearing from view before he could recover.

Joshua felt as if he'd been poleaxed.

JESSIE'S PURPLE-AND-PINK parachute floated over the vineyard toward the eucalyptus tree windbreak on the south side of the clearing near Simon's house. Joshua shaded his eyes against the sharp winter sun and scowled. He'd had precious little sleep the night before. Thinking about her, knowing she slept under the same roof, had caused him to toss and turn. So near and yet so far.

In his imagination she'd appeared larger than life somehow. Vibrant and intoxicatingly *alive*. She had what the French called *je ne sais quoi,* an indescribable *something*.

Joshua didn't consider himself a fanciful man, but he needed to see Jessie Adams again. Needed to assure himself that what he remembered from the night before was as simple as her unmistakable sex appeal.

Joshua enjoyed sex. He considered himself a considerate lover. He wanted Jessie. It seemed simple enough. And yet… He narrowed his eyes trying to put his finger on it. There was more to her. Something complex. Something intriguing. Something, damn it, that called to much more than his libido.

Which was, of course, a ridiculous assumption based on a few minutes of conversation the night before.

He wanted to chat with her once more before he left to drive back to San Francisco. Get rid of this stupid fantasy he'd built up during the night. Frankly, he reminded himself grimly, he didn't have the emotional fortitude to deal with a woman for more than companionship and sex.

They didn't call him The Glacier for nothing.

High above him, a gust took hold of the thin silk, and Jessie's slender arms madly manipulated the controls against the sudden shift in wind direction. She was losing the battle.

"Hell." Joshua started to run as her feet skimmed the treetops. Behind him, the follow vehicle revved, then bit a wheelie into the dirt road running alongside the vines behind Simon's house. Joshua sprinted to the other side of the trees just in time to see the billowing silks covering Jessie's prone body.

Roughly he gathered the fabric, flinging it behind him until he unveiled her. She looked up into his face and grinned.

"God, that was fabulous!" She sat up, brushing twigs and dirt off her arms. A skintight purple and fuchsia spandex bodysuit clung to every sleek, tight inch of her long body.

"You little idiot," Joshua said furiously, his heart still pounding. "You could've been killed."

Jessie's hand stilled and her smile slipped a little as she unbuckled her fuchsia helmet and tugged it off. Something he didn't recognize flared in her eyes.

"Yeah, my landing left a little to be desired." She tossed her braid over her shoulder. "I'll have to work on that." She stuck out a hand. "Pull me up."

He hadn't imagined it. She seemed to inhale life, to eat it with a spoon, relishing each delicious moment at a time. He knew she'd be like that in bed. Eager. Hot. Passionate and wild. He could drown in those hot, brown eyes. "You like living dangerously, don't you?"

"You have no idea," Jessie managed to say breathlessly as he suddenly tugged on her hand, drawing her to her feet and against his chest in one quick move.

"I want to taste it on you." Joshua breathed in her already familiar scent that even dust and eucalyptus couldn't mask.

"Taste what?" she asked, a hairsbreadth away from his mouth. She looked up at him, her hand in his against his chest. Her fingers flexed under his but her eyes were steady. "Taste what?" she repeated, her husky voice low.

"Danger." He brought his mouth down on hers like a starving man at a banquet. He knew after he'd slept with her a few times the gnawing want would lessen and become manageable enough to ignore.

Jessie's lips held the sheen of his kiss as he stepped away from her. Joshua handed her the helmet. "I'll call you January first," he told her. Ignoring her bemused look, he turned and walked away. It was one of the hardest things he'd done in years.

He walked faster.

2

As promised, Joshua called Jessie on New Year's Day.

Jessie made sure she wasn't home.

He called again on the second, the third and the fifth. She'd let the answering machine pick up while she sat in her kitchen listening, his tone getting progressively cooler and more impatient with each call.

Joshua had left half a dozen imperious messages in the last two weeks. She had no intention of falling over herself to call him back. Obviously he wasn't used to being ignored.

She knew she was playing a dangerous game. There was a fine balance as she waited for the timing to be right without causing Joshua to lose interest.

Soon. Very soon, Jessie thought as she drove onto the narrow road leading up to the gatehouse. She'd been startled, no, *stunned,* when Joshua had admitted he was a married man. His honesty, not only in acknowledging his marriage, but the *status* of that marriage, had confused her.

If she hadn't been his wife she would've politely walked away. Her mother had had plenty of married lovers. The ending was always sad and messy.

She sighed. His honesty had disarmed her and made her feel a little guilty about what she was about to do. But he was still The Glacier. Cold. Hard. Ruthless. He was still her absentee husband. He was still the man who was going to give her her heart's desire. A baby. Born in wedlock.

It was the second week of the new year and cold for Northern California. The wind cut through her jacket as Jessie got out of the car. It was after three and she'd missed lunch looking for a particular wallpaper sample at the design center in the city. Her stomach growled.

The little cottage welcomed her with warmth as she quickly closed the front door behind her and headed for the kitchen. She loved the carriage house. It was home. Safe, warm, welcoming, and as permanent a home as she'd ever had. Joshua's lawyer, Felix Montgomery, had taken her under his wing and introduced her to his son Conrad that dizzying day seven years ago.

Con had offered her not only the use of the gatehouse, but also a job in his architectural company while she went back to school. Conrad and his partner, Archie, had converted the gatehouse cottage into a charming home for her, then later incorporated the studio when she'd gone to work for Conrad full-time as an interior designer.

They'd helped her transform her life and, in the process, the two men had become her dearest friends and the brothers she'd never had.

The phone rang. Jessie turned off the machine. "Hello?"

"Where in the hell have you been?"

She dragged in a breath. "I believe you have the wrong number," and hung up.

The phone rang again. Jessie tossed a tea bag in a mug of water and stuck it in the microwave. The phone continued ringing. The microwave dinged. She squeezed out the bag and poured in a little milk. "Hello?"

"This is extremely time-consuming," Joshua said with a great deal of annoyance.

"Who is this?"

There was a pause. "Joshua Falcon."

"Oh. Sorry. I've been getting a lot of crank calls," Jessie told him sweetly. She sipped her tea and burned her tongue. She sat down at the small round table in a weak ray of sunshine and unhooked the calendar beside the phone.

"I've been calling you for weeks."

"Darn. And I kept missing you." She didn't bother trying to sound too sincere. "I've been *so* busy."

"So have I," he said coolly. "I just returned from an important business trip, but I made time to call you anyway."

Jessie grinned. "Where did you go?" Her stomach growled.

"Ireland."

"I've always wanted to travel. Tell me about it." She dragged the cord over to the cupboard and scanned her soups.

Talking to him on the phone was easier, safer, than in person. She couldn't see his eyes. Or his mouth. Or smell his cologne. She wanted a baby from this man. She did *not* want to fall in love with him.

Jessie refused to go there. That path was rocky and filled with potholes. Fortunately, she'd outgrown the gigantic crush she'd had on him years ago. She'd seen what love had done to her mother. No, thank you very much. That wasn't for her. Mutual attraction would get the job done. Quick. Painless. Satisfying. No fuss. No muss. It might be cold-blooded, but *she'd* know who her child's father was. No one would get hurt. Everyone would get what they wanted.

It was a good plan.

She prayed she'd get pregnant immediately.

She held the phone between chin and shoulder as she found a bowl, opened a can of tomato soup and added water and milk to her late lunch.

Joshua gave her the *Reader's Digest* travel tour of Ireland while she mumbled "Hmmm" and "Fascinating" at appropriate moments. And it would have been if she wasn't so uptight about seeing him again. At this rate, she'd develop indigestion.

She was sure as soon as she saw him the panicky feeling she'd been experiencing would pass. Between her "schedule" and his business travel, she'd managed to avoid him since Simon's Christmas party. Unfortunately January was a slow month in the interior design business, and she could've used the distraction of being genuinely busy. She'd have to see him soon, even if the timing wasn't right.

"All right. Enough about my trip." He sounded exasperated. "When the hell am I going to see you?"

"How about tomorrow night?" Jessie glanced at the calendar where the next night had been marked with an X. She'd calculated just how long she could keep him dangling. She didn't want to see him one second more than necessary. Her attraction to him was already putting a crimp in her plans. She had to stay focused, no matter what.

"Tonight," he insisted.

"I'm busy tonight." She lied cheerfully, getting up to place her empty bowl and spoon in the sink. "I'm free tomorrow night or next Wednesday. Your choice." Next Wednesday was circled in red. And underlined. She closed her eyes and prayed he'd pick door number two.

"I'll pick you up tomorrow night at seven."

"I'll meet you at Noble's, near Fisherman's Wharf, at seven-thirty," she said, resigned. There was a long pause. Jessie held her breath. Had she pushed him too far?

He laughed sardonically. "God, you're ornery. All right. Noble's. Seven-thirty." The dial tone buzzed in her ear.

She collapsed back in her chair, eyes closed. She'd done it. She picked up the calendar and ran her finger tenderly around the dates she'd marked in red and underlined. The nights for conception. All she had to do was hold him off a week, until her next ovulation. The prize was worth any discomfort she might feel, any small niggling twinge of conscience she might have. All she had to do was stick to her plan without deviating and she'd walk away with the grand prize.

JESSIE WAS COOL, calm and collected when she walked into Noble's restaurant at precisely seven-thirty the next night. She wore a simple royal-purple dress with a jewel neckline and cap sleeves. Sophisticated and sexy enough to hold him off while beckoning him closer.

Joshua rose to greet her. The hem of her dress suddenly felt way too short, the silk far too thin, clinging to her body in a way it hadn't done at home.

"Hello, Jessie. You're more gorgeous than the last time I saw you." His pale eyes gleamed in the candlelight as he took her hand, and drew her onto the banquet seat beside him. A sizzle of electricity arced up her arm.

"The last time you saw me I was covered in dirt." God, but he smelled good. He looked virile and alarmingly masculine. And he was sitting far too close. Jessie tried to scoot up against the window.

"You were covered in skintight Lycra." His breath

fanned her mouth. She struggled to draw in air, mesmerized by his silvery gaze as he whispered huskily. "I've dreamed about peeling you out of it for weeks."

Jessie paused a beat for her nerves to steady, then reached for the menu. If she handled this right, she could make the next date for the following week when it would count. One dinner for one night in his bed. Two dates. *I can do this. I can.*

"The seafood here is fabulous." Her pulse throbbed in her ears. She willed herself to relax. She knew the outcome of tonight. He didn't.

The waiter arrived. "Two specials," Joshua said, neither consulting her nor taking his eyes off her for a second.

His broad chest, covered in shirt, tie and jacket, was inches away. She had a lustful vision of it quite naked. Would his chest be sleek and smooth, or sprinkled with hair? It was alarming how badly she wanted to touch him to find out. "Perhaps I'd like something else."

"So would I." Joshua brushed a wisp of hair away from her cheek. His touch was electrifying. "But I'm not going to get it before we eat." She must have looked as blank as she felt. He gave her a wry smile. "I don't give a damn what the specials are, as long as it's served fast."

Jessie controlled a bubble of hysterical laughter. "We could've gone to McDonald's."

"This was your choice."

"I'm starving." God. If they were this hot for each other they'd burn each other to cinders.

He slid from his seat and held out his hand.

"Where are we going?" Jessie took his hand automatically.

"To dance," he said thickly. "I have to hold you."

He pulled her up, then maneuvered her to the small, empty dance floor and tugged her into his arms.

It felt good pressed against the length of him like this. *Far* too good. Jessie tried to put a little space between them. Joshua's arms tightened in a firm, inexorable embrace.

The solid width of his chest felt like heaven beneath her hand. She looked up at him. Would her baby have Joshua's nose? His pale-blue eyes? His mouth?

The small band in the corner played something soft and bluesy. Lord, this is dangerous, Jessie thought, as Joshua moved her expertly around the floor. And expertly against *him*. She should have been shocked by the hard length of his erection pressed against her. Instead her heart leaped, and her skin heated. Her nipples puckered and rubbed against the inside of her bra. She moved a little closer, allowing the slide and sway of their bodies to ease the ache a little. He brought his hand up between their bodies, and clasped her hand against his chest. The backs of his fingers brushed against her nipple making her shudder with longing.

It was no accident. Of course it wasn't. He kept up the slight friction, until Jessie wanted to scream.

His hand felt warm through the thin silk at the small of her back as he pulled her more snugly against him. His thumb moved in a maddeningly light caress. Goose bumps spread from her back to her breasts in a slow, sweet rush that heated her skin another few degrees and made her heart pound.

Oh, boy. Definitely dangerous.

They were practically making love while vertical. Joshua brushed his mouth across her forehead and Jessie felt dizzy with longing. She struggled to find a topic of conversation to keep herself sensible. "Noble's was the first commercial interior design job I ever did on my own. I'd never done any commercial work until Con convinced Charlie to let me do—"

She glanced up while she was speaking. Why did he have to look at her like that? She licked her bottom lip, losing her train of thought.

Joshua's eyes smoldered; he drew her closer. "You did a superb job." He caught her nipple between the backs of two fingers and exerted gentle pressure. Moisture pooled between her thighs and her eyes glazed.

Her skin felt overly sensitive, almost electrified. *Get a grip, Jessie.* "How would you know? You haven't even looked." She managed a smile, and covered his eyes with her hand. She was demonstrative by nature and didn't give the impulsive act a moment's thought. But touching his bare skin, no matter what part of his body, was a mistake. A huge mistake.

"Tell me what you like about it." Her voice sounded strangled. Joshua's hot breath fanned the edge of her palm, his hips moved in a lazy, age-old rhythm that was making her insane, and his tweaking fingers had her libido at fever pitch. Jessie shifted slightly and rested her elbow high on his shoulder, feeling the play of muscles and the tantalizing brush of his hair on her overly sensitized skin as they swayed to the music. When had their feet stopped moving?

"I like the plaid carpet. And the mahogany paneling, the subtle lighting on the seascapes." He was very observant. The thought gave her a chill. *Watch yourself, Jessie.* "And the brass lighting and the dance floor." She felt his eyes move beneath her fingers.

"Lord," he said roughly, nuzzling her temple. "You smell like sin."

She withdrew her tingling palm and vowed to keep

her hands to herself from now on. His lips skimmed her cheek.

"Would you make those sweet little moans for me in bed, Jessie? Would you whimper?" His teeth teased the shell of her ear. "You'd be hot and so sweet." He paused, breathing as raggedly as she, and when he spoke again his words were a fragmented whisper against her cheek. "Do you lie in bed at night and wonder how you'd move beneath me? How incredible it would feel to have me deep inside you?"

The picture came to her in vivid Technicolor and her mouth went dry. She gave him a cool look. "Actually…no."

"Liar." His pale eyes looked as hot as lava. "I can see how much you want me. I can see your heart pounding." He used the tips of two fingers to measure the pulse at her throat. "Right here." He dropped his hand, satisfied as her pulse throbbed even harder.

"I don't like the way I behave around you, Jessie Adams. It's completely out of character and I don't like it at all." He said it like a caress. Like a curse.

She smiled, but inside a frightened little voice silently echoed his sentiment. "I thought I made you hot."

"Oh, you do. Make no mistake about that." A muscle jerked in his jaw. "Hell, right now I wouldn't give a damn if half the press corps sat at the next table. That's how much I want you."

His face was just inches away; she could see herself reflected in his eyes. Jessie dug her short nails into her palms until she regained her senses.

"Wow," she said dulcetly. "That much?" She'd observed men play the game of "I want you until I have you" all her life. "Then it's a good thing we're in a public place."

"Which is why I'm not stripping your clothes off."
His brows drew together in a frown. "As a rule, I'm a
patient man. Congratulations, you've managed to try that
patience to the limit." His fingertips ran along her jaw
and left a trail of heat in their wake. His thumb glided
over her lower lip.

"You and I have different priorities, Joshua." She
struggled to control her own libido. "Satisfying your
expectations is on the very bottom of my list. I happen
to have a life of my own and you're only a very small
part of it."

"That's going to change, Jessie. Very soon I'm going
to be a major part of it."

His arrogance and self-confidence were bred to the
bone. "Don't be too optimistic, Mr. Falcon. This is our
first date and I don't like having a man tell me what to
do, or when to do it."

His gaze rested on her mouth before he looked her
right in the eye. "Are you telling me we *won't* become
lovers?"

"I haven't decided one way or the other—yet." She
ignored the little thrill of excitement skimming her
nerves. She fought the unwelcome, insidious attraction
with a reminder it was a physical ailment, like a cold or
the flu, and would pass.

"You'll be the second person to know once I make
up my mind." She glanced at the table where the wait
staff hovered. "Oh, our dinner's arrived." Her hand slid
down his arm and caught his as they returned to the
table.

Joshua sat down and flicked his napkin onto his lap
with controlled irritation. "Are you always this stubborn?"

"Let's say I'm extremely selective. I don't jump into

bed at the drop of a hat. And, frankly, the thought of tossing my underwear into your collection is something I have to think about.''

''Will I see you tomorrow?'' he bit out, his expression savage. Desire dilated his eyes. Clearly part of him loved the challenge; the rest of him wanted her. Now.

Please God, next Wednesday was the next and last time she planned to see him. She'd see how Mr. Impatience liked waiting another week. She groaned inwardly. At the rate she was going, he might become a vapor trail before *tonight* was over.

''Let's see if we manage to complete this evening unscathed first, shall we?''

Amusement flared in his eyes. Jessie was afraid he knew exactly what she was experiencing. He leaned back in the booth, his expression bland as his hot gaze raked her face. ''We'll see just which of us raises the white flag first then, shall we?''

Jessie relaxed the tense muscles gripping her spine. She didn't even *own* a white flag. He had no idea just how stubborn and determined she could be.

Neither of them was getting any sex tonight, she reminded herself. After dinner she would drive herself home. Alone. It made a world of difference to her nerves when she leveled the playing field. The balance of power was in her hands tonight.

He might *wonder*.

But she *knew*.

THE SUN SHONE BRIGHT as a spring day, but there was still a nip in the air as Joshua strolled beside Jessie at the antique street fair one Sunday afternoon. She wore blue jeans that did marvelous things to her long legs and heart-shaped butt, a short, screaming orange sweater, and a brightly patterned silk scarf. The outfit was so Jessie, as he was finding out. She hadn't worn the bold colors to attract attention, Joshua knew, although several men had turned to look at her. Jessie loved bright colors. *Happy* colors she'd informed him, eyeing his tan slacks, pale-blue shirt and navy windbreaker with disfavor when he'd met her downtown earlier.

The streets were crowded and noisy. Not the kind of place he'd ever have chosen to spend a Sunday afternoon. And certainly not where he would have chosen to be with Jessie. He preferred his surroundings slick, modern and new. And he wanted this woman to himself. Preferably in his big, black lacquered bed.

An unexpected business trip had kept him out of the country and he hadn't seen her in a week. Her face had come to mind at the most inappropriate times. It annoyed the hell out of him.

Jessie paused beside a table laden with junk. She ran her hands over chipped cups and tarnished silver, all the while chatting comfortably with the vendor, an older woman with improbably red hair and a tired face.

Joshua admired the way the sun tangled in Jessie's dark hair, and the sweet curve of her cheek and mouth as she spoke. She talked with her hands, too. Animated, alive, interested in strangers. He felt a pang he grudgingly admitted was jealousy.

He wanted her to himself. Yet each time he saw her he became more intrigued by her interaction with others. She put people at ease. The things that drew him to her were the same traits that drew other people. Jessie's obvious joy for life, her enthusiasm, her sheer pleasure in everyday things. He glanced at the elderly lady's face as Jessie asked about a particular item on the overcrowded table.

The woman was brought to life by Jessie's animation, by her interest. It wouldn't have surprised him if she gave Jessie anything she wanted from her table of wares.

"She expected you to bargain, you know." Joshua told her as they strolled away with Jessie's purchase, a beaten-up, tarnished teapot for which she'd paid the asking price. A ridiculous amount for a piece of junk.

Jessie cradled her purchase to her chest. "She's raising her two grandchildren. Oh, look at that!" She grabbed his hand, dragging him through the crowd to look at a sideboard on the opposite sidewalk.

Joshua looked at their clasped hands. Her skin looked pale and soft, her hand small. He liked the feel of it in his. He liked the joining. And he wanted her more than his next breath.

Not just the wanting sexually. Although, God only knew, he urgently wanted her naked beneath him. But he wanted some of her joy, some of her zest for life.

He didn't ever remember having Jessie's...*zing,* for want of a better word. She crackled with energy. Was gloriously, unabashedly *alive.*

"What?" She glanced up to find him staring at her.

The milling crow faded as Joshua bracketed her face between his hands and brought his mouth down on hers. Her lips felt smooth and soft beneath his. He eased his tongue into the warm wetness of her mouth. She tasted of the caramel corn she'd eaten earlier. He'd never cared for the flavor before, but, on Jessie, the too sweet flavor tasted like ambrosia.

He stroked down her back and held her lithe body against him in an agony of want. The sun shone brightly on Joshua's closed lids, bathing him in gold. *I've lost it. We're in the middle of the street for heaven's sake! Surrounded by hundreds of people—* A magnitude-ten shudder traveled from his face to his groin when Jessie used both hands to hold his head steady, then lightly stroked his cheeks with her thumbs as he kissed her. Her agile tongue played with his, darting and playing tag until Joshua felt weak and stupid with desire.

Once. That's all he'd need. One time in Jessie's bed. One time in Jessie. Surely to God that was all that was required to get her out of his system. Jessie Adams was just too much hard work. He was used to picking up the phone and having his woman available immediately. With Jessie he had to watch the ball.

Her tongue slipped from his mouth, and an ache of disappointment pressed against his chest. No. His arms tightened about her slender waist. But his Jessie wasn't done with the kiss, after all. She brushed her damp lips across his, once, twice, then nipped his lower lips between strong, white teeth, and all the while her soft hands stroked his face.

Joshua had never experienced anything like it. Hell, he'd been horny before. He'd been turned on before. Sex was fine. Gratifying. A stress reliever. But with Jessie he wanted... What? More? Joshua went hazy for a moment as Jessie's body shifted against him.

She was dangerous...lethal. Damn it, he didn't do commitment. He wanted her to be the same as other women he'd dated and slept with. He *needed* her to be just like them. He wouldn't have it any other way.

She finally pulled her mouth away. "We're going to be arrested if we don't stop."

Joshua looked at her through dazed eyes. "What?"

Jessie smiled, her mouth blush-pink, damp and swollen from his kisses. Her unruly hair flew about in the warm spring breeze, strands stuck on the front of his sweater. Bonding them.

Joshua took a step back and stuffed his hands in the front pockets of his Armani slacks. "I don't do public displays of affection."

"Really?" Jessie's brown eyes danced. "I'll have to remember that the next time you grab me for a kiss in public."

ANOTHER DINNER DATE. Joshua vowed he wouldn't see this woman anywhere dangerous. Like a street fair. Or a parking lot. Or standing beside her car outside the theater in broad daylight.

There was something wrong with him, Joshua knew. He was incapable of feeling true emotion. Oh, he could fool most people, and he was quite proud of his ability to project the illusion. But the reality was he didn't experience emotional highs or lows like other people. He had some sort of missing gene.

He could claim it was because unemotional, uncaring parents had raised him. But he was an adult now, capable of seeing their selfishness for what it really was. No, the failing was his and his alone. It just wasn't in him to have any depth of feeling. It wasn't a problem. He'd managed perfectly well without it for thirty-three years.

It was easier to move on and not linger when he had an affair. No one got hurt. He was upfront and always told the woman that he had no intention of getting involved. Hell, fact was, he *couldn't* get involved. It just wasn't in him. It was always her choice if she decided to stay or go. He never admitted he didn't have the emotional fortitude to sustain any kind of relationship.

Take it or leave it. This was who he was. The Glacier.

Joshua had coldly analyzed his obsessive attraction to and fear of being with Jessie. He didn't want her to get close enough to see through him to his empty heart. He didn't want her to know that what she saw was merely the shell of a man going through the motions. Like Pinocchio, he wanted to be a real boy. Unfortunately he had a wooden heart. If he had a heart at all.

Fortunately Jessie would never know just how much he relished basking in her joie de vivre.

"Are you angry because I went to Paris without you?" he asked, reigning in his thoughts. She'd been quiet all evening.

"*A.*" Jessie broke a small loaf of sourdough bread and absently handed him a chunk. "I'm far too busy to go gallivanting off to Europe at the drop of a hat. *B*, I wouldn't have gone even if you'd asked me."

"Then why are you so annoyed?"

Her brown eyes were so dark they were almost black as she gave him a waspish glare. "You were gone for *ten days.*"

Joshua bit back a satisfied smile. "Not a lifetime, surely?"

There was a pregnant silence when she said, "I hate playing games," and she suddenly looked frustratingly lost. Some of the heat left her eyes.

"You do it remarkably well," he told her.

She stared up at him, her eyes huge. "I won't sleep with you tonight."

"*A.* I haven't asked you to." He smiled coldly. "And *B*, when we're in bed, we won't be sleeping."

Jessie made a low growling sound. "The reason I agreed to meet you tonight was to tell you to go to h—" She paused to look up as a family settled themselves noisily at the table next to them.

"You were saying?" Joshua ground out over the child's shrieks as its mother stuffed its flailing legs into the high chair their waiter had pulled up. "Jessica?"

She turned back, her expression dazed. "What?"

"You came here tonight to tell me to go…?" He knew damn well what the little shrew was going to say. He wanted to inform her he would go to hell *after* he had taken her to bed and made love to her until she couldn't remember her name, let alone give him so much aggravation.

"To tell you…" She looked at him blankly, glanced back at the fussy baby, then in a split second recovered herself. She smiled. Lord, he had never seen anything more captivating than Jessie's smile. "To tell you I missed you," she said huskily.

The waiter must have been trained to wait for the most inconvenient moment. He chose right then to deliver their entrée, then fussed with salad and plates and refilled water glasses. Joshua sent him off with a glare.

Before he went to hell, before he was driven out of his mind, he was going to have to spend at least a week in bed with this infuriating woman. He didn't like this sensation of not being quite in control. She smiled a sweet, gentle smile before picking up her fork.

Joshua had never experienced anything like this in his life. Not when two people's desire for each other was so palpable. Jessie Adams was just as turned on by him as he was with her. And *still* she held him off.

Half of him was annoyed by her reticence. The other half admired her restraint. When they did finally have sex he'd better alert the fire department.

He glided his fingers up her thigh. Jessie shivered, then grabbed his hand and set it back on the table. For a split second, her eyes flashed. The child at the next table broke into a high-pitched babble capturing Jessie's attention again for a moment. When she looked back at him she gave him a dulcet glance and picked up her water glass. Her cheeks were flushed.

She laid her napkin on her lap. A fraction of a second later, her eyes met his, a warm, soft smile touched the corners of her lips. A jolt of pure desire sizzled through him.

His heartbeat sped up as he said gruffly, "I want you very much, darling, so if you don't stop looking at me like that—"

She laughed, that deep, throaty, sexy-as-hell laugh of hers. A couple of heads turned, people smiling reflexively with her. "Behave," she told him sternly.

Her mouth, pale and free of lipstick, tempted him beyond endurance. Damn her. "Impossible. You wore that red dress expressly to make me crazy. It did its job. Now you have to pay up."

He leaned forward for a brief taste of her smile, slanting his mouth over hers briefly. He felt the quick, unexpected flick of her tongue. Perhaps he'd better place busy restaurants on his dangerous locations list. Electricity shot through him and he jerked away from her potency. After a quick glance his way and a raised eyebrow, Jessie resumed eating.

Joshua enjoyed the delicate greed with which she consumed her meal. A silky strand of hair trailed down her shoulder. He was sorely tempted to pull out the rest of the pins and see how it would look tangled after their lovemaking. He grew harder just at the thought.

"Tell me about Paris," Jessie demanded, leaning forward. "What you like about it. What you hate. What does the city smell like? Did you walk along the Seine in the rain? What's the food like?"

Joshua laughed at her outpouring of questions. So Jessie. Having her focus her entire attention on him was intoxicating. In the flickering candlelight, her skin looked translucent and incredibly soft. Her long, elegant legs were hidden beneath the table, but he could feel the erotic brush of her foot against his calf.

Once the honeymoon part of the relationship ended, he wouldn't have to invest as much time and energy into getting her into bed any time he wanted her. He didn't like wasting the time *thinking* about sleeping with her. He wanted to *do* it, and then go back to concentrating on Falcon International.

He bought failing businesses, put a competent manager in place, and when the business was once again in the black, sold it off. Much like not having the emotional fortitude to bond with a woman, he didn't form emotional attachments to the companies he purchased either. Everything about his life was controlled, planned and had a finite ending.

An ending of his own choosing.

It had been years since he had taken the time to slowly seduce a woman. It had been even longer since he had wanted a woman as much as he wanted Jessie. In fact, when he thought about it, he couldn't remember ever wanting another woman as much as he wanted Jessie. Nor could he remember one who actually listened without trying to impress him—which might explain his excruciating patience.

And the fact that he was still around. And very aroused.

Over the past several weeks, and mostly during transatlantic phone calls, he'd discovered they had many things in common: old movies, Japanese and Italian food and skiing. Joshua had no interest in skydiving, bungee jumping or spelunking. Jessie's love of dangerous sports appalled him. Not sure why, but wanting to understand this complicated woman better, he brought the topic up again.

"I don't get the fascination," he finally said, after she'd told him about a recent rock-climbing excursion. "What is it about the danger that turns you on?" Her skin looked soft, the bones in her slender hands almost fragile. He refrained from touching her. He wasn't a hand holder. Had never even thought about it before. He frowned. Even the idea of just holding this woman's hand had appeal.

"Everything." Her eyes looked mysteriously dark in the shimmering light. Her gaze skittered to the table next to them and back. The toddler was banging a spoon on the high chair tray.

"I suspect it's the same surge of adrenaline you get when you…when, you know, you're going to attempt a merger. That heady rush that tells you you're alive. That feeling of power can't be duplicated. I feel invincible…." She shrugged one slender shoulder. "It's hard to explain. Why don't you come with me the next time I go?" She gave him that mysteriously limpid look he couldn't fathom.

"Thanks," Joshua said dryly, picking up his wineglass and taking a sip. "I'll stick to mergers and acquisitions. At least I won't have any broken bones."

"Luckily, I haven't had any of those. Believe me, I'm not into physical pain. Just the rush."

"I don't like you doing anything that has the distinct possibility of leaving you dead or paralyzed." He didn't like the thought *a lot,* he thought scowling.

"I'm always careful." She viewed his concern with a strange expression in her dark eyes. "I've never had anyone worry about me before." Her lips curved in a poignant smile for a moment before she looked down at her lasagna, then back to meet his eyes. "I'll probably stop soon anyway." Something flickered behind those fathomless brown eyes again, then was gone.

"Somehow I doubt anyone could make you do something you didn't want to do." His tone was dry.

She picked up her wineglass. "With the right incentive—" she toasted him "—you'd be surprised."

"I LOATHE THAT MAN!" Jessie slammed the kitchen door at the main house and stormed into Conrad and Archie's family room.

Conrad hid a grin. "Another amicable dinner date?" He folded his newspaper on his lap.

"Grrr." Jessie started pacing. "This isn't in the least bit funny, you know. I've missed out a *gazillion* times because he keeps going on these blasted business trips. Damn it. I'm starting to *like* him!" Jessie flopped down in an easy chair cradling a cushion on her lap. "I don't want to like the blasted man. Don't look at me like that, Archie. I don't!" She grimaced. "At this rate I'll be old enough to be my baby's *grandmother* before we do it."

Archie hid his grin behind his book. Conrad managed to look mildly interested by keeping his expression bland. "Good Lord," he said, tongue-in-cheek. "Sounds like you might have to have a relationship before you fall into bed with each other. How novel."

Jessie stuck out her tongue at him. "How droll." She kicked off her shoes and pulled her legs under her. "Neither of us wants a *relationship*." She said it as if it were the plague. "I just want him to be in the right place at the right time, damn it."

3

THE LAZY DRIFT of fog gave an otherwordly charm to Pier 39, a picturesque tourist mecca of shops and restaurants down on Fisherman's Wharf. Jessie tucked her hand into the crook of Joshua's elbow and matched her stride to his. Moisture speckled Jessie's dark hair like liquid diamonds. Their footsteps echoed on the wooden boardwalk as they strolled companionably between tubs of brilliant early-flowering spring perennials and the inevitable camera-toting tourists.

Jessie tugged on Joshua's hand. "Come on. I want to go and see the seals."

She leaned over the railing to get a better look as the animals lolled about on custom-made platforms in the water. "Cute, huh?"

Joshua chuckled. "Yeah, really cute." He turned up the collar of her scarlet wool coat, his hands warm on her icy neck. "You're freezing." He tugged off the soft, warm scarf about his own neck and wrapped Jessie in it up to her eyebrows. She giggled. "How about a couple of gallons of hot coffee?"

"And pie?"

"And pie."

They walked quickly, and found a small coffee shop down a little jog in the boardwalk. The restaurant smelled warm and yeasty and was almost empty. They selected a tiny, rickety round table with a view of the boats ferrying tourists out to Alcatraz Island and ordered their coffee before removing their coats.

"There are only about thirty choices. We could always order a slice of each," Joshua suggested politely as Jessie scanned the menu for the pie selections. She stuck out her tongue at him.

Joshua's eyes darkened. "I can think of more productive things to do with that."

"Wicked man." She turned to smile up at the kid who'd come to deliver their coffee and take their order. The young man almost stumbled into their table. Joshua sighed. Jessie had that affect on men of all ages.

Pie ordered, coats removed and coffee doctored, they lazily discussed the art show they'd seen together the week before, Joshua's recent trip to Japan, and a large commission Jessie had just started, a bed-and-breakfast in Marin.

The waiter delivered their order and faded away. Jessie picked up her fork, and then put it down again. She pressed a hand to her midriff.

"I'm terrified I'm going to let Conrad down." Absentmindedly, she began to tear a paper napkin into shreds. "The people who own the B-and-B also own a small vineyard in Napa. They're influential, and there's a good chance they'll send a lot of business Con's way if I do a good job." She fiddled with the strips of napkin she'd torn.

"I've seen your work, Jessie. You're a fine designer. They're lucky to have you."

Her cheeks pinked. "Really?"

"Really. But if worry is preventing you from sampling the delights of that lemon meringue p—"

"Oh, no you don't." Jessie pulled her plate closer and picked up her fork again.

She glanced up and, smiling, offered him a bite. He closed his lips around the tines of her fork. She was going to be under him tonight. She was going to feel the fires he'd been keeping banked explode into a fury of passion that was going to leave them both too weak to move.

"Thanks for sharing that with me." He was so turned on he felt feverish. He'd been on a slow boil for months. "I can see how much you enjoy your food. You consume enough for a linebacker and look like a nymph. God, where do you put it all?" His eyes traveled down her slender body to rest for a moment on her small breasts.

"Well, obviously not *there!*" Jessie blushed. "Look at the baby seals or something. I can't eat when you're staring at me like a lion about to devour his Bambi du jour."

"Hmm. Soft, succulent and tender pink."

Jessie rolled her eyes. Joshua calculated they'd be out in the cold another hour at the most. He had an excellent bottle of Cristal chilling at home. He regrouped. "Tell me how adorable you were as a child."

"I wasn't an adorable child at all. I was a homely, gangly child." She smiled. "Which made it tough to make friends. My mother and I moved constantly. We'd move from apartment to apartment, town to town, sometimes state to state, so I was always being shoved into a new school."

"Military?"

"Collection agencies," Jessie said dryly.

He frowned. "You were poor."

"I suppose so, although I didn't think about it at the time. Things were how they were."

"When did you start this love affair with food?" He

couldn't wait to feel that avid little mouth all over him. Certainly, thinking of her sexually beat thinking of Jessie as being poor and wanting and having no one to care for her. For some reason picturing her that way pissed him off and made him feel…uncomfortable, damn it.

"Oh, way back. I learned to cook when I was six or seven because it was the only way I got to eat. My mom tended to forget little details like that. At one apartment, we had a wonderful Italian neighbor, sometimes she'd let me sit and watch as she prepared the family's evening meals. The stairwells used to smell incredible." She closed her eyes and inhaled deeply. "Garlic. Tomatoes. Yum. Hot, homemade sourdough bread. I used to sit on the bottom step outside their door and salivate. Just the *smell* of garlic is enough to make me remember that apartment on Ninth."

"God, Jessie." He'd never imagined her as a child, just a sensual woman, born to be made love to.

She waved away his sympathy. "Oh, don't feel sorry for me. Trust me, when I was a kid, it was all a wild adventure. I thought being hungry was normal. And I learned to make a mean spaghetti."

"That's child abuse."

"My mom? No. She didn't hurt me. She just—"

"Neglected you." Christ, no wonder she ate as she did; there would never be enough food in the world to a little girl who was starving. It explained her insistence on always getting a doggie bag even in the finest restaurants.

"It was a bit more complicated than that." Jessie paused and bit her lip. Her eyes met his. "My mom hooked on the side to make ends meet. There. I said it. Phew. As a teenager, I began to hate her for what she was doing. For how we were forced to live. Basically, I was a huge oops. She never knew who my father was.

"She died six years ago. I didn't like or approve of her lifestyle, but I loved her." She looked at him, her eyes unusually bleak. "In an odd way, now that she's gone, I miss her. Family is important, Joshua. No matter what."

"Family," he repeated dispassionately, his eyes flat. "I thought mine was bad, but my life was a cakewalk compared to yours."

"Tell me. You never talk about anyone but Simon and your cousin, Paul the Playboy."

"Want another slice of pie?"

"Does the Pope wear a beanie?" She mouthed "Apple" to the waiter across the room, then turned back to fix Joshua in place with her chocolaty eyes. "Tell me all the Falcon family's dirty little secrets."

"Read the tabloids. They seem to have everything covered."

"Poo, they make up stuff. Thanks," she said as an aside to the waiter, who'd cut at least half the apple pie onto Jessie's plate. She picked up her fork. "Unless the story about you having an alien's love child is true?"

Joshua smiled. "I missed that one."

"They had pictures," Jessie mumbled around a mouthful of pie.

"Yeah?"

"Uh-huh." She swallowed. "No family resemblance. Talk."

I could've used someone in my life just like you, Jessie Adams. Looking back, it seemed now to Joshua that he'd always been cold, physically and emotionally. "I was pretty much brought up by the servants before I was shipped off to boarding school,'' he said shortly, less comfortable when he was the one in the hot seat.

''Poor little rich boy.''

Joshua stared at her for a moment before shaking his head. ''Not at all. I had everything I wanted.''

''Not quite. I bet you missed your mother.''

''I missed her when I was *home*. She was always off somewhere. No, what I *wanted* was a Lionel train,'' he said, annoyed by her misinterpretation of his childhood. ''What I *got* was a track that ran the perimeter of our thousand-acre estate with a train that required an engine driver and a full-time staff to keep it running. Not quite what I had in mind to take up to my room.

''Naturally I wanted what I perceived the 'normal' kids had. A yo-yo, or a blue Swiss Army knife, or the brown leather bomber jacket owned by one of the servant's kids. Stupid. I could've bought a hundred of each out of my allowance. But perversely it just wasn't the same. I finally figured out that none of that was the least bit important. I was well taken care of, had an exceptional education and learned, *eventually,* to relish hard work and responsibility instead of growing into a dilettante.''

''Oh, Joshua…''

''On the other hand, what I'd really like, right now, is for you to come home with me.''

Jessie smiled almost sadly. ''Sorry, Romeo. Bad timing.''

''Damn.''

''You can say that again. How about another slice of pie?''

''WHEN'S THE NEXT DATE?'' Archie asked her.

''Tonight. Listen, guys. Don't romanticize this. It's

sex. Plain and simple." Except it was getting more complex every time she saw him. She shook her head as Archie started refilling her cup. "None for me, thanks." Jessie withdrew her palm from the rim of her cup then rose and rinsed it at the sink. Drying her hands, she said over her shoulder, "We're going to Noble's in the city. He said he has something special to celebrate tonight."

"Valentine's Day," Archie said cheerfully.

"He's going to get you into bed," Conrad said morosely, running his fingers through his blond hair.

"No, he's not," Jessie said grimly, hanging the towel she'd just used on the rack. "He can huff and puff, but he won't blow my house down." Then she smiled. "Not for two weeks, that is. Won't need to dig out the good underwear until then."

"Better run out and buy some *bad* underwear," Archie advised mischievously, giving her a wink.

Conrad walked over to Jessie and tilted her chin up. "Don't for a moment think The Glacier is going to make an honest woman of you. It isn't going to happen. You know it, we know it, and you can bet your sweet patoot the thought hasn't crossed his mind. I doubt the guy has ever eaten meat loaf in his life."

"In this case, I *am* an honest woman. I'm his wife. At least I am until I hand him the divorce papers. I don't want, or need *either* of us to fall in love," Jessie reminded him. "I just want my baby." *And to get out of this with my heart intact.*

"Then I'd suggest, love," Conrad said softening his tone, "that instead of buying undies, you go back home and reread Falcon's press clippings before you take your temperature."

JOSHUA GAVE HER pink diamonds for Valentine's Day. He watched her reaction as they sat in a dim, candlelit booth at Nobel's.

"Thank you so much, Joshua. These are beautiful. But I don't want you buying gifts for me." That unfathomable look came and went in her eyes.

"You don't like earrings?" he asked sardonically, it was clear she was delighted with the way the pendants brushed her neck.

He'd begun to realize that every gift he gave Jessie was a test. She couldn't possibly pass every one. Couldn't possibly be so genuinely pleased every time. No one was that good. He needed to bring what he was starting to feel when he was with her back down to a manageable level.

"I love earrings, the bigger, the better. And these are absolutely gorgeous." She touched a finger to one large pink drop. "What are these stones?"

"Diamonds."

Jessie flushed and he felt a need to taste the heat. He imagined warming his mouth against the fire in her cheeks.

"I mean the big pink stones."

"Diamonds," he repeated.

"Diamonds." Jessie went pale. "Oh, my God. Joshua! They must be…they're huge."

"Five carats." The receipt had been left in the bottom of the box, as he always instructed his secretary to do. He'd probably see them once more before they got "lost."

"Please, I love them, but I can't accept them." She yanked one off her ear with enough force to bruise. "I adore big, flashy *costume* jewelry. I'd be paranoid I'd lose these." She placed the earring on the table between them as if it would shatter.

Joshua picked it up and reinserted the post in her earlobe. After affixing the earring back, he stilled her other hand. "Keep them. They're insured." Conversation closed.

He felt the warmth of her thigh beside him on the banquet seat. She'd swept her hair up off her neck into a sexy chignon that defied gravity. The pink diamonds glinted in the soft lighting, casting rainbow prisms on her smooth cheeks. Candlelight danced in her eyes as she watched several couples moving slowly around the pocket-size dance floor. The pink jacket she wore rustled as she turned inquiring eyes up to his.

"Don't even ask," he murmured huskily, his breath making a curly tendril of hair dance against her cheek. He had no intention of dancing with her again until he had satiated himself with her body in bed. He was a ticking bomb as it was. "Hell, if I held you that close right now, I'd take you on the floor. Hard and fast."

She smiled that annoying as hell little enigmatic smile of hers. The one that turned the neurons in his brain to live wires and prepared his muscles for action.

"I want you," he murmured. "Right now." He restrained her fingers as she tried to pull away. "You've been holding me off far longer than I've ever waited for a woman."

The soft candlelight flickered on her face, bathing it in an apricot glow that made her dark eyes brilliant and drew his gaze to the sheen of wine on her mouth. She ran the tip of her tongue across her bottom lip and Joshua suppressed a groan. She leaned forward, her elbows on the table. The movement made the neckline of her jacket gape just enough to reveal the soft upper curve of her breasts. He dragged his eyes upward with reluctance and she made a small, low sound deep in her throat.

"I think you must put that stuff in my food when I'm with you." Her voice was so low he could barely hear her. "I've never felt like this in my life."

Joshua cleared his throat. "What stuff?"

Jessie's eyes were liquidly slumberous, and she blushed a velvety pink. "Spanish fly."

Joshua thought he would explode. "Spanish fly is actually cantharides made from the skeletons of beetles."

She grimaced.

Joshua held a laugh. "It causes itching all right, but not necessarily for sex." If possible, her blush got deeper, and she gave a small embarrassed groan. His body vibrated with need. "What we both have is an overdose of good old-fashioned lust." Then he lifted his glass. "To new beginnings."

"To new beginnings." Jessie clinked her glass against his, her smile brilliant before she blithely finished her shrimp.

Half her hair had escaped the pins, tangling with the heavy diamond drop earrings. Reaching out, he freed the silky filaments. His fingers lingered on her neck. "You know we're going to be lovers, Jessie. God knows, I've been patient and waited long enough. I won't wait any longer. I'm not a man who waits very long for anything. I need an answer."

Jessie laid her hand on her purse, something she did often, almost as if it were a talisman. "You haven't asked me a question." She pushed the last bite of lemon meringue pie around her plate.

"I'm asking now."

"I'm not sure what the question is."

He pulled a folded document from his breast pocket,

sliding it across the table. "I want you as my mistress, Jessie." Joshua's voice dropped another octave, his eyes kindling as he watched her mouth. He nudged the papers closer to her coffee cup.

Jessie eased her dry throat with a gulp of ice water. "What's this?"

"A contract. A legal, binding agreement." The sharp focus of his eyes reminded her of a bird of prey. "Read it."

"I'd rather you gave me a brief summary." Her hands balled into fists under the tablecloth. A contract! The bastard. And she'd been feeling guilty at how cold-bloodedly *she* was going about this.

"From now until the end of the year as my mistress," he said baldly, "I pay your rent. Buy your clothes. In exchange, you give me exclusive rights for the duration." Cut and dried. No mention of *his* fidelity.

She remembered Frankie, the fifteen-year-old who'd lived next door to them when she was thirteen. She'd had a huge crush on him. When she'd tried to steal a kiss, he'd called her a whore, like her mother. It had taken three other kids to pull her off him. She'd broken his nose and given him a black eye. She wondered how many people would be needed to pull her off Falcon.

"I'll think about your offer." She coolly pushed away her plate and reached for the leftover bread sticks. She filled her doggie bag then snapped two folds in the top to close it.

"You want me just as much as I want you."

Yes. And if I'd slept with you months ago this wouldn't hurt. "I can't tell you how sorry I am about that."

"Don't apologize for wanting me, Jessie. You're a sophisticated woman. You know the score. You want me and I, God knows, want you. You won't be sorry. I can be a generous lover.'' He tapped an earring with his finger. It grazed her neck and she felt the chill travel across her skin. ''You won't want for anything in my care.''

She took a calming breath. ''You want me to sign a contract.'' It wasn't a question.

''What did you expect?'' he asked, his face impassive. ''A handshake and a gentleman's agreement?''

Jessie's laugh sounded brittle, even to her ears. ''I can see why that wouldn't work. Neither one of us is a gentleman.'' She paused. ''What happens after my time is up?'' Her voice sounded oddly flat. ''Do I just disappear, no questions asked, to that great graveyard for all your old mistresses?''

Joshua merely watched her. Suddenly angry—he was too damn cool!—Jessie shoved the papers back across the table. ''I hate to be the one to disillusion you, Joshua, but not every woman finds you irresistible. I thought I could do this but, no, thank you.''

This was too impersonal, too calculating. She'd thought she could handle this part of it, but she'd been wrong. Dangerously wrong. *A little late in the day, Jessie,* she taunted herself.

''I want more than this. I deserve more than this.''

''Ten thousand a month.''

''W-what!''

''Ten thousand a month, tax free. An apartment and your clothes. And a car.''

Jessie gritted her teeth. ''I wasn't talking about mon—''

''Twelve thousand. And that's my final offer.''

Black dots blurred Jessie's vision. ''You can take those papers and shove them—''

Grabbing her purse and paper bag, she stood. Joshua

gripped her wrist tightly as she tried to sweep past him. With his other hand, he picked up the contract. "Take this. Read it. I'll give you two weeks to decide."

Jessie stared down at him, her breathing erratic. "One of my best qualities," she said frigidly as she tugged her hand away, "is that I make up my mind quickly. You're a self-righteous bastard, and I'm immeasurably grateful that I didn't fall into bed with you. You're a cold, arrogant—" her breath came out in a rush, her heart pounding so fast she thought she might faint "—jerk," she finished.

She had to get out of here. Now. Her cold hands took the papers from him, folding and then refolding them. Then she twisted them into a tight tube. "Here." She shoved them against his chest. "Try this for size!"

The contract slowly unfurled and dropped to his lap. His fingers tightened painfully on her wrist. "Jessie…"

She shook off his hand, removed the earrings, laid them carefully next to his coffee cup, then walked swiftly out of the restaurant.

BLAST THE MAN. Couldn't he do *anything* right! On each of her fertile days in January he'd been out of town. In February, he'd been gone at the wrong time again. In a couple more weeks all systems would've been go. With any luck, they would've been in the same place at the same time.

Instead he had to go and irritate her so darn much she'd almost punched his arrogant nose. Jessie wanted to throw up her hands in disgust.

She turned into her driveway. This was a case of "be careful what you ask for." And, God, had she asked for this. An icy wind rattled the car. Jessie laid her arms across the top of the steering wheel and stared sightlessly at her cottage. The ache in her chest made her lay her forehead down and squeeze her eyes shut.

She had been so close. So damn close. Tears of frustration and disappointment seeped between her eyelids. She slammed her fist down on the steering wheel. "I want my baby." Her voice broke and she pounded the wheel again. "You promised me my heart's desire. You *owe* me my baby, damn you."

She lifted her head and stared at the dark, swaying treetops beside her cottage. Joshua Falcon approached a personal relationship exactly as he did a business merger. Why had she been surprised? For him, they were one and the same.

She had two more weeks to calm down. She'd go to him on her first fertile day, she thought grimly, gritting her teeth.

She'd seduce him.

If she didn't kill him first.

4

JESSIE RANG the ornate bell outside Joshua's downtown San Francisco condo. He'd mentioned he rarely went home during the week, preferring to stay in his penthouse apartment in the Falcon building to driving the forty minutes to his house outside of town.

She'd dressed with care in a short, moss-green ultrasuede skirt suit that did flattering things to what few curves she had, and high heels of the same color. She'd swept her hair away from her face with combs and left it to fall down her back in a tumble of natural curls. On her ears, she had her lucky four-leaf clovers. In her purse, her lucky divorce papers. She was all set.

Her heart thudded as she heard approaching footsteps. The front door opened. Joshua surveyed her without expression, his sexy mouth grim.

Jessie's heart sank to her toes, that is, until she noticed his eyes fixed on *her* mouth. For a moment, their gazes locked. Her temperature immediately spiked.

"You took your sweet time." He pushed the door open. Without seeing if she followed, he turned and strode across the wide marble entry. He disappeared into another room, leaving Jessie to close the door and follow him.

The living room was expansive, with a breathtaking night view of the city and the necklace of lights on the Golden Gate Bridge. During the day, the panorama would be just as spectacular. A black granite fireplace took up space between the wide windows, pewter andirons reflecting a blazing fire.

Papers and file folders were spread across a granite-and-chrome coffee table the size of a small room. A plate with an untouched sandwich had been pushed aside and replaced with a telephone and notepad. Joshua stood at a built-in bar across the room. He turned as she moved across the thick carpet. "White wine?"

"I'd rather have a Coke."

He added ice to a glass and poured her drink. They both seemed fascinated by the building foam.

"Thanks." Jessie took the glass he handed her, pleased by how cool her voice sounded. *How very civilized we are.*

Without invitation, she sat down, the glass pressed between her palms. The leather quickly warmed to her body temperature as the upholstery enveloped her. Too comfortable. She shifted to the edge of the plump cushions as Joshua lounged on the plush sofa opposite, watching her with disconcertingly hooded eyes.

Jessie's experienced eye took in the vast room. Everything was technically correct. The paintings and sculptures were expensive and well showcased beneath discreet spotlights. The wine-colored carpet, bordered with alternating bands of cream and black, stretched across the enormous room to the windows. Stiffly formal tied-back drapes matched the carpet. No one could see into the windows twenty-two stories above the city. Three butter-soft black leather sofas made a U, facing the fireplace and the two windows with an incredible view of the downtown lights.

There was absolutely no life in the room.

"Conrad did a fantastic job, but whoever did your

decorating must have been an android.'' Architecturally, Conrad had had carte blanch, unlimited funds and a client who had no interest in the project until it was finished. In other words, as far as Con was concerned, a perfect client. Unfortunately, Joshua must have given the designer the same blank check.

Jessie, however, preferred her clients' involvement with the project from start to finish. She wanted them to invest more than their money. When Jessie was done with a house, it was a home. *Their* home. Stamped with *their* personality.

Joshua's eyebrow rose at her android comment. ''This is a business residence.'' He didn't glance around. His attention was one hundred percent on Jessie. ''It suits me perfectly.''

They *were* talking about interior design...weren't they? ''I didn't mean to disturb you.'' She lifted her chin a notch, intending to do just that—disturb this man of ice until he melted. If she didn't do him bodily harm first. She gave him a limpid glance from under her lashes.

At first glance, his gaze could give her frostbite. *This* was why he was called The Glacier. His expression had not changed one iota since she'd walked into the room. With that icy glare, he'd unknowingly just declared war. She smiled inwardly, because Jessie knew that just beneath that hard, frigid exterior lay the real Joshua Falcon. And she was determined to chip away the solid ice to unearth the lava below. Not enough to get burned herself, of course. But enough to keep Joshua hot and bothered until she had what she wanted. Then he could freeze over again.

''You've disturbed me since I met you, Jessie,'' Joshua admitted dryly. ''You better have come to tell me yes. If not, run like hell.'' His voice was low and rough.

His eyes met hers—*Oh! Not so cool, after all*—pale and hot, as he scanned her body as though she were naked. ''I'm not waiting another second for you.''

''No?'' Her cheeks flushed as she struggled to regulate her breathing, and she covered the rapid pulse beating at the base of her throat with her hand. It was hard to remember that *she* was the one in control when he looked at her like that. The air between them heated another fifty degrees. Her nipples pressed against her bra, and her skin felt sunburned as her temperature rose.

Their gazes locked as he lifted his glass to his mouth. ''Why *are* you here?'' The muscles moved in his throat as he swallowed, his pale eyes unblinking as he watched her. That stare was as primal as being pinned in place by the hypnotic stare of a large, dark panther. *I'm going to have you,* it said. *I'm going to devour you from heart to toes. I'm going to start right there at that frantic pulse in your throat and work my way down....*

Foolish imagination. Wishful thinking.

Jessie heard the thudding beat of her heart in her ears. *Down, girl.* This was purely business and biological for Joshua. She had to remember that.

Well, so what? It was the same for her, wasn't it?

Then why was her heart beating much too rapidly? And why were her palms damp? And why were her nipples aching with longing? And why, God help her, could she feel moisture gathering between her legs?

''You gave me two weeks, Joshua,'' she answered mildly, *and the timing is perfect.* She crossed her legs, and noticed Joshua's hand tightened on his glass as his eyes followed the movement.

"Have *you* changed your mind?" She held her breath waiting for his answer. It was slow in coming.

"No. But I am curious as to why you've changed yours."

Jessie shrugged, and her nipples rubbed against the inside of her bra, sending a shudder rippling through her body. She swallowed hard and held his gaze with some difficulty. How had she ever thought his eyes were cold? They smoldered, hot and clear. She swallowed again and managed to say calmly enough, "It's a woman's prerogative."

"I'm still a… What did you so aptly call me the other day? A self-righteous bastard?"

"And a cold, arrogant jerk." Jessie filled in helpfully. "But I'm here anyway."

"Why?"

"I'm *madly* in love with you." *Madly in love with the idea of walking out of here pregnant.*

"Don't be." His voice was ice cold, in marked contrast to his eyes and the pulse leaping at his strong tanned throat.

Jessie opened her eyes wide. "Okay, I'm not madly in love with you." *And I plan to keep it that way, too.* A woman would have to be insane to allow herself to become that vulnerable around him. And, Jessie knew, if she didn't have this powerful desire to have closure with her husband, if she didn't want to have his baby, if she had any sense at all, quite frankly, she'd be running as far and fast as she could. And she'd mail him the divorce papers from Timbuktu.

But she *needed* closure.

She *wanted* her baby.

Nobody was going to get hurt.

Joshua would have what he wanted.

She'd have what she needed.

And, God only knew, their attraction was undeniable.

"Have you ever been in love?" she asked, curious if anything had ever dented this man's heart.

"I love my business."

"That's not the same thing."

"It's all I need," he said shortly. "Can we get on with this?" He gave her a penetrating look, then rose to cross the room. Opening a drawer in the desk, he returned with a crumpled sheaf of papers. "Is this what you came for, Jessie?" His gaze fastened on her mouth, then slid, tactile as a caress, up to her eyes. "To sign this?"

Jessie kept her gaze steady by changing her focus so he was a blur. It was hot in here. She wished he'd open a window, or put the fire out…or touch her. Why did she have this sudden compunction to touch him? To taste those stern lips? To run her fingers through his neatly combed hair? She curled her fingers against her palms. What had he asked? *Contract.* "Actually, no."

"Then what the hell are you doing here?" Joshua abruptly came back into focus as he tossed the rolled-up contract onto the coffee table. It unfurled slowly.

Jessie drew a deep breath and said calmly, "I won't sign that contract, but I will sleep with you." Now. Immediately. Soon? Oh, please make it *soon.*

"I won't marry you."

Jessie raised her brows. "Who asked you to?" She made a moue of distaste. "I have no desire to get married. We can sleep together until I…" *conceive my baby* "…we tire of each other. A few days or weeks…" She shrugged. The movement rasped her hard nipples against the silky fabric of her bra. She couldn't control the shudder this time.

"A year."

"Too long-term for me."

"Long-term?" A muscle ticked in his jaw. "*Twelve months?*"

"That's *far* too long." Jessie's laugh was sophisticated and light, with just enough mockery. "Besides, we both know that kind of contract wouldn't hold up in a court of law anyway."

He let that ride, watching her with sparkling hot eyes. "Don't you at least want to know the terms?"

Jessie sipped her drink, letting the sweet fizz slide down her throat as she watched him over the rim of her glass. "No." Anticipation sang in her veins, giving her a rush of warmth that made it hard to keep up the casual facade. Now that the hard part was out of the way she should feel more relaxed; instead her nerves were stretched to the snapping point. He wanted her just as much as ever.

Her mouth went dry despite the soda, and she swept her tongue over her lower lip. His gaze fastened on her mouth and his eyes grew heavy lidded. Jessie felt that look in every pulse point of her body.

"Why are you doing this, Jessie?"

"I told you I'm madly in lo—"

Joshua ran his fingers through his hair in utter exasperation. "You're not in love with me, for God sake!"

Almost drunk with desire, and giddy with triumph, Jessie was starting to enjoy herself. "Oh, yes. I forgot. I'm definitely *not* in love with you." She choked back laughter as his fingers clenched on his knee. Carnal-induced adrenaline raced through her, her skin humming with it. She relished the stroke of fabric across her nipples, and craved Joshua's mouth there. Hot and wet…

"I have a dinner date in an hour," she told him casually. "Is there anything I should know before I go?"

His jaw clenched. *Direct hit.*

"The contract was supposed to be twelve months. January 1 to December 23. It's March. We've wasted time."

Hey, not my fault. Jessie looked at her glass instead of glaring at him. If he hadn't kept going out of town at the most crucial moments, this conversation would've been history. She could be home right now with her feet up, knitting something adorable.

"Darn, we've missed two months. No extension for good behavior?" Jessie asked with a little bite in her voice. She wished he'd stop talking and touch her. She might not be in love with him, but she was definitely in lust. Who knew lust could be this big? This overwhelming?

Her fingers dug into the soft leather and she crossed her legs again, then quickly uncrossed them. God, she'd never experienced anything like this in her life. Surely it wasn't natural. He hadn't even touched her and her body was on fire. She tried to focus. "What if *you* want to extend it?"

"I won't," he answered unequivocally. "The agreement gives us each exclusive rights. No one else. So forget your dinner date tonight," he inserted in a hard voice.

"Fine." She wanted his hands on her bare skin, on her fever-hot breasts, on her aching nipples. She wanted his mouth…everywhere. She felt the flush of heat rise to her cheeks and swallowed a moan. What was he saying…? "As long as you understand that *I* won't share you, either."

A wicked gleam flared in his eyes. "Jealous, Jessie?"

"No," she said firmly and drank the last of her soda before setting the empty glass on the table beside her chair. "Just fastidious. I want to be sure we understand each other clearly. I won't cheat on you, and I expect the same from you. One slip, and I'll consider the arrangement over."

Her gaze was steady, her heartbeat off the chart.

"I'll take care of birth control."

"I've already taken care of it," Jessie said calmly.

"Fine. I have a condo in the Sunset district. I want you to move in there immediately."

"No, thank you. I have a perfectly nice cottage. And my studio is there. I'm not going to disrupt my whole life for just a few months." *Once,* Jessie thought longingly. *Just once should do it.*

The air around them shimmered with sexual arousal. He was leaning forward, his elbows on his knees as he watched her through hooded eyes. He had the sexiest mouth. She pressed two fingers to her lips. A muscle throbbed in his cheek.

"I won't sleep with you there. Not under Archie's and Conrad's overprotective eyes. You'll have to come to wherever I am."

Jessie saluted smartly. "Yes, sir." She held back a scream of frustration. *Hurry up, for heaven's sake, I'm internally combusting here!*

"I don't like actually sleeping with a woman in my bed. When the alarm goes off, Barlow will take you home."

"Wham-bam, thank you, ma'am?" *Yes! Wham me. Bam me. Anytime in the next ten seconds would be fine.*

"Your choice."

Jessie sighed. "What time will I have to get up to go home?"

"Three."

"In the morning."

"Your choice."

"You said that already. Fine—3:00 a.m."

"I'll concede the point of your staying at your cottage, as long as you're available when I need you."

"I sincerely doubt that you'll ever *need* anyone, Joshua." *And at the rate we're going, I'll have to wait another month before we do anything, in which case I'll go stark raving mad.*

"And don't get any romantic ideas about love," he said crisply. "This is merely a business transaction."

"It certainly looks that way. I've never met anyone who keeps his emotions so tightly under wraps. No wonder they call you The Glacier." Jessie wondered what he'd do if she grabbed him by the collar and pulled him onto the floor.

"You're not required to understand me. All I want is a mutually satisfying sexual arrangement."

Jessie wanted to throw up her hands. It was easy to believe the man was made of solid, mile-deep ice—if one didn't see his eyes, which were as hot as laser beams. His control was absolutely phenomenal. "I'd feel more…comfortable if you showed at least a little emotion about this. I know I'm not the only one whose hormones go into overdrive when we're together. Do you feel nothing emotionally at all?" Her feet were starting to get decidedly cold. Oh, Lord. What had she been thinking?

"I feel damn primitive about you."

"You don't show it." Jessie put a little taunt in the words.

"If I lost control, you wouldn't be able to walk for a week."

Jessie was determined he would not only not be able to walk for a week, she was now bound and determined she was going to push this coldhearted man right over the edge. She almost rubbed her hands in anticipation, but instead she kept her casual demeanor. "So, let me recap this so we both know where we stand. Fidelity for the duration. For both of us. We'll have sex at your place and the chauffeur will take me home at three in the morning. Does that about cover it?" Jessie asked, not giving a damn, because at the outside that would happen twice.

"As long as I don't have to wear corporate colors." She glanced around the burgundy, black and silver room.

"I buy your clothes."

"I'll buy my own clothes."

"Consider the wardrobe I furnish a uniform then."

"I don't suppose this job has a pension plan—401K maybe? How about medical, dental, profit sharing?"

"You're damn cool about this," Joshua snapped, torn between admiration and irritation. When had he lost control of this conversation? Forget all this damn *talking*. The arrangement was a fait accompli. God, he wanted to go over there, grab her and carry her off to the bedroom like a primitive caveman.

The material of her dress looked butter soft, but not as soft as her pale skin. He could clearly see the sharp points of her nipples through the fabric. He controlled the burning need to leap across the space separating them and feast on her breasts through the fabric. He wanted to rip away her clothes and taste her body. He needed to plunge deep inside her, and feel her hot, wet heat close around him.

He felt as hot and horny as he had at fifteen when he'd seen his first naked woman. He could control himself. God help him, he could. But it had never been this difficult. He was scared to move in case he lost it.

"Yes, I am, aren't I?" Jessie folded her hands loosely in her lap and looked at him with dark, steady eyes. She tapped her fingers on her purse. Her control sent his blood pressure soaring. He'd been restless and edgy the moment he'd opened the door and seen her there. So much for his being The Glacier. What the hell was it about this woman that brought out this latent, primitive need to ravish her? He had been sexually attracted to women before. It had taken very little willpower to control his urges around them.

"Are we done talking?" he demanded through clenched teeth.

"I guess…"

With a swift move that took her completely by surprise, Joshua rose, stalked the three steps between his seat and hers, grabbed her by her shoulders and dragged her from her seat. He crushed her little yelp of surprise beneath his mouth.

It started as a kiss of mastery and domination. He wanted her to know that he was the one in control. She was his, damn her. But the moment Jessie realized what he was doing, her body relaxed against his. Her arms came up around his neck, one hand threading through his hair.

Her action softened the kiss. God, her mouth felt so damn good. He forgot just what it was he was trying to prove. She tasted sweet, her lips soft, her tongue aggressive. The suede fabric beckoned his hands. She smelled of fresh air and Joy. Enticing, and so female. She felt so incredibly good in his arms. He buried one hand in the silken mass of her hair, alive beneath his questing fingers. His other hand caressed the slender dip of her waist, the slight curve of her hip, the enticing firmness of her behind, pulling her more tightly against his agonizingly aroused body.

Joshua sighed against her mouth as her tongue came out and, as delicate as a cat, traced his lips. His hands tightened against her back. "The deal is made," he whispered hoarsely against her throat as his fingers found the concealed buttons of her suit jacket and started undoing them with fervent haste.

"There's one more thing," he growled against the fragrant curve of her throat. Her hands were driving him wild as she struggled to rip his shirt from his pants. He gently bit and she made a jerky little moaning sound that drove him wild.

"W-what?" Jessie's voice was a mere thread of sound, then faded completely as her hands encountered the naked skin of his chest. One hand slid up his back, trailing her short nails down the deep groove of his spine. The other hand slipped lower. Down his belly, her nails cool against his hot skin. She managed to unzip his pants. Her pale skin was flushed, her eyes heavy lidded and as dark as chocolate as she held his gaze.

"Don't ever... My God, Jessie," he groaned as her fingers cupped his sex. "Don't ever...ah, woman!... don't ever look at another man. I'd kill him."

"Fine," Jessie replied weakly as she helped him tear the buttons off her jacket.

"Twelve thousand dollars a month."

Her mouth inched over his face back to his lips. "Ten...thousand. You...said...ten..." She used her tongue to open his lips while her jacket fell unheeded to the carpet behind her.

Joshua cupped her bottom, pulling her hard into the cradle of his thighs and firmly against his erection. Unable to stay away from her succulent mouth, he kissed her again. "Twelve," he groaned, and she bit lightly at his lower lip.

Her knees buckled as he stripped off her skirt.

"I...don't...need your..." His fingers slipped beneath her panty hose. "Money." The nylon slithered down her legs and she swayed against him. "I—" she punctuated each word with a nibbling kiss wherever she could reach "—have...my...w-work." The words came out against his navel.

Joshua groaned. "Fine." His fingers tangled in her hair. "Fine," he said again, distracted as her fingers dragged down his shorts, deliberately skimming his rock-hard erection on the way down. Too gentle. Too fleeting. "Oh, God. That's just fine."

They dropped to the floor in a tangled heap of clothes and limbs, him on top of her. Joshua pulled her face up to his for a searing kiss that rocked them both. "You're going to kill me."

Jessie kicked herself free of the skirt and panty hose tangled around her ankles and tugged his shirt over his broad shoulders. Now he was gloriously naked, too. "Can't," she said fiercely, her hands skimming his wide, hair-roughened chest. "I'm...not...finished...with...you... yet!"

His laugh was muffled by the fascinating silky texture of her right breast, small and perfect. He brushed his lips over one tight nipple, then opened his mouth and closed his teeth around the hard point, and sucked it into the hot, wet cavern of his mouth. Jessie's back arched off the floor.

She twisted her head to nip his shoulder. He tasted of soap and salt. The scent of him went to her head like fine wine. The carpet scratched her naked back, but she didn't care. It was far more fascinating to feel Joshua's chest hairs scraping the sensitive nerves of her breasts and belly.

"Is there…any…thing…ah!…else?" Her lips parted, and she inhaled deeply, her eyes almost closed as she felt the damp heat of his mouth laving her breast. Suck. Lick. Suck… A sharp, sweet sensation shot to her groin. She panted for breath. His fingers felt slightly rough, *hot,* on her skin as he caressed her other breast with his hand, while devouring her with his mouth, teeth and tongue.

"Not…that…I…can…think of…at…the moment. God, you taste sweet." He shifted his head to pay tribute to her other breast. His soft, dark hair tickled her skin as he shifted, and Jessie got goose bumps. She slid her fingers through his hair, feeling the heat of his scalp through the cool, silky strands as she held his head to her breast.

Jessie sighed with pleasure as Joshua licked a path between her breasts. Hot and slick, his tongue traced a sensuous path down the center of her body, making her burn and shiver by turns.

He looked up the length of her body. "Touch your breasts, Jessie. Close your eyes. Play with those pretty nipples, and pretend your hands are mine."

Jessie squeezed her eyes shut and cupped her aching breasts in her palms. Her nipples felt exquisitely hard. She pressed down. God, it felt good. Relieved a little of the urgency. She felt Joshua's smile against her tummy, and took her nipples between her fingers, squeezing and rolling as Joshua's hot mouth slid down her body. His hands trailed a burning path down her sides, a beat slower than his lips.

Jessie's body quaked, and she groaned softly as his mouth brushed the nest of curls at the juncture of her thighs. She felt a brief moment of panic and clutched a handful of his hair. But what he was doing was so incredible that her fingers sifted through the silky strands, anchoring his head in place instead.

His strong hands cupped her hips, and her body trembled as his tongue parted her. She shifted, murmuring with intense arousal as he sucked and licked her clit, his shoulders keeping her legs apart. Her head thrashed on the floor. She needed more. Less. *More,* damn it. She grabbed handfuls of his hair as he plunged his tongue deep.

The pleasure was sharp and riveting and left her breathless. His fingers would leave bruises on her hips tomorrow, but she didn't care. She couldn't quite catch her breath. Couldn't quite get her mind to work.

A low throbbing began in her belly, then spiraled hot and delicious when he moved his hand around from her bottom to slide to the inside of her thigh. His finger filled her. Her muscles convulsed around it. A second finger joined the first, Jessie moaned low at the sensation of fullness. His damp mouth returned to her clit, and tongue and fingers worked together in a magical, maddening dance that had her breathless and poised on the brink.

His fingers rotated, he sucked harder, and Jessie let out a wild cry as she came in a hard, sharp spasm that lasted an eternity. Her fingers fisted in his hair, and for a moment everything went black.

When she managed to open her eyes, she saw his face above her. She raised a leaden arm and looped it around his neck, drawing him up. His body was heavy, damp with exertions.

The slide of his body against hers made her pulse leap higher and faster. He kissed her, and she tasted herself on his lips. His tongue bladed into her mouth, hot and

slick, demanding and insistent. Jessie had never been
kissed like this. Never been the focus of anyone's attention to this degree. It was intoxicating. He was intoxicating. She slid her tongue against his, mimicking his
movements.

He braced his elbows on the floor on either side of
her, but his lower body, and thick pulsing shaft, lay
heavy and welcome between her legs.

Snap out of it! Jessie cautioned herself, horrified at
her response to him. She hadn't wanted to enjoy his
lovemaking quite that much. "More," she demanded,
when she was finally capable of speech. She shifted her
hips.

"More?"

Terrified by the depth of emotion she'd just experienced, Jessie's heart started pounding for an entirely different reason as she started to panic. She couldn't afford
to form any sort of emotional attachment to Joshua Falcon.

She couldn't. Wouldn't. Must not.

She was here for one thing. And one thing only. Oral
sex wasn't going to cut it.

*Please don't bind me to you. Just have sex with me,
and keep it impersonal. Please. Ha, fat chance!* As her
mother used to say, "*Be careful what you wish for. You
might get it.*" Jessie was getting far more than she'd
bargained for when she'd taunted the devil into making
love to her.

"Finish it," Jessie begged. She had to have sex and
get out. She wanted to run far, far away.

"Patience." Joshua smoothed her hair back from her
damp brow, his eyes softer than she had ever seen them.
"I want to look at you. You're so beautiful. Beautiful
and so damned responsive. The perfect mistress."

Yes, Jessie thought, an odd twinge pinching her heart. *That's what I am, a mistress. A business arrangement. Give me what I want, and I'll give you what you want. A fair trade...*

Oh, God. Please don't take more than my body.

Jessie tugged at his shoulders until his heavy, welcoming weight covered hers. She reached down and closed her fingers around the hard length of his penis. It felt thick and long, silky and...alive. "I want you deep inside me," she begged, not at all sure that her body could accommodate him now that she felt the size of him. Oh, God. What if it didn't fit?

"It'll fit just fine. Trust me," Joshua murmured against her throat, and Jessie realized she must've said her thought out loud.

With a hoarse cry, he slid into her slick heat. Jessie gasped as he filled her, stretched her slowly. Oh, so slowly... "Oh, yes...give...me...baby," she panted hoarsely.

He plunged deep.

Jessie hissed out a surprised breath at the sharp sting, froze, then tried to arch away. For a moment the pain was so intense she gave a keening cry, her nails digging into his bare back. He didn't stop, and she was fiercely glad. "More. More. More," she chanted as she adjusted to his width and length. "I want you. I want you. I want you."

His large hands clamped on her hips, and he gave her a feral smile, filled with triumph. "You have me." He began to move again, his thrusts sliding her body on his shaft in a slick, thrilling roller-coaster climb of sensation.

His thrusts grew stronger, deeper, harder. Jessie wrapped her legs around his pistoning hips, and dug her heels into his lean flanks, feeling the bunch and clench of his muscles.

The sensation was too intense to bear. Jessie's head thrashed on the carpet. Her body felt too tight to remain whole. "I can't..."

"You want more?" he demanded, jaw tight with the strain, dark hair sticking to his sweaty forehead. His pale gaze ate her whole.

Jessie tried to focus her eyes. "No. Yes."

He slid in deeper. "Yes?"

She moaned.

He slid out almost all the way. "No?"

She wrapped her arms more tightly around his shoulders and held his hips in place with her legs. "Bastard."

"True. But is that a yes, or a no?" He thrust deep.

"Yes, yes, yes," she panted. Her hips met each plunge, her body straining for release. Her long hair tangled across her damp face and chest. She ran her hands down the slick, hard plane of Joshua's back, feeling the flex and twist of his muscles beneath the satin of his skin. She dug her short nails into his hips. "Now," she begged, hoarse and breathless, body on fire. "Please. I can't take any more."

"No." He kept moving. Changing the rhythm, changing the speed, changing the depth of his thrusts until she was about to come. Then he'd back off slightly until the moment passed, leaving her body screaming for release.

"Now. Now. Now," Jessie gasped, breathless and dizzy.

"Now?"

"Yes, damn it! Now!" she said hitching her hips and clamping her heels down to bring him in harder. One more deep thrust, she thought, just one more...

He slid a hand between their sweat-slick bodies and touched her, rubbing a finger in her moisture.

"Joshua!" Jessie's body immediately convulsed, and she cried out as she climaxed hard and fast.

Joshua continued his deep pounding rhythm until his cry echoed hers.

He collapsed against her, turning their joined bodies so they lay side by side on the plush carpet. Then he cradled her trembling body to his, his hands making broad tender sweeps down her naked back. His breath was harsh in her ear as she melted under his touch.

"Is it always like that?" Jessie was caught unaware by a yawn, and snuggled into the safe harbor of his arms. His laughter vibrated through her. Her eyes were too heavy to open as he brushed a kiss across her hair.

"No, usually it's not quite as hard and fast. Sometimes it's long and slow." Amazingly he felt himself swell inside her again. Joshua moved his hips slowly, enjoying the sleepy warmth of her.

"Give it to me, baby?" he asked, amused, and her eyes narrowed before she shrugged and glanced away.

She closed her expressive eyes and relaxed beneath him. "I watch a lot of movies, what can I say?"

"The dialogue is vast and varied." He assured her dryly, "We'll have time to explore every nuance of post-coital conversation." He glanced down to see the steady rise and fall of her beautiful breasts and realized with amusement that, contract or not, she was his new mistress, and she was fast asleep.

Using a gentle touch, he traced the perfect symmetry of her face, still flushed and damp from their lovemaking. With gentle mockery, he whispered softly, "Nice of you to forewarn me you were a virgin, Jessie."

JESSIE WASN'T USED to answering to anyone. Especially someone who had sent her home at an ungodly hour the morning after with his stony-faced chauffeur, then called her the next day as if nothing earth-shattering had happened. Her car had been delivered back to the cottage by invisible pixies in the middle of the night.

Joshua had called to tell her he would be in New York for two days. He'd left two messages on her answering machine while she'd been out seeing clients. She'd wanted to ask him if sex with her had been so bad he had to flee the state. She hoped to God that their love-making had taken. She didn't think she could go through it again. The intensity of climax with him had been almost terrifying. It had left her shattered and shaky and not quite as confident about her own control of the situation.

Jessie pulled her car into the narrow road leading up to the gatehouse. She'd been single-mindedly concentrating on a hot, steamy bath for the last hundred miles.

It was midnight, and she was absolutely exhausted. She'd gone to see a client in Redding, three hours away, leaving early enough to beat the commute traffic in San Francisco and arriving at the client's small ranch just in time for breakfast.

After she and Karen King had talked drapes and case goods, the two women had wandered outside to see the show horses Karen and her husband bred. Their animals had won competitions from Canada to Brazil. Peter's den was filled with trophies and ribbons.

The last time she'd been out here, Karen had put her up on a placid cow pony and she'd laughingly complained. She'd expected a nice, civilized ride this time, too. But Karen, knowing her preference for a challenge, had put her up on Billy. By the time she realized that she and the horse had completely different ideas, it was too late. She had the bruises to prove it.

Jessie was surprised to find Joshua parked outside her cottage—hadn't even noticed his car at first. She'd forgotten to leave the porch light on. The bitter cold hit her as she got out of her car. The wind snapped the bare branches overhead, and moaned around her solid little stone cottage.

The windows of his Jag were steamed and so, apparently, was he.

"Where the hell have you been?" he demanded, slamming out of his car and following her to the front door.

Jessie unlocked the door but didn't push it open. "I *beg* your pardon?" She had a feeling he was going to be the last straw of her day. Joshua stretched over her, pushing the door ajar and following her inside where it was blessedly warm.

"You heard what I said." He started unbuttoning her kelly-green wool coat as soon as the door slammed shut behind them.

"Yes, but I didn't believe my ears," she said crossly, too tired to move. He was awfully quick with those buttons. The back of his fingers brushed her breasts and her nipples stood up to attention. "Did you need me today?"

"What's wrong with…" he started, obviously perplexed by her waspish attitude. Until he saw the condition of her jeans and sweater as he drew off her coat. His pale eyes narrowed. The jeans had been old to start with. They had merely attained an extra patina of real hard work this afternoon. The poor sweater was another matter. Ripped and mangled, it was going to be fed into the trash as soon as she had the energy to do it.

"Who did this to you?" Joshua demanded with deadly calm, carefully drawing the tattered sweater over her head. Jessie couldn't hold back the wince as the sleeve pressed against her arm.

For the last several hours, on the drive home, Jessie had fantasized about a long soak in a hot bath, not an interrogation. She looked up at his hard face, curious to see his reaction. "Billy," she said sadly.

"Billy?" Joshua repeated coldly as he paused in his perusal of her Technicolor ribs.

Jessie sighed. "Bucking Billy. The cad. The *horse*," she emphasized, only because she was too tired to clobber him. "He has no idea how to show a lady a good—"

"Billy is a horse?"

Jessie gave him a dirty look. It was weak, but still, she hoped, conveyed her feelings on the subject. "Didn't we make a verbal agreement the other night?"

"Yes," Joshua ground out.

"Well then, why would you think I'd be the first to break it?" *You big jerk!*

"Excuse me," he said stiffly. "I forgot your propensity for danger."

The most dangerous thing Jessie could think of right now was their proximity to the kitchen with its myriad sharp instruments. She sighed. Murdering him now would make life so complicated. Besides, she'd need energy for that. She heaved another put-upon sigh.

Joshua gave her an odd look. "Have you seen a doctor?" He did both a visual and tactile search, his hands cool and unbelievably gentle as they skimmed her body. His eyes were hot and hard. "Do you *need* to see a doctor?"

"No and no." She needed more than his impersonal

fingers on her skin. Jessie looked up at him. "I don't know the procedure here. What am I supposed to do when I want you to hold me? Do I have to wait for sex?" She saw his lips twitch. "Because, believe me, as much as I loved what we did on Saturday night, I have to tell you I don't think…"

"Oh, I think I can handle a little light touching without resorting to my basic animal instinct to throw you down and have my wicked way with you."

His touch was gentle as he wrapped his arms around her, but Jessie had never felt anything as wonderful in her life. His firm lips brushed hers. Too lightly, too slowly.

Jessie deepened the kiss herself. What she lacked in experience, she made up for with enthusiasm. Her tongue explored his mouth, and he groaned, holding her more tightly. Jessie moaned. In pain. He quickly let her go.

"I heal quickly," she promised.

"I hope so," Joshua said dryly as he carefully swung her up in his arms and headed for the stairs. Jessie gave a muffled squeak as she went from vertical to horizontal.

"Why do you think I stayed away from you for three days?"

Jessie rested her aching head against his chest. *Because you're so darned perverse?* "I thought you'd lost interest," she said so quietly that when he didn't answer right away she thought he hadn't heard her.

"I left town before I was reduced to mauling you on the floor again."

"You didn't maul me." Jessie was indignant. How like a man to take all the credit.

Joshua turned on the landing, heading for the bathroom. "If I'd known what you'd get up to while I was gone I'd have—"

Jessie stiffened. "Yes?"

"I'd have said, be careful." He'd backtracked. Smart man. Jessie relaxed against his broad chest. She'd never been carried anywhere in her life. It felt wonderful.

He leaned over, turning the handles, and water gushed into the claw-footed tub. "Damn. You're black and blue all over. Why can't you have a nice, quiet little hobby like...needlepoint?" He sighed.

"That doesn't say a whole heck of a lot about my charms," Jessie said, imagining what her battered body must look like, yet too exhausted to move as he undressed her as if she were three years old. The bathroom rapidly filled with steam. "The water's going to overflow."

"I'm not making love to a woman who can barely stand." He turned off the taps when the tub filled to the perfect depth. The man could be annoyingly precise.

"I could lie down," Jessie offered. "The bath mat's soft and fluffy."

Joshua shook his head in amusement. "I'll take a rain check. Tell me about Bucking Billy. In."

She stuck a finger into the water. "Too hot." He turned on the cold. Jessie stood there, letting him look at her bruised, battered, goose-bumpy body, thinking perhaps she'd fallen on her head. Because having Joshua look at her like this was more arousing than embarrassing.

"Unfortunately Billy had seen my likes before. He was no gentleman. I managed to stay on for three seconds. It *felt* like three years. *He* couldn't resist a challenge, either."

Joshua frowned. He was very close, and she noted

how the steamy bathroom intensified the scent of his cologne. Her pulsed started throbbing. She hoped he'd kiss her. She hoped she had the energy to pucker up when he did. The timing was still right, maybe she could work up the energy…

At some point he'd shut off the water. "Bucking Billy won." Jessie wanted to enjoy the hot, steamy water; unfortunately, she was just too darn tired to move. She gave Joshua a pleading look, and he took her hand and assisted her into the high-sided tub.

"Ow-ow-ow," Jessie wailed as hot water met abraded skin. She didn't feel the least like being brave tonight.

"Needlepoint," he said grimly, picking up the washcloth slung over the spout. Jessie slid inch by inch under the water, and watched him froth the terry with peach-scented bubbles.

"Boooring."

Joshua ran the soapy cloth over her chest. She glanced down. Her hard nipples poked out of the water. She glanced up. Joshua had noticed. Would he do anything about it?

"Close your eyes."

Jessie looked up at him. "Why?"

"I'm going to wash your face. Close, you stubborn woman."

Jessie closed her eyes. The peach-scented cloth drifted across her cheeks, over her nose, climbed her forehead, then brushed down to her throat.

"Wait," he warned before she opened her eyes.

Jessie kept her eyes closed. It felt nice this way. Warm water lapped at her skin as Joshua carefully rinsed her face. She didn't bother opening her eyes again.

She could feel each one of his strong fingers beneath

the soapy terry cloth as he washed her throat, then slid down to sweep across her collarbones.

He swore, obviously coming across more bruises. "I hope they sent this nag to the glue factory."

Jessie's lids weighed a million pounds each. She had throbbing parts and colored parts and scraped parts, and they were all telling her to shut down and sleep. "He's a nice horse."

"Yeah, right." His hand shifted to her nipples. *Ah.* Her nipples perked right up at the attention. Other body parts started coming to life, too. She shifted without opening her eyes, water lapped the edge of the tub. She didn't hear any water splashing the floor, so Joshua must've absorbed the overflow. Her lips twitched. "Are your pants wet?"

"Yes." He sounded amused.

Jessie blinked her eyes open. He was very close. His pupils had dark blue around the edges. "You could get naked, and come in here with me." It sounded a lot more needy than she liked. "Never mind. I'm not up to any fun and games tonight anyway—oh, that feels great." The washcloth was gone and his slick bare hand was doing cleanup duty on her, apparently, *very* dirty nipples.

"Like that, do you?"

"Hmmm," she moaned. Her lax body slid farther down into the hot water. Joshua's steadying hand braced at the back of her head was the only thing preventing her from drowning. The fall from Billy, combined with the long drive back in the dark, had drained all her resources. She felt punch-drunk and silly and overwhelmingly glad Joshua was here with her.

"This is the second time I've been naked," Jessie mumbled sleepily. Joshua chuckled as his soaping hands

smoothed across her breasts and did an intoxicating slip
and slide over her nipples. She wanted to purr.

"In your whole life?" He sounded so amused, she
opened one eye.

"In *your* whole life." She yawned. "You've only
seen me naked once before. Mmm, that feels wonderful." She spat out a soap bubble as he scooped water
over her skin. Runnels of hot soapy water tickled her
breasts.

"I'm going to be seeing you naked a million more
times, Jessie," he promised. "Preferably without these."
Underwater, his finger traced a bruise on her ribs. It was
a sweet sensation.

"He took me literally, darn it."

"Who?"

"God. When I was a kid I prayed my boobs wouldn't
get as big as my mother's. She was *huge*." Jessie
yawned as Joshua chuckled. "I should have waited a
few more years until I was a little bit bigger before asking."

"You're perfect just the way you are," he said huskily, his breath fanning her damp face. "Any more
would be excessive."

There was something she'd wanted to tell him, but the
steamy combination of the water and the unbearably
gentle touch of Joshua's hands made her forget what it
was. She'd wanted to say...

She was asleep.

Joshua watched her face as he finished bathing her.
He'd showered with women before. He'd bathed with
women before. But they'd always been wide-awake and
responsive. Washing Jessie as she slept was a novelty.
Her cheeks had pinked up from the steamy heat. Her
ridiculously long, black lashes lay still and spiky on her

damp cheeks. Her sweet mouth curved with a faint smile.

Joshua bent his head and brushed his mouth over hers. Her lips were moist and softer than anything he'd ever touched. Sleeping Beauty, he thought fancifully.

Her sweet breasts seemed to float on the water, the nipples soft and as petal pink as her lips. He brushed a finger across one velvety nub. It tightened in response. "Damn it, Jessie—"

Never before had he wanted a woman so much. So why did it feel so good simply to watch her sleep?

SHE LOOKED her usual bright and perky self the next morning as she walked into the kitchen, haphazardly rolling up the sleeve of a man-style white shirt she'd tucked into her jeans.

Her eyes widened when she saw him sitting at her kitchen table. "Well, good morning," Jessie said cheerfully, clearly surprised to see him. She was no more amazed than he'd been. He couldn't remember the last time he'd spent the night beside a woman, *not* making love. And despite three cups of coffee this morning, he was *still* trying to figure it out.

"Let me," he said standing up and crossing the room, just wanting to touch her. She extended her arm, and he brushed the sleeve down before neatly folding it up to her purple elbow. Jessie's eyes twinkled as she extended the other arm. Her skin felt warm from her shower and she smelled of shampoo.

She'd put her damp hair up in a lopsided ponytail, which had dripped a damp spot on her shoulder. He noted her total lack of makeup. Any other woman would have rushed to the pots to cover the bruises. For just a second he contemplated Jessie's clear skin and candid brown eyes. There was not a shred of artifice about this woman.

"How do you feel?" He traced her cheek with a stroke of his thumb. She smiled.

"Terrific."

"Terrific?" Joshua handed her a cup of coffee. She gingerly sat down, easing her body into the ladder-back chair. The pine table wobbled, despite the matchbook under one leg.

"How can you feel anything but god-awful? You're black and blue and must hurt like hell."

"Oh, this is good." Jessie almost inhaled her coffee. "Of course it hurts. But I still feel terrific. The bruises and stuff are just a blip on the screen. I had so much fun yesterday, it was worth it." She splashed more caffeine into the purple mug with a red ladybug on it, before she got up to hang on the open refrigerator door like a kid after school. "Wanna share cold pizza?"

Joshua glanced at his Rolex. "It's 7:15 a.m."

Jessie grinned over her shoulder. "And that means…?"

"Usually people eat cereal in the mornings."

"I eat cereal at night." Jessie took out a large rather greasy box, sliding it onto the table between them. There was one slice left. She looked up at him, her eyes dancing. "How do you feel about leftover spaghetti?"

5

IT WAS A GOOD THING she wasn't prone to excessive drinking or tantrums. Jessie swallowed two aspirin, more for the Joshua-size headache than for her cramps, and glared at the calendar.

She wasn't pregnant.

Her cycle had always been erratic, but there was no mistake. The disappointment felt like a physical blow to her chest. Her throat had felt tight with unshed tears for hours.

The times with Joshua were becoming more and more like real dates. She didn't want to *date* the blasted man. It seemed Fate conspired against her, as if the gods were challenging her to get to know him before they allowed her a child.

Jessie walked downstairs into her studio. She knew all she wanted to know about Joshua Falcon. He was impatient, arrogant, dictatorial and rude. He was also generous, insightful and an incredible lover. She groaned. She had told the guys the relationship with Joshua wasn't personal, but it was becoming more personal by the day.

She didn't like it. He had one purpose for being in her life, and one purpose only. She couldn't lose sight of the whole point of this exercise. There was no use weeping and wailing and pounding her breast. If she wasn't pregnant, she wasn't pregnant. Yet.

She'd keep doing it until she got it right.

She stepped back from the samples she'd propped on the three-hundred-year-old refectory table she'd bought for a song and refinished herself. Arms folded, she critically eyed the wallpaper and fabric combination, visualizing it all in conjunction with everything else in the client's living room.

Her own home was decorated in the primary and secondary colors she loved. The sunshine-yellow canvas sofa was strewn with plush pillows in blues and reds and parrot green. Various clay pots held grasses or twigs. A large brass spittoon on her drafting table held the mixed bouquet of iris and daffodils Joshua had sent her a few days ago. The cottage was a comfortable blend of antiques coupled with a very modern drafting table and her computer, which she'd used to prop up the enormous wallpaper sample book.

The client, a retired dentist, wanted Victorian and Laura Ashley. Jessie slowly walked backward, her hands framing the still life on her desk, her head tilted. "Perfectomundo!" She stepped back and walked smack into a hard body. "Joshua." She turned into his arms, lifting her face.

His mouth came down hungrily on hers as he angled her head for a perfect fit. Jessie wound her arms around his neck, pulling him closer. She made a soft sound of pleasure as his hands slid under her flannel lumberjack shirt and found bare skin.

She'd given him a key last month, the day after Billy, although this was the first time he'd used it.

She savored the feel of his fingers against her skin as his large hand skimmed up her back. "What are you doing here?"

"If it's not obvious then my technique is lacking

something,'' Joshua said dryly. "I came to invite you to dinner. How about Japanese tonight?''

"Great." Jessie unwound her arms. It was becoming too easy to be touched by him. Far too enjoyable to have his mouth explore hers. She strolled across the room, then plunked down in her seat and hit the save button on her computer. "I love Japanese." She looked up at him. "I actually thought it would be hard to fit in with your rarefied lifestyle, but it's not all bad."

"You'd put up with the paparazzi and other hoopla for the food alone."

"The travel benefits aren't bad, either." She wanted to touch him but rested her fingers on her keyboard instead.

"Good, because we'll be eating that Japanese meal I was talking about in Tokyo."

She should have realized, with Joshua, nothing was quite that straightforward.

"Not *we*, Joshua." Jessie closed the wallpaper book before turning from her computer, resting her arm along the back of her chair. In a dark business suit, with a teal tie and his hair brushed back, he looked immaculate, efficient and cool. As usual. She knew she must look like hell with her hair haphazardly piled on top of her head and anchored with a couple of pencils. She wore no makeup and was dressed in black leggings and her favorite red-and-black plaid shirt which came to her knees. She hadn't expected him. Usually at this time of the morning he was entrenched in his office in the city.

She'd left him sleeping at 3:00 a.m. and now, seven hours later, he was insisting she pack for a trip to Japan and leave within hours. He hadn't said a word about it last night.

His eyes went cool, aloof. She knew he was ticked

off by her refusal to go. His lips tightened. "Part of our agreement, Jessie, was that you would be available to accompany me on my business trips. I'm leaving out of SFO in two hours. Don't bother packing much. You'll have ample time to shop in Tokyo."

"Please don't tell me what to do, Joshua. I said no, and I mean it." Joshua used shopping trips like a carrot at the end of a stick. Shopping had obviously been an inducement to his other mistresses. She supposed she should be grateful he wasn't observant enough to realize she wasn't enticed by the same baubles as his former mistresses.

He hadn't liked it when she'd refused the BMW he'd had delivered a few weeks ago either. He hadn't understood the charm of her ancient Celica.

"I have plenty of clothes—that's not the point. You'll have to give me more than a couple of hours notice for these trips. I have clients who require my attention and two bosses who depend on me to carry my share of the work."

His face rigid, Joshua dug his hands into the pockets of his coat. In the bright morning sunlight streaming into her downstairs studio, Jessie could see how tired he looked. Not a hair was out of place and no wrinkle marred his impeccable suit or crisp white shirt, but lines of fatigue were clearly visible on his face. The man worked too long and too hard.

She softened her tone. "I enjoy being with you, you know that. But we only got back from Greece ten days ago—"

"This is strictly business. It won't be a repeat of the yacht."

"It will always be a repeat," Jessie said with sardonic amusement. They'd spent seven days on his yacht in the

Aegean. "I only saw you after sundown." While the men talked business in the luxurious stateroom, the women had tanned up on deck. There were plenty of hot-and-cold running waiters, the Greek sun had baked out the last of her Billy bruises, and she'd been amused by the other men's trophy wives or mistresses. But the time was wasted if she wasn't spending it in bed with Joshua. They had gone during peak conception days. Taking advantage of the golden opportunity was the only reason Jessie had hurriedly juggled her schedule.

"As much as I enjoyed it, taking a week off unexpectedly like that threw me off. I have to finish this before my meeting with Dr. Low on Friday."

"Send Conrad."

"Con's an architect, not a decorator. Besides, Jenn is *my* client, Joshua." She rose and put her arms around his neck. Despite his obvious reluctance to be cajoled, he dipped his head and accepted her kiss.

There was one place Joshua Falcon was not one hundred percent in control and that was in the bedroom. She needed him to respond to her without restraint, and he did. Jessie didn't want to analyze why it had become important but with every breath she took, she wanted to know that, in this, she had power over him. That she could make him melt in her arms. She felt the stiffness in his shoulders gradually ease. His lips felt warm, alive. Her body jolted with the erotic touch of his tongue against hers. His arousal was even more potent; she felt his erection through her Lycra leggings.

She moaned into his mouth and, after a minuscule pause, Joshua's arm tightened around her back, drawing her up and onto her toes, one hand buried in her hair. She heard the anchoring pencils fall onto her worktable as Joshua bent her backward like a bow, his teeth nipping ravenously on her lower lip.

Suddenly he gripped her wrists and brought them from around his neck taking a step back. His fingers imprisoned the delicate bones. "Come with me, Jessie."

"No. I'm sorry you're disappointed, Joshua. But I have a life, too. My business is important, and when I make a commitment to a client, I damn well keep it."

"You *have* a commitment…" he said harshly, his fingers flexing on her wrists. "To me. Which is far more important."

Jessie twisted out of his hold. His grip hadn't hurt and he let her go immediately. She leaned her hip against her desk and gave him a cool look. Still struggling for a breath, her heart pounded. He was as cold as the spring breeze whipping the trees outside.

"I'll be seeing these clients again next year, and probably the next." His mouth tightened. He got the point. Jessie forged on. "My clients are a long-term commitment, Joshua. By next January you won't even remember my name. I'll be mistress number—" she waved a hand "—whatever." She crossed her fingers behind her back for implying she'd still be around then. By next *month* she wanted him out of her life.

"I'll be gone fourteen days." Joshua searched her face. Jessie had no idea what he was looking for. Capitulation?

"Have a safe trip."

There was a long pause. "I'd like you to do the interior design on the resort I'm buying in Tokyo."

Jessie closed her eyes and sighed inwardly. The multibillion dollar resort in Tokyo was a very big carrot to dangle indeed.

"I prefer residential to commercial." She hardened

her heart. She had a bad habit of believing she knew
what he was thinking and invariably ended up being
wrong. There wasn't a needy bone in this man's body.
If Joshua wanted her in Tokyo, it was for his convenience.

He'd told her what a good hostess she was, how well
she fit in with his business associates and their wives
and mistresses. Fine. Well, this time, he could do his
entertaining on his own. She had other things to do and
people who needed her immediate attention. Besides it
was *his* fault she had PMS.

She leaned over her desk and snagged her day plan-
ner. "Let's coordinate this trip and I'll make time—"

"By the time you've thought about it," Joshua stated
in a voice sharp enough to chip ice, "I'll have contracted
Evelyn Van Roosmalen to do the job." He fastened the
buttons on his navy-blue cashmere coat and strode to the
door. "I beg no woman, Jessie." He reached for the
doorknob. "You only had to tell me once. I won't ask
you again."

"Joshua—" The door shut quietly behind him.
"Damn!" Jessie spun her chair around before sprawling
inelegantly in it. "Damn and double damn."

JOSHUA PUSHED AWAY the paperwork he'd been trying
to concentrate on for three hours. Damn her. She was
his mistress, for Christ's sake. What in the *hell* did she
want? He'd never had a mistress who made him feel as
if he were jumping through flaming hoops. And she did
it seemingly without guile.

She never complained, usually complied and rarely
caused even a ripple in his normal workday. He'd become used to her waiting for him at his house in the
evening. Used to the novelty of helping her prepare a

meal in his kitchen. Damn well complacent about having her in his bed at night.

He felt annoyingly uncomfortable making Jessie get up to go home. Usually *he* left the woman right after sex. But she refused to let him sleep at her place.

Somehow, spending the entire night with a woman had always implied an intimacy he'd never wanted, a level of trust he'd never experienced. This way the sex act was easy—fast, satisfying and impersonal. Intimacy was different. Intimacy required vulnerability, loss of control.

It was probably a good thing the affair with Jessie Adams was over.

Joshua stared at the clouds drifting by the window of his 727. The pressurized cabin was cool, the way he liked it. Except that he could smell the faint scent of Jessie's perfume on the still air. She hadn't been on his plane since the trip to Greece. The aircraft had been cleaned several times since then and yet her fragrance lingered still. That annoyed him. Joshua scrawled a note to himself to inform the flight crew to make sure the plane was scrubbed down after every flight. His pen pressed so hard he gouged the paper.

He'd been forced to be emotionally independent early in life. He'd learned the lesson well. It was damn hard for him to trust anyone. But, damn it, he wanted to trust Jessie. He wanted it badly enough to relax his guard once in a while, like a dog belly-crawling for a pat instead of the stick.

From the hidden speakers came the faint sound of a dreamy Brahms waltz. Something Jessie would love to dance to, her tall, slender body pressed against his chest, her arms stealing up around his neck, her fragrant hair tickling his chin as she hummed along, out of tune, with the music. Joshua laid his head back against the velvety nap of his seat and squeezed his eyes shut against a headache starting to throb in his temples.

How dare she presume that he would come running back when she clicked her fingers. Like a goddamn lapdog. He didn't need her. He didn't need any woman, least of all her. She was too tall, her breasts were too damn small....

Joshua wished to God he hadn't thought of her breasts. Which, of course, like everything else about the woman, fit him to a tee.

He wished he'd never met her. Never tasted her soft, pouty mouth, never held her in his arms or felt her velvety skin beneath his hand. Never had her slick and panting under him, crying his name as her slender body convulsed time and again.

He hadn't become a millionaire by being dictated to by anyone. He called the shots and people obeyed or were eliminated from his equations. He made a thousand competent decisions a day. Had thousands of people working for him who considered his word law. Jessie Adams was dangerous. She reminded him of things he'd never had.

He'd left Jessie five hours ago and already his body ached for her. Joshua gripped the armrests with fingers that turned white. He was getting too involved. It wasn't emotional, of course. But his body craved hers like a drug. He'd never before bedded a woman as sexually compatible. That was all it was.

If any one of a number of other mistresses in the past had done to him what Jessie had done today, that would have been the last time he'd have seen her.

Hell, he hadn't seen his *mother* since she walked away from him when he was kid. And he was a lot less forgiving now. He'd been shunted between two hedonistic, uncaring people who had the misfortune to be parents. His mother's pregnancy had been cold-bloodedly calculated to snag Joshua's very wealthy and totally unromantic father. Wife number five, the only wife to give him a child. The marriage endured for three years. Joshua had been the pawn in their power-play game of revenge.

Neither wanted him. Both fought over him. He wasn't being volleyed from parent to parent for anything other than power and money. If his father had him, his mother toed the line. If his mother had him, her expenses skyrocketed as she squeezed his father mercilessly. Until his Uncle Simon and the family lawyer had insisted young Joshua be sent to boarding school where he wouldn't expect anyone to care and therefore would never be disappointed.

He'd never seen his mother again. His father had died of a massive coronary when Joshua was seventeen.

Joshua pushed himself upright and drew the papers on his desk closer. To hell with Jessie. She wasn't worth all this introspection. When he said jump to a mistress, she sure as hell better ask how high.

He paused, his eyes on the phone at his left hand. He could call her and give her one more chance. He'd make sure she understood she'd been given a reprieve. It was damn inconvenient when he was so busy to be looking for another bed partner.

Joshua picked up the phone.

JUGGLING TWO BAGS of groceries Jessie managed to open the back door into her kitchen as the phone started ringing. Rushing, she set the bags down. Her heart gave an illogical leap. *Joshua.* Apples rolled from the bag and her eggs landed, box open, to splatter on the tile floor. The second her hand touched the receiver the ringing stopped.

Jessie picked up the phone anyway. For a moment she stood there in her kitchen, eggs slithering across her clean floor as she clasped the phone and its dial tone to her chest. Her heart was beating much too fast for a short sprint across her kitchen.

Jessie carefully hung up phone.

MAY

JOSHUA HAD NOT called once in the three weeks he'd been gone. There had been an unusual amount of hang-ups—people not leaving messages. But Jessie knew that Joshua would always have something pithy to say to her machine when she wasn't there. The hang-ups were just coincidences.

Joshua's absence was intolerable. Once again her *C* days had come and gone while he was somewhere else. Damn him, the least he could have done was call. He'd been gone a week longer than he'd said.

The enormous black wrought-iron gates slid open, the gold Falcon, wings spread, parted in the middle as she drove her five-year-old Toyota up the herringbone brick driveway to the house.

Joshua's home was a two-story English Tudor set on six acres of prime real estate just south of San Francisco. Behind the stone wall surrounding the property, emerald-green lawns and deep flower beds, filled with a brilliant profusion of spring bulbs, lined the long entry to Joshua's very private estate.

The weeks he'd been gone had crept by, no matter how busy she kept herself. He hadn't even bothered to call her himself this morning. One of his secretaries had called and set up an "appointment" for Thursday evening at seven. Typical Joshua. He was still ticked off that she hadn't gone with him. Jessie wasn't going to tell him how close she'd been to hopping a commercial jet and surprising him in Tokyo.

She was starting to get desperate. Perhaps she shouldn't limit their sexual encounters to just her fertile days. Perhaps she should go with what her body was telling her and have sex as often as she could. The law of averages made a compelling argument for increasing her chances of conception.

She parked beside a brilliant bed of pink parrot tulips, right over the drip pan Barlow had discreetly supplied weeks ago. She grinned.

The crisp breeze played with her hem as she hopped out of the car. Perhaps she should have worn something a little more conservative. She looked like a wild gypsy with the brilliantly colored, ankle-length, ruffled skirt and off-the-shoulder blouse. Hardly appropriate clothing for May, but she'd changed so many times before coming, she finally decided she needed the added confidence of the bright colors.

Her hair was its usual wild, curly tangle around her shoulders and the air currents ruffled through it as Jessie sprinted up the shallow brick steps curving up to the massive black front doors. She shivered. The spring air felt crisp on her bare arms and caused the gold charms on her hooped earrings to tinkle softly as they brushed against her cheeks.

The doors were slightly ajar. She rubbed her arms briskly as she stepped into the dim entry hall checkered in black-and-gray Italian marble. She'd been here so many times, she knew her way around the mansion by heart.

She'd love to redecorate the house out of its official, cookie-cutter, corporate mold. Bold colors, she thought, her skin adjusting to warm air as she closed the front door behind her. Teal and sienna, gold and royal purple. She'd strip the tall windows of their fussy layers of draperies. Let the sunlight pour in to warm both house and man.

Jessie's heels clicked across the marble, dulled a little on the polished parquet of the corridor and then became muffled on the thick burgundy carpet of the formal living room. Every one of his homes carried the same corporate colors as his office, planes and yacht.

Joshua stood at the Palladian windows at the far end of the room overlooking the rose garden. Outside, the gardeners had turned on the sprinkler system. Water sparkled in lazy swoops across the freshly mowed lawn. Other than dropping the sheer back across the window, he didn't acknowledge her arrival.

"I'm here," she said unnecessarily, tossing her purse onto the white brocade sofa and stepping up behind him. Her heart suddenly pounded with anticipation, her mouth dry. Obviously her body had made up her mind for her.

More sex, more often.

He didn't turn around as she slid her arms around his waist. His stomach contracted, his only acknowledgment. Rock hard under her fingertips, his skin felt warm, alive. Jessie rested her cheek against his broad back. "How was your trip?"

"Profitable."

"Did you get any rest?" Jessie felt the exhaustion dragging at his shoulders beneath her cheek.

"I'm not a child. I know my own limitations."

"No, you don't," Jessie scolded as she felt his stomach clench under her hands. "You push yourself to the very edge. One day you should play hooky with me and smell the roses."

"I suggested that, you declined."

"Japan?" Jessie tried to turn his large body. He remained like a blasted rock. "Tokyo wouldn't have been playing hooky, Joshua. You probably worked eighteen-hour days, and I would have been sightseeing and waiting in a hotel room for you to come to me. Come upstairs, and I'll help you relax." Jessie ran her hands up his flat stomach, pressing a series of kisses on his back.

"Is sex all you think about, Jessie?"

Jessie gave a soft, incredulous snort of laughter. "Talk about the pot calling the kettle black." He had no idea how close to the truth he was.

"We've been apart for three weeks, and all you can think about is going upstairs and having sex."

The smile died on Jessie's face. "Good Lord. You're serious." She moved a step away from him. "Joshua, I can tell how exhausted you are. I just wanted to help you relax. That doesn't always mean we have to make love."

"Have sex."

"Make love, damn it. I missed you more than you'll ever know. And that has nothing to do with sex." *Oh God. Where had that come from?* Jessie thought, panicked.

"I don't want you to love me."

"I know." Jessie squeezed her eyes shut. *I'm trying not to.*

"And I'll never love you. From observation, love isn't all it's cracked up to be. It binds you, strips away your pride and strength with nothing in return."

"You've had more experience. I'll take your word for it," Jessie hedged. "But I did miss you holding me. Turn around. Kiss me. Please, Joshua." Her voice sounded thick. Her heart took up a dull, heavy beat as he remained facing the window before turning around slowly. He looked down into her upturned face, using a finger to trace the curve of her cheek.

The feel of his fingers on her face was unbearably tender. A contradiction to the rock hard look in his pale eyes.

"*Did* you miss me, Jessie?"

"Yes. Very much." She ached for him to wrap his arms around her, to hold her close to his broad chest. She uselessly yearned to have him welcome her into his arms. Every time they were apart, it seemed to Jessie as if they had to start again from square one. The man had the worst timing of anyone she knew.

He dropped his hand from her face, reaching into his jacket pocket and withdrawing a glossy black paper bag with gold corded handles. "Here."

She looked at the bag. Jewelry wasn't what she wanted from him. "I told you I don't want you to keep buying me things, Joshua." She refused to take it from him. "Don't make me feel…cheap."

He ran his knuckle down her cheek as he stared down at her meditatively. "No, you're not cheap, are you, Jessie?"

"I'll stay for as long as it suits us both, but I won't be bought." Her cheek was immediately cold as he dropped his hand.

"Just open the damn thing. It's no big deal."

Jessie didn't care about the present. Why hadn't he kissed her? Was this his way of punishing her for not joining him on his trip? She absently took the bag from him, and inserted her hand into the iridescent, gossamer-thin paper inside.

She pulled out a delicate rose quartz box the size of her palm. It was crusted with pearls, what looked like pink diamonds and intricately woven gold leaves. It was feminine, delicate and quite unlike anything he'd given her before.

"It's exquisite." Jessie looked up at him. *Please don't just stand there with that hateful cold look on your face.* "Thank—"

"Open it."

Jessie clicked open the lid. Inside, nestled on a bed of blush-pink satin lay two pale green spheres, each about three quarters of an inch across. Earrings. She lifted one from the box. It moved in her hand. Jessie stared at it. Not an earring. It had no back to it.

"Marbles?" she asked, puzzled. She flattened her palm, and the small ball rolled across her hand.

"Benwa balls," Joshua told her.

Jessie put the thing back into its box, then gave him a puzzled look. "Benwa balls?"

"You insert them into your vagina," Joshua said, watching her face. "You'll have continuous orgasms when we're apart."

Jessie pulled a face. "Sounds exhausting. Think I'll pass."

"These particular benwa balls were hand carved over a thousand years ago." He removed both balls from the box. "Give me your hand. See how they move? That's because they've been carefully weighted so that they'll continually shift inside you. They're made from white jade found in Myanmar, Burma. This particular jade is called moss in snow—see the little flecks of darker green? They're said to have magical powers."

"Well, anything that can give a woman multiple orgasms without human contact, must," Jessie said with a small smile. "But if these things are over a thousand years old I'd hate to think how many women have…used them. Ew. Thank you for the gift, but I'll *definitely* pass."

Joshua took the box from her and inserted the jade balls. He snapped the lid closed then shoved the box in his pocket. "They're nonporous and sterilized. Do you think I'd give you anything that would harm you?"

"No. But I'd still prefer to have something as intimate as that in its original, sanitized, shrink-wrapped packaging, thank you very much."

"Go upstairs and wait for me," he said coldly. "I have to make a few calls."

Jessie gave him a narrow-eyed look before turning on her heel and leaving the room. She left a drift of Joy and disappointment in the room behind her like an invisible ghost.

He should have given her more diamonds. She'd liked the earrings he'd given her for Valentine's day. The benwa balls had been too intimate, too personal. He'd been thinking of her pleasure. The antiquities had cost enough to support a small nation, and she'd dismissed their value as casually as she would a Cracker Jack box toy. He'd seen the disappointment in her eyes when she'd opened the damned box. She'd expected jewelry. Something she could wear and show off. Damn. He rubbed the ache between his eyes.

Once when he'd been about twelve, he'd given his mother a purple leather coat. It had cost him his month's allowance and humiliating hours trying to choose the one he knew she would like. The memory of her laughter made him cringe to this day. The color, of course, had been all wrong with her skin tones and didn't he know that she had wanted a red fox fur, for God's sake?

His mother had returned the coat and kept the money. The look on Jessie's face had frozen his marrow in exactly the same way as it had frozen all those years ago. Joshua hadn't liked it then, and he sure as hell wouldn't tolerate it now.

He'd watched her bounce in, her bright figure reflected in the small baroque mirror on the wall beside him. He'd squeezed his eyes shut as her fragrance drifted closer and closer. God, when she'd walked in, he hadn't been able to turn around without making an absolute ass of himself.

If he had, he would've grabbed her and held on tightly. He would've inhaled the sweet familiar fragrance of her hair and brushed his mouth across her velvety check. He'd ached so, missing her.

His need for her was alarming. Jesus. What the hell *was* this? It was more than sex. He was addicted to the taste and feel of Jessie. Addicted to the touch of her hands. Hell, he didn't care where she touched him. Didn't care whether it was sexual or not. He wanted her hands on him.

He'd just realized since meeting her that the only time anyone had touched him in his life had been purely by necessity, for sex, or by accident. Who would have thought that touching could become so damn addictive? When he was with Jessie he felt as uncontrolled as the boy he'd once been trying to hug his mother without blubbering like an infant.

It was easy for Joshua to express himself with sex. Sex was physical, immediate, the meaning unmistakable. His insatiable desire for Jessie was a clear indication of his… Joshua grit his teeth. *What?* God only knew, noth-

ing as clear cut and simple as physical desire described
what he felt for the infuriating woman upstairs.

He didn't understand this emotional churning, or the
mental upheaval of titanic proportions he'd been experiencing in the months since he'd met her. Instinct
warned he was in way over his head and sinking fast.

He glanced at his watch. Eleven minutes had passed.
He turned for the stairs, warning himself to slow down
and not appear more eager than was financially advisa-
ble. The woman turned him inside out, but she didn't
have to know it.

Joshua winced when he recalled his crude question to
her about just thinking about sex. Christ. *He* was the one
who thought of nothing else. He walked slowly up the
curving staircase, his footsteps as heavy as that frozen
rock in his chest.

Only the light beside the bed broke the darkness. The
room was empty. He could hear water running in the
bathroom. Joshua shrugged out of his jacket and loosened his tie. He and Jessie had never taken a bath together. Their coupling was always too fast and hard to
waste a moment. Joshua felt his arousal despite the bone-
weary exhaustion that dragged at his shoulders and made
every step seem a mile.

He envisioned Jessie up to her pink nipples in foaming
water, holding out her arms to him wearing bubbles and
a smile. She'd be slick with water and desire. He moved
into the luxuriously appointed bathroom.

She was still fully clothed. The brilliant orange, red
and yellow skirt trailed onto the black-carpeted floor as
she sat on the top step near the edge of the tub, her
fingers testing the water.

"You're not naked," he said more harshly than he

intended. Steam had made her hair curl more tightly and filmed her face and neck with a pearlescent glow.

"Not yet." She stood and wiped her hands on a towel she'd draped on the heated rack next to the sunken tub. She moved toward him with that lithe, catlike grace that made his mouth water and his penis stand to attention. Her fingers finished loosening his tie, tossing it behind him where it landed in the doorway.

She stripped off his shirt, tossing it the way of his tie. Her hands felt cool against his stomach as she unbuttoned, unzipped and managed to draw down his shorts with his pants.

"What d—"

Jessie stopped him midword. "Joshua?" She curved her palm against his cheek.

"What!"

"You're behaving like a jerk." She reached up on her tiptoes and gently kissed his mouth. "I know you're tired. Just don't say anything for a while, okay?"

His forehead dropped to rest on hers, and his arms looped around her slender waist. "Jesus, Jessie," he groaned. "What are you doing to me?"

"Tonight, let me be a friend, even if you are behaving like an ass." She methodically removed the rest of his clothing. "The closer we get, the harder you try to push me away. Sometimes you push too hard and it hurts. So, tonight, we'll just be friends."

Joshua bracketed her face with both hands, closed his eyes as if in pain and then opened them to look down at her, a half smile curving his mouth. "What will my 'friend' do when she sees how aroused I am?" he asked on a huff of air.

Jessie grinned. "Oh, I'm friends with that part, too. Don't worry, I can control my baser side."

"Shoes?" he asked, amused by her enthusiasm. "The shoes come off before the pants, darling." Joshua buried his fingers in her hair as she knelt at his feet. Impatient with how methodical she was being, he cupped her face. "Stand up, Jessie."

She rose slowly, hitching up her blouse where it drooped off one slender pale shoulder. Her dark eyes grew heavy lidded as he stroked the warm, damp skin of her neck, then slipped the elastic farther down her arm.

"I know I don't always respond to you appropriately," he said softly as she looked up at him warily. The woman turned him inside out. "But can we be 'friends' later?" he murmured roughly, "As much as slow turns me on, I need you hard and fast right now. It's been too damn long."

As he talked, he stripped her naked. Despite the blustery weather, she hadn't worn much. Her gypsy-girl outfit was more color than substance. She wore no underwear. Joshua groaned, kicking off his shoes as his mouth hungrily sought hers.

Jessie pulled his head closer, kissing him openmouthed. He swiftly turned the kiss into a prolonged, nonverbal apology.

He felt *very, very* apologetic.

They sank onto the carpeted steps running the length of the deep Jacuzzi tub. Joshua lay back, and Jessie straddled his hips, holding herself over his erection until she was comfortably situated. "You don't get to call the shots tonight. It's my turn. Just lie there and let me do my thing. Now, put your arms out on either side of you where I can see them, and don't touch."

Joshua's mouth watered as he let his gaze travel from her wild hair, down the smooth satin of her skin. She lifted her arms to shake back her hair, baring the slender length of her throat and the gentle slope of her breasts. He reached for her, but she gently pushed his hands away. "Uh-uh. Tell me what you want. I'll give it to you."

He stretched his arms out along the step. "I want to taste your nipples."

She arched her back, leaning forward, hands braced on the step near his head. Her dark, fragrant hair fell in a silky curtain around their heads. Her nipple was hard and puckered as she brushed his lips with first one and then the other. God, she was responsive. Joshua latched on to one hard point on her next pass and gently closed his teeth around the bud, then laved it with his tongue. She moaned low in her throat, and he felt the shudder run through her body. He nuzzled his face between her sweet breasts, inhaling the heady fragrance of an aroused Jessie.

"Go down on me, Jessie," he begged, his voice almost unrecognizable.

"Kiss me first," Jessie said thickly. "Kiss me as if you're thirsty, and I'm water." Her slightly parted lips brushed his mouth. Eager to taste her, Joshua allowed Jessie to take the initiative. Her tongue slicked along the seam of his lips and he opened his mouth to her. She tasted achingly familiar. For a moment, he couldn't bear to move as she brushed her soft lips over his and tasted him with her tongue.

"I'm dying of thirst here, Jessie. More."

Her husky laugh tickled his lips. She angled her head and tunneled her fingers through his hair, holding him where she needed him, not that he was going anywhere. Joshua dug his fingers into the thick pile of the carpet, resisting the overwhelming need to touch her velvety soft skin.

She kissed him back boldly, aggressively. Her tongue mated and dueled with his until his erection jerked and bobbed against his leg.

They were both breathing hard when she lifted her head. Their eyes met for a moment, then, keeping eye contact, Jessie slid down his body, supple and eager.

Joshua's head fell back on the thickly padded stair as her hair flowed like summer rain across his chest. Stomach. Groin. *Ah, Jesus…* She knelt between his legs, naked and glorious, her pale body luminous against the matte blackness of the carpet.

Jessie.

Her fingers were cool as she tested the weight of his balls in one hand, while with her other she brought the tip of his penis into contact with the slick, wet heat of her mouth. And, all the while, her big, brown, beautiful eyes watched his face.

As delicate as a cat, she licked the bead of moisture from the tip, then ran her tongue down the length of his erection as though it were a Popsicle. She wrapped her cool fingers around the base, and his nostrils flared and teeth gritted at the exquisite sensation. He bit back a groan and dug his fingers into the carpet to anchor himself.

Jessie.

Her lips worked the swollen head of his shaft as though she'd done this a million times before. Her eyes lost focus as she concentrated on pleasuring him.

She drew her slick tongue down the length, and then took the head into her mouth and sucked hard. Joshua's shoulders came up off the step, and he let out a feral growl of pleasure.

He grabbed Jessie's slender shoulders and pulled her up the length of his body.

"Not good?" she asked crawling up the rest of the way on her own.

"Too good." His erection demanded relief, it bobbed and stroked her flat belly with a mind of its own. "Top or bottom?"

"Top," Jessie decided, voice thick. She took his shaft in one hand and guided it home.

6

JESSIE GLANCED at the clock on her nightstand as she finished dressing for the party. For once she might be ready when Joshua arrived. Grabbing the yellow clutch that matched her dress, she dashed downstairs to her studio to put the finishing touches on the presentation she'd been working on for the past week. It was a nice commission, one she wanted to close.

Despite Archie and Conrad being good friends, they were also her bosses. She'd hardly been bringing in enough to cover her paycheck in the past few months, and she was starting to feel guilty.

When Conrad had hired a new designer for the team a month ago, he'd been quick to assure Jessie that she still had her job. The architectural design firm was simply growing.

It was. Jessie knew that, but she felt guilty all the same. Getting out of bed at 3:00 a.m and then getting out of bed to go to work again at 7:00 a.m. was hardly conducive to a good night's sleep. She was starting to feel the strain.

But neither by word nor deed did she intend Joshua to know that. She'd just have to become more organized.

They spent almost every night together, and every morning at three, Jessie drove herself home. It was ridiculous, not to mention inconsiderate, to wake the chauffeur to have him drive her back to the cottage at the crack of dawn. She didn't care how much he was paid.

That time of the morning was the loneliest Jessie ever felt. If sometimes she needed to cry on the drive home, she wanted to do so in private. Almost five months of being Joshua's lover, and she still wasn't pregnant. The spare room was overflowing with baby stuff. A white wicker crib, a high chair, toys, clothes, books.

She'd tossed out the calendar and the basal thermometer. If rabbits could do it then so could she. The fact that she wasn't pregnant wasn't for lack of trying. Joshua couldn't seem to get enough of her and Jessie was afraid to analyze too closely what was going on in her own mind.

She stuck her client's paperwork, which she hadn't even glanced at, back in the file so she could get up and pace. High heel sandals picking up speed from the doorway to the far wall and back again.

"What am I doing?" she asked herself in disgust before flopping inelegantly into the comfortable chair by the window. There was no point anticipating failure. It wasn't over yet. She still had more than half her "contract" time left. She'd just never thought she'd *need* this much time.

TONIGHT THEY WERE attending an engagement party and Jessie was curious to meet his friends.

"How do you know this couple?" She leaned against the brass handrail in the elevator; it felt cool on her bare back. She wore a bias-cut, silk charmeuse dress and huge dull gold earrings that dangled almost to her bare shoulders.

"Guy works for me. I've never met Ginny."

"How long—" Jessie's eyes widened as Joshua took

two steps to close the space between them the moment the elevator doors closed on the parking garage.

"There can't be a yard of material in that dress."

She clasped her hand around his wrist in warning, glancing at the flashing numbers above the door. "Behave yourself."

"You look absolutely delectable in yellow, Miss Adams," Joshua said huskily, surveying her from very close up. His hand went to the back of her neck. "What happens if I undo this little button right here?"

Undoing the halter neck would get him a pair of naked breasts against his chest. Which was exactly his intention. Jessie's fingers tightened around his wrist. He grinned wickedly, hesitated, then removed the threat of his hand.

"You're creasing me," she admonished, grateful the party was in the penthouse, seventy-two stories up, and they were alone in the elevator. She wasn't sure she would have stopped him.

"Silk doesn't crease," he assured her, nuzzling her neck. Her short, sassy skirt rustled over net petticoats. Jessie trembled as he pressed her gently against the elevator wall, her breasts flattened against the hard plane of his chest. He'd been in New York for the last three days and arrived home barely in time to change and pick her up tonight.

"We have about forty seconds before this elevator door opens. I'm just making the most of them," he murmured, a breath away from her mouth.

"I wish we'd stayed home." Jessie fluttered her long eyelashes. "Why'd we have to come to this dumb old party anyway?"

Joshua grinned. "For a bright brunette, you certainly do a great dumb blonde."

"Hey," she said indignantly, leaning into him. "I was flirting."

"You were asking for trouble."

She smiled seductively. "Have I come to the right place for it?"

Joshua made a sound deep in his throat as he lowered his head. Jessie tilted her chin, offering her mouth. He brushed his open mouth against hers, then stroked her lips with his tongue.

She had a vague thought that she was playing with fire, but his mouth was so seductively sweet all thought of propriety fled. He exuded pheromones like a musky cologne and her body chemistry always responded.

Jessie slid her hands beneath his jacket to stroke his back. He kissed her harder, tilting her head back so he could slant his mouth and deepen the kiss. She whimpered helplessly.

He lifted his lips from hers a fraction of an inch, his breath warm on her face. "One more taste before the doors open."

"Living dangerously, Mr. Falcon?" She could feel how much he wanted her. His need was in the depth of his kiss, in the press of his body against hers, in the urgency of his hands. The rigid length of his arousal pressed hard against her.

When the elevator jarred to a stop and the doors slid open, Joshua straightened the halter straps, used his thumb to remove her smudged lipstick from her mouth and then his own.

A dozen laughing, talking people got into the elevator on the next floor of the garage. They were clearly going to the same party. The fragrance of expensive cosmetics and perfume filled the small space. Jessie moved closer to Joshua and he pressed her back into the corner, a wicked gleam in his pale eyes.

"Hold the elevator!" a voice yelled.

Joshua slid his hand up Jessie's thigh. Under her skirt. Eyes opened wide she shot him a startled look. He gave her a sexy smile and kept on going.

Jessie grabbed his wrist and tried to pull his hand away.

"Thanks," the guy said, ushering three more people into the already crowded car.

What do you think you're *doing?* Jessie's eyes demanded as Joshua's fingers slid inside the elastic leg of her panties. He gave her an innocent look back. He stroked a finger in the crease between leg and mound. Her knees went weak. "Stop it!" she mouthed.

Everyone in the elevator was laughing and talking and watching the numbers above the door. Joshua was the only one turned her way. Still… His finger slid inside her.

Jessie's knees went weak. His foot came between hers, and gently spread her feet apart.

Jessie licked her lower lip, then squeezed her eyes closed as he inserted a finger deep between her slick folds. Oh. My. God. Her petticoats rustled around his arm.

All it needed was one person to turn around…one person to look…

A second finger joined the first. She bit her tongue to prevent the moan from escaping, and leaned back into the corner. His thumb brushed her clit. Jessie shuddered. *Brush harder.* She felt the coils tighten. His fingers were deep inside her, and her muscles tightened and spasmed around them as he played her clitoris like a master. Her body throbbed, her nipples clearly, visibly aroused behind a thin layer of silk. She was beyond ready to come. How could so many people just be *standing* there, oblivious to what he was doing to her?

His fingers slid in and out. Faster. Faster. Faster.

Jessie came in a dizzying rush. Her back thumped against the wall, and she pressed her hand over her mouth so she didn't shriek with pleasure.

Everyone around them continued chatting and laughing.

Jessie's muscles tightened as Joshua removed his hand. She flashed a glance at the numbers over the door. Seventieth floor.

His hand was back. No way. In a few seconds that door was going to open and everyone would spill out. She was not going to get caught with Joshua's hand up her skirts and down her panties.

Something cool rolled passed her clit...and again something. She felt a weight deep inside and her muscles automatically tightened in response. She met Joshua's eyes. "What...?" she mouthed.

He smiled.

The door dinged, then slid open.

Everyone poured out, leaving Joshua and Jessie behind.

Joshua had his handkerchief in one hand. He offered her his other hand. Jessie took it, and stepped forward. Oh, my God.

The benwa balls shifted and slid inside her. She stumbled, holding on to Joshua's hand for dear life. Her vaginal muscles clamped down hard. She shot him a narrow-eyed look.

"I'm operating these things without a license, and without instructions," she said between her teeth. "I'm going to get you for this, Falcon."

They followed the noise to the open doors of the penthouse. He smiled, tucking his damp hankie back in his pocket. "All you need to know is muscle control. You can do it."

"Easy for you to say," Jessie groused. "You're not the one walking like a duck."

"I am walking with a limp, however. I haven't seen you in seventy-two hours. God, I missed you."

The unexpected flash of a camera captured Jessie and she started to laugh. "Oh, no, the paparazzi are here." She got the giggles. "Oh, Lord. What if these damn things fall out and roll across the floor?"

"They won't." Joshua squeezed her hand against his body. "Everyone's going to see that picture and want to have you."

"I'll have to tell them I'm taken 'til December." Jessie looked around for a familiar face, trying to concentrate on anything but what was happening to her body. Those benwa balls certainly produced an odd sensation. The more she walked, the more they slid around and the hornier she became.

"Rat," she grumbled under her breath as a nice little aftershock traveled up her spine and she pressed their clasped hands against her aching breast.

He smiled. "Thank me later."

The balls did a slow shimmy. Jessie tightened her pc muscles. Oh, brother. Wasn't this going to be an interesting evening?

There were several of her clients and a few other people she recognized. She turned back to him. He had the strangest look on his face. His playful mood of moments ago evaporated. Once again he was The Glacier. Now what?

Raising her voice above the noise, she stepped closer

to Joshua as people surged around them. The balls danced around a bit, then settled when she stood still. Good. Stay that way. "Which is the engaged couple?"

"The joyous couple over by the ice sculpture." Joshua indicated with a nod. He slid his arm around her waist, anchoring her to his side.

"The blonde in the blue dress and the tall guy?" Jessie observed the newly engaged pair as they gestured angrily, oblivious to their guests. In the din, it was impossible to hear what they were saying, just observe how they were saying it.

"That's a photograph I'd put in the dictionary under *divorce*."

"They're not married yet," Jessie reminded him. He *was* in a strange mood.

"Yeah, well, it won't last if they already argue in public like that."

"Not all marriages end in divorce."

"Just more than fifty percent."

"That means almost fifty percent are *happy*."

Joshua touched her cheek. "The half-full glass theory?"

"Works for me."

"Let's agree to disagree." Joshua's hand lingered on her cheek. Jessie searched his face for a clue to his mood. "We'll drink some of their, no doubt, excellent champagne then go home. How does that sound?"

Every opportunity sounded promising to Jessie. "I'd rather have you in me than these million-year-old balls."

Joshua chuckled. "Me, too."

She looked wistfully at the elegantly draped tables groaning under elaborate canapés and soaring ice sculptures. "The food looks good." She shot him a mischievous grin. "How about this, we grab something to eat *before* we push our way over there, say congratulations…or offer condolences, whichever is more appropriate, and then go home?''

"Smart as well as beautiful. How unusual—damn.''

Jessie followed his gaze and recognized the busty blonde making a beeline toward them. Her photograph had accompanied Joshua's in the press for twelve months the previous year. "Stick by me. I'll protect you," she said dryly.

Joshua looked as suave and debonair as a man could, caught between this year's and last year's models. "Perhaps we should save time. You go and congratulate Guy and Ginny, and I'll tackle Megan.''

Jessie shot him a reproving glance just as the other woman stepped closer. "Megan, hi." Jessie gave her a cheerful smile, stepping a little in front of Joshua, which was a mistake because moving made her little friends dance happily inside her. "I'm Jessie Adams.''

Joshua placed a hand firmly on her waist and eased her back to his side again. Out of clawing range, Jessie presumed. He kept a proprietorial arm around her.

Megan Howell narrowed her baby blues as she glared up at Jessie. "Do I know you?''

"No," Jessie said gently, seeing the high emotion under the other woman's flush. "I recognized you from that great photo of you in the *Inquirer* last December.'' Jessie carefully removed her hand from Joshua's. "I'm sure you want to talk privately with Joshua, so I'll go over and—''

"You might as well hear this." Megan's tone was pure hostility. Jessie moved closer to Joshua, her eyes narrowed on the blonde.

The Glacier was back in full force as Joshua bit out icily, "Say what you have to say and leave Megan.''

"I'm pregnant," Megan said defiantly in a too loud voice as she crossed her arms over her plastic bosom. A very elegant tent dress effectively hid any hint of a baby.

Jessie felt an immediate surge of anger. How dare this woman be carrying Joshua's child! Jessie wanted to rip her lips off.

She felt sick with jealousy and heartsore with disappointment. *Megan* was pregnant. Damn it, it wasn't fair. A heavy lump in her throat made swallowing impossible. She looked up at Joshua. He had a very nasty smile on his face.

"Congratulations. Who's the father?"

"You are, you bastard!" Flashlights popped. "What are you going to do about it?" the blonde demanded, not missing a beat.

"Ask you to lower your voice, for a start," Jessie cut in, for a moment hating them both, "unless you enjoy having your private life speculated about over breakfast. Guy and Ginny have invited every tabloid in the universe to their party. So smile nicely and behave like a lady."

Joshua looked at her as if she had sprouted another head. He turned back to his ex-mistress, his pale eyes frosty. "It's taken you an inordinate amount of time to come up with this, Megan." Joshua tsked. "You used to be much faster than this at cooking up money-making schemes."

"I've talked to your lawyers," Megan snarled, her cheeks scarlet, eyes flashing him a grim warning.

"Wise idea." Joshua rested his hand on the small of Jessie's back. "They no doubt told you about the mandatory DNA test?"

"I refuse to harm my baby just because you don't believe me," she said caustically, glaring up at him.

"DNA testing can be done at twenty weeks, Megan, without doing any harm to the fetus. I'm sure Felix gave you the facts." Joshua rubbed his thumb on Jessie's bare back.

"This is obviously a private discussion," Jessie inserted. "I'll wait for you over by the bar," she added to Joshua over her shoulder. She turned on her heel and walked away.

As if the world hadn't come crashing down around her.

HER LIGHTLY TANNED BACK was very straight when Joshua found her on the other side of the room minutes later. She was by herself, ostensibly looking at one of Guy's nightmarish paintings. She made a spectacular picture herself in the barely there little number that showcased her gorgeous long legs and the sweet curve of her spine.

"Let's go." Joshua came up behind her, resting his hand on her naked back. Her skin was silky smooth, shimmering with vitality.

"Let's say our goodbyes to our hosts first. I think they're done with round nine."

He glanced down at her set expression. "Can you walk okay?"

She shot him a look. "I took them out," she said under her breath. "I had ninety-nine orgasms without you. I didn't like it."

He didn't talk all the way down in the elevator. The paparazzi had gotten off several dozen shots of the three of them, he knew, in just about every configuration. Jessie was going to have a million questions. Hell, if she wanted to know what he and Megan had discussed she only had to buy one of the tabloids in the morning.

She rested her head on his stiff shoulder as he drove. Of course, she wouldn't pull away, Joshua thought bitterly, leaning back against pliant burgundy leather. She was his mistress. Another woman was threatening her cash cow. What the hell, she only had to put up with him another few months and she'd be free as a bird.

Joshua exited the parking garage, staring straight ahead before he said grimly, "She was lying—"

He felt her exhale before she said calmly, "I know."

Joshua looked down at her. The passing streetlights dappled her face, making her expression hard to read. "Did you hear what I said?"

Jessie yawned. "Mmm. The baby isn't yours."

There was a heavy weight in his chest. "How do you know?" His voice almost cracked in the middle of the question. Far from being concerned, Jessie was almost asleep.

She squeezed his waist, snuggling closer. "You just told me."

"You believe me?"

"Of course," she mumbled matter-of-factly, although her voice sounded thick. "You're a man of your word. If you say the child isn't yours, it isn't."

He stared at her. There was no doubt in her voice, or on her even features. She believed him. No ifs, ands or buts. She just…believed him. Unequivocally. A wave of emotion swept through him. Disbelief. Acceptance. And something else too powerful, too impossible, to believe.

Jessie rubbed her cheek on his upper arm, sweetly drowsy as she settled her arm across his waist, eyes closed. "As a matter of curiosity, what would you do if she was pregnant?" she asked in a soft, casual voice.

"Thank God that can be proven one way or another in this day and age—"

"But what if—"

"She just got greedy."

"She's trying to blackmail you?" Jessie asked indignantly, sitting up straighter. "That little b—"

"Felix will take care of her." Joshua tucked her back against his side.

"If he doesn't, *I* will," she said firmly, then snuggled against him again. Her hand stroked lazily up and down his side under his jacket.

Jessie tucked her thumb under his belt as Barlow made a hard right at the corner. When Joshua looked down, her long lashes were casting shadows on her cheeks. He tightened his arm around her slender shoulders and held her close.

"I wish—"

"What do you wish, Jessie?"

He felt her small shrug as she whispered dreamily, half asleep, "A little girl. I'd dress her in clean, pretty clothes and keep her safe. She'd never ever be hungry or afraid." Jessie covered a yawn. "But most of all, I'd just love her."

Joshua felt the ache in his chest tighten a notch. Jessie seemed unaware of what she'd just revealed. He knew firsthand a mother's neglect, but at least he'd had someone to care for his most basic needs. Housekeepers and nannies may not have provided anything more than necessities, but he had been clothed and fed and had never known cold, fear or hunger.

As a child Jessie had known real hunger and very real fear. She seldom spoke about those years. She'd never known if or when her mother would come home. According to Felix, Jessie's mother had been picked up for solicitation a dozen times or more. Where had Jessie gone when her mother was in jail? How had Jessie, who

HOW TO PLAY:

1. With a coin, carefully scratch off the 3 gold areas on your Lucky Carnival Wheel. By doing so you have qualified to receive everything revealed—2 FREE books and a surprise gift—ABSOLUTELY FREE!

2. Send back this card and you'll receive 2 brand-new Harlequin® Blaze™ novels. These books have a cover price of $4.50 each in the U.S. and $5.25 each in Canada, but they are yours ABSOLUTELY FREE!

3. There's no catch! You're under no obligation to buy anything. We charge nothing—ZERO—for your first shipment. And you don't have to make any minimum number of purchases—not even one!

4. The fact is thousands of readers enjoy receiving books by mail from the Harlequin Reader Service®. They enjoy the convenience of home delivery...they like getting the best new novels at discount prices, BEFORE they're available in stores... and they love their *Heart to Heart* subscriber newsletter featuring author news, horoscopes, recipes, book reviews and much more!

5. We hope that after receiving your free books you'll want to remain a subscriber. But the choice is yours—to continue or cancel, any time at all! So why not take us up on our invitation, with no risk of any kind. You'll be glad you did!

A surprise gift

FREE

We can't tell you what it is...but we're sure you'll like it! A

FREE GIFT!

just for playing LUCKY CARNIVAL WHEEL!

Visit us online at
www.eHarlequin.com

LUCKY Carnival Wheel

Find Out Instantly The Gifts You Get Absolutely FREE!

Scratch-off Game

Scratch off **ALL 3** Gold areas

YES! I have scratched off the 3 Gold Areas above. Please send me the 2 FREE books and gift for which I qualify! I understand I am under no obligation to purchase any books, as explained on the back and on the opposite page.

350 HDL DNW2   150 HDL DNWR

FIRST NAME	LAST NAME

ADDRESS

APT.#	CITY

STATE/PROV.	ZIP/POSTAL CODE

Offer limited to one per household and not valid to current Harlequin® Blaze™ subscribers. All orders subject to approval.

(H-B-08/02)

If offer card is missing write to: Harlequin Reader Service, 3010 Walden Ave., P.O. Box 1867, Buffalo, NY 14240-1867

BUSINESS REPLY MAIL
FIRST-CLASS MAIL   PERMIT NO. 717-003   BUFFALO, NY

POSTAGE WILL BE PAID BY ADDRESSEE

HARLEQUIN READER SERVICE
3010 WALDEN AVE
PO BOX 1867
BUFFALO NY 14240-9952

NO POSTAGE
NECESSARY
IF MAILED
IN THE
UNITED STATES

had never known security or trust as a child, grown into a woman who trusted so easily?

He was basically a solitary man. He had a few men he called friends, but they were really just business associates he trusted. He had never had a woman trust him as much as Jessie did, understand him as Jessie did. It was a novel experience. Joshua savored it as Jessie's body relaxed against his. He brushed a strand of hair off her cheek.

She was asleep in moments, her fragrant hair tickling his face as it blew about in the warm breeze through the open window. Well, hell, Joshua thought, wanting to laugh out loud. She believed him. No fuss. No muss. He leaned his head against the plush leather upholstery, closing his burning eyes. How the hell could such an uncomplicated woman be so damned difficult to understand?

When she'd said earlier, oh, so casually, that she was taken until December, he'd checked a surge of anger. She didn't have to be so damn complacent about the temporariness of their arrangement. Joshua scrubbed his face with his hand. She turned him inside out, then left him swinging. And somehow she made him think he liked it!

As the gates to the estate skimmed open, Joshua recalled a conversation he'd had with his lawyer just before he'd left for New York last week. Apparently his wife wanted more money. The only time Joshua ever heard from her was when she contacted Felix to up the ante. A small price to pay for a trouble-free invisible wife.

"Jesus, Felix," Joshua had griped. "What's she trying to do, squeeze me dry?"

Felix had looked serious as he'd handed the paper-

work over for Joshua to sign. "Hardly. You'd give an
employee an annual raise. Why not your wife?"

"I'm giving her enough to support a small country
now, for God's sake!"

He might not remember anything about the girl, but
she *had* served her purpose. He'd made her a promise.
"All right, Felix. Give her what the hell she wants."

He was a man of his word, as many people had
learned to their regret.

Joshua carried Jessie into the house and upstairs without disturbing her sleep. She would be awake soon
enough.

JOSHUA HADN'T MENTIONED Megan Howell all week.
He'd been more intense than usual, more serious. Jessie
thought he watched her as if he were trying to read her
mind.

He called her in the middle of the day several days
after the party and told her to pack a bag. They were
going to Tahoe for a long weekend.

Jessie nibbled the cap of her pen, wrapping the telephone cord around her hand. "How many bedrooms
does your cabin have?" she asked innocently.

"One." Joshua sounded amused. "How many do we
need?"

"That depends on if I have to haul my butt out of bed
at 3:00 a.m.," she said carefully. The cord left red marks
on her fingers and she unwound herself, listening carefully to his tone.

There was a slight pause, so slight that if she hadn't
been listening for something, she wouldn't have heard
it. "I'll throw away the alarm for the weekend."

Jessie laughed. "How soon can you pick me up?"

They flew to Tahoe in Joshua's Lear. He didn't want

to waste time driving. A shiny black Range Rover waited for them at the airfield when they arrived.

The cabin was far from a log shack in the hills. It was built of cedar with a wall of glass facing the north shore of Lake Tahoe. It was luxurious, with an enormous bedroom cantilevered over a naturally terraced lawn. The living room and kitchen overlooked towering pine trees and the shimmering blue lake.

Despite the corporate colors, the cabin was less decorated than his other residences, more casual and conducive to relaxing. And there was only one phone. Jessie was thrilled.

Joshua carried their suitcases into the bedroom and came into the kitchen for a snack. "You know what the best thing about you is?" He nuzzled her neck.

"What?" Jessie ran short nails through his silky, dark hair as he pressed her lower body against the stainless steel sink behind her. She nibbled at his chin.

"You never ask me for anything."

The one thing I want, you haven't been able to give me, Jessie thought, turning her face up for his kiss while her heart squeezed hard. There was no use dwelling on it. When it happened it happened.

His open-neck blue shirt was the exact color of his eyes and she had ogled him the whole time she fixed the cheese-and-tomato sandwiches. "Actually, there is something I want," she teased, her finger trailing to the top button of his shirt.

"Lord, woman, you're insatiable."

"I can't help myself." Jessie pretended to pout. "I just love it." She fluttered her lashes, trying not to giggle. "I think...yep, I think it might be one of my most favorite things in the world."

"Take me, I'm your..." He started dramatically then

narrowed his eyes suspiciously. "Just what *is* it you love, you little tease?"

Jessie laughed. "Gambling." She stood on her tiptoes and twined her arms around his neck. He smelled of pine and clean air, the stiffness had eased from his shoulders while they were in flight, and the lines of strain had left his face by the time they landed. He smiled down at her indulgently, obviously amused and perfectly relaxed. Her eyes sparkled as she lured him closer, still laughing as she avoided his tickling fingers. She danced backward. "Can we go gambling? Can we, huh, huh?"

Joshua laughingly agreed. It was only after they were in the car and halfway around the lake that Jessie said mildly, "I think it's time you bought a pair of jeans. You look as if you're ready to play polo."

"One does not wear summer-weight wool slacks to play polo, Jess. One wears breeches to play polo," he pointed out drolly as he pulled into a frighteningly large shopping mall at Jessie's urging. He couldn't remember when last he'd shopped for clothing for himself. Years. Normally his secretary called a clothier in London or Milan, and they'd send him what he needed.

Clothes shopping with Jessie was a surprisingly pleasant experience. She didn't dawdle about making selections. She knew exactly what she was looking for and didn't linger if the shop they were in didn't have it. Two hours later, Joshua was the recipient of three pairs of jeans and several shirts he wouldn't have looked at twice if he'd been on his own. He'd tried to tell her he only wore blue or white.

Jessie had coerced several mall-walking senior citizens to come into the store to give him *their* opinions. How could he win against Jessie Adams at her best, and several blue-haired little old ladies?

After depositing his new purchases in the hands of the owner of the local laundromat they went to lunch.

"I hate to ask—" Joshua toyed with her fingers on the bare oak table as they waited for their spaghetti to arrive "—but why did we just purchase clothing that needs to be laundered before I wear it?"

"The jeans have to be prewashed a couple of times before they feel slouchy," Jessie said absently as she watched a toddler across the room trying to get into his baby brother's high chair. She smiled at the ensuing drama.

Joshua glanced over his shoulder to see what Jessie was smiling about. He'd never seen quite that look on her face before.

She gave the waiter a soft smile as he set her plate down. The guy almost tripped on his own feet as he became the recipient of the smile Joshua should have gotten. He shot the hovering kid a pointed glare and almost had a plate of pasta and marinara deposited in his lap as the guy gulped and scurried to make himself scarce.

"I love kids, don't you?"

"I don't know. Probably not." Joshua unwrapped his silverware from the paper napkin. "The only ones I've been around seem...disorganized."

He looked up as Jessie burst into peals of laughter. "Disorganized?" She choked. "Of course they're disorganized!" Her eyes were sparkly with mirth. "They're just learning everything. Even *you* were disorganized when you were a little kid."

Joshua thought if he could bottle and sell that laugh he would quadruple his money. "Actually, I wasn't." He pushed the limp spaghetti around his plate. A pool of watery sauce made a moat surrounding the unappetizing lump of his pasta. "I was a well-disciplined, clean, respectful and organized child from as far back as I can remember."

Her eyes got more liquid as that sweet, soft smile quivered then died.

"Good Lord. Don't start crying, for God's sake." He leaned over and wiped away the mascara under her right eye.

Jessie blotted her eyes with her own napkin. "You had a shitty life," she said fiercely. "I wish I could make it all up to you, Joshua."

"My childhood was perfectly acceptable, Jessie. Don't overdramatize it."

"Your mother was a real bitch."

He smiled. "No arguments there. Are you done poking that revolting mess? I'd like to go somewhere and get some real lunch. Then I'll take you to some den of iniquity so you can throw away my money."

Somehow the glow seemed to have gone from Jessie's face. After playing a few hands of blackjack, with the money she had brought for the purpose, thank you very much, she wanted to go home. Joshua liked the sound of that.

"How about going for a walk?" he asked after parking the car in the carport beside the house. He held out his hand for her and she handed him the laundry and an arch look instead.

"Go put on your new jeans and shirt first." She followed him into the house, immediately throwing open all the windows to let in the warm, scented air before she followed him into the bedroom.

"I just love this house." Jessie flopped down on the king-size bed, watching him with hot-chocolate eyes as he changed. "If I ever have a summer house, this is what it would be like. Far enough away from city noises. Nice, clean air.'' She fell onto her back as he struggled with the unfamiliar closure of the jeans. "That fabulous smell of pine and lake water. Fishing. Boating. *Gambling—*"

"Jessie?"

"Hmmm?

"Do you think you could help me with this?" He walked toward her sprawled legs.

Without moving and not bothering to hide the smile tugging at her lips, Jessie asked seriously, "Which do you need help with, sir? The buttons or the erection?"

She was bonelessly relaxed against the burgundy spread. Her left knee rose to bracket his leg as Joshua leaned down so his braced arms framed _er head. "Which do you think?" he asked huskily.

Jessie reached up and gave him a quick peck on the lips before she pushed at his shoulders, her eyes devilish. "I think you need help with those pesky darn buttons so we can go for that walk."

"Touch these buttons and I won't be *able* to walk, woman."

Jessie lectured him on self-control, all the while her nimble fingers enclosing him tighter than a straitjacket behind the row of metal buttons.

"I don't think I like jeans, Jessie," Joshua confessed pitifully as she dragged him outdoors.

Jessie grinned. "They look ma-a-avelous on you, dahling." She hung back then patted his behind. "Great butt." She linked arms with him and gave him a sultry look. "We'll keep them at my house. I don't want you wearing these when I'm not there to beat the women off with a stick."

"That good, huh?" he asked, highly amused. She

gave him a sultry look, and he wondered fleetingly what he had ever done to deserve her and how he had managed for thirty-three years without her.

They walked hand in hand on the lakeshore. The smoldering fire of the sun melted into the water, leaving a dancing, shimmering reminder as dusk stole slowly over the lake. Purple and royal-blue faded into black ridges and ranges, spiked with the suggestion of forest. There was an anticipation of things to come as stars started shining more brightly and the velvety sky darkened to reveal a wisp of a moon.

He took her hands, pulling her against him. She'd changed into black leggings and a thick, white cotton sweater with a wide neckline that kept slipping off her shoulder. Her skin felt cool as he caressed the back of her neck, his thumb finding the vulnerable hollow at her nape. He felt her deep shudder through his bones. God, she was responsive. He touched his lips to her temple.

Jessie turned in his arms, rising up on her toes as she gathered handfuls of his hair in her fists. With a little pressure she brought his face down to hers. "Don't play with me, mister," she warned in a tough voice, and she kissed him, her lips insistent and ravenous.

They eventually had to come up for air. Jessie's dark gaze stayed riveted to his face. "I can hear your mind whirring," he said, amused at her intense scrutiny. "What are you thinking about?" Her lips looked soft and slightly swollen from the kiss. The moonlight loved her face, sculpting it with silver.

She opened her mouth as if to say something; Joshua held his breath for a painful heartbeat. Then she shook her head. "Nothing." She touched his face with a small, cool hand as her eyes seemed to memorize his features. "You make me very happy, Joshua."

He couldn't explain his disappointment. Didn't even try. He dipped his head and feathered a kiss on her closed mouth. She tasted of the rich coffee ice cream they'd bought on the way home. Jessie had eaten more than half the carton in the car and then claimed that the bites she had spoon-fed him had been way bigger than the teeny ones she'd had.

A banner of geese flew across the moon. He turned her and braced her back against his chest. Wrapping his arms about her, he rubbed his hands up and down her arms. "I had no idea," he said into the deep pool of silence, "that I could feel this…content." Jessie stroked her head against his chin, resting more fully against him as he leaned against the trunk of a ponderosa pine, looking at the shimmering lake through a veil of her frothy hair. He added softly, "You make me happy, too, Jessie."

Around them the gentle silence of night drifted as soft as a breeze. The air was warm and fragrant with her floral perfume and the scent of woods and water.

There was nowhere on earth he would rather be than right here, with Jessie in his arms. There was no need for conversation. Even his sexual desire seemed tamed and manageable. He felt…calm. For the first time in memory, he felt strangely at peace with himself.

He had learned his lessons of self-preservation as a child, but with Jessie he found his emotions blatantly *out there*. Sometimes he felt so raw and exposed with her, he wanted to flee back into that same protective, rocky shell he was almost ready to cast aside. And other times, like now, she brought him more joy and contentment than he had ever known.

He didn't want her to know just how vulnerable he

was to her vibrant spirit, her gentle eyes and soft mouth. He felt raw enough as it was.

THE NEXT MORNING Jessie went swimming in the lake. Her suit was perfectly decent. Red. Plain. Skintight. Joshua watched her from the window in the kitchen as she played in the shallows like a child. She wasn't a child. As the three kids in a speedboat noticed, making ever smaller circles closer to shore.

The waves were lapping at Jessie's calves when he came out to join her. "Hi." Her smile was brilliant, white and directed solely at him. "I thought you had calls to make."

"Made." He dragged his eyes from her sun-kissed face to the three teenagers who were a little less cocky now.

"You look good enough to eat," he told her as the boys took off, the wake making her sway against him. The tight Lycra of her suit flattened her breasts, but he could clearly see her hard nipples.

"Finished swimming?"

Jessie looked at him under her lashes. "Got a better idea?"

"How does grabbing a blanket and taking a walk deep into the woods sound?" He wiped away a droplet of water from her temple with his thumb, her skin was sun warmed and damp.

"Why do we need a blanket when we're going for a walk?" His lady had very expressive eyebrows.

JESSIE ROLLED HIM OFF the blanket. A pinecone or something jabbed him in the back as she straddled him, her eyes determined, her hands firmly planted on his chest.

"I don't know why we brought the blanket," Joshua

said mildly, as he shifted his hips and Jessie's off whatever was under his bare back.

"'Cause you thought I'd be on the bottom.'' Jessie pointed out reasonably, her knees nudging his sides.

He reached up to gather her loosened hair back into the scrunchie and out of her face. "Why aren't I on top?"

"You were being too darn fussy." She leaned forward to nibble a damp path up his chest as she spoke. "Everybody knows…one…*never*…bothers to fold their… clothes in the woods."

She reached his jaw, while behind her she slapped at the hand he was using to try to get her hips and other body parts aligned where he wanted them. "I don't want you rushing me," she groused against his throat. "In fact," she took a sharp nip and every nerve in his body stood at attention, "don't touch me at…all."

She gave some attention to his lower lip. "At all?" His hands itched to caress her smooth, damp skin.

"At all," Jessie whispered when they were nose to nose.

"You don't like me to touch you?" he asked. In answer Jessie slid her sweet breasts sensuously across his chest. "Because, darling, I sure as hell love to touch you."

"You will lose control."

Joshua huffed. "Are you telling me or hypnotizing me?" It was damn hard to be amusing when he felt like taking off like a rocket.

"I want to see you lose control. Don't touch." When she paused, he could feel the rush of her blood through her veins as she pressed him down. He closed his eyes, letting his arms fall over his head. "You have too much control," she added.

"There's no such thing as too much control, Jessie," he murmured, using every scrap he had. "Although I must admit, with you I seem to have less control than ever before...."

She looked down into his eyes. "Let me see you lose control, Joshua. Don't think. Just close your eyes and feel." Her small white teeth closed in to give a sharp love bite on his neck before she dragged her body up his and took his mouth in a kiss so sensual, so erotic Joshua had to give himself up. He wanted to howl with the pleasure of it.

He sighed, slitting open his eyes. "Have your wicked way with me." Her nimble fingers slid unfairly up his sides. "I'll only touch if you beg me to."

"I won't," Jessie assured him with false confidence as she nibbled his mouth.

The air smelled of the pine needles she was crushing under her knees. Dusty sunlight filtered through the tall trees, dappling her tanned, lithe body as she drove him wild with a deep, wet kiss. He allowed her to believe she was suppressing him with her small hands pressing his above his head into the leaves and needles that made up their bed.

He had never seen her like this. She tormented him with her mouth. Slowly. Maddeningly. Joshua lay where she had pushed him, half on, half off the blanket. Her eyes got so dark there were almost no pupils. She kissed his cheekbones, his nose, his eye sockets and his forehead before she got down to some serious lip action.

He could smell her sensual woman's essence as she broke contact. He thought he would explode without her moist heat surrounding him. Her breasts heaved as she gulped in air, her hands braced on his chest. She must be able to feel his heart thundering beneath her palm.

Her hair, never tamed, slipped from confinement and tumbled into a dark cloud around her shoulders as she kept her hot center inches away from his straining flesh. She slid slowly down his body, kissing a path toward very dangerous territory.

"This is torture, you know," he groaned as her tongue discovered his navel. He sank his fingers in her hair. She tasted lower. "Jessie—"

"I'm busy!"

He laughed on a huff of frustration as she finally did something about his agony. They probably heard his groan as far away as Sacramento when she skimmed that clever little tongue around his erection.

Joshua gritted his teeth and he closed his eyes, fisting his hands against her scalp. Nothing in his life had ever felt this good.

Cool air blew on a hot place. His eyes shot open. Jessie looked up the length of his body. "Uh...what now?" she asked uncertainly, her short nails digging into his flanks as though if she let him go he would disappear.

Oh, God, she had been doing just fine. Joshua closed his eyes on a prayer before pulling her to sit astride him.

"Whatever you want. Just don't stop," he panted, seconds before she sank home to the hilt. No testing the waters for Jessie. His vision blurred as she started to move. Hot, slick, tight. Agonizingly perfect. He held her hips long enough to start the rhythm.

"I can do it, I can do it," she said through clenched teeth and he let go and left her to it. She was doing a damn fine job.

Her breasts were slick, her nipples dark and fully aroused. "Touch me!" she demanded. He slid his hands up her slim hips to her rib cage, feeling her heart fluttering beneath his fingers like a frantic bird. Fascinated by the absolute concentration on her face, Joshua lost track for a moment. Sweat glistened on her skin, sticking her hair to her cheeks, making her skin glow. Eyes narrowed, her concentration complete, she growled ferally as his hands closed over her breasts. He knew exactly how Miss Adams liked those pert little breasts touched, and he did his humble best.

She rode him with a fierce and beautiful savagery, her rhythm perfect. Her primal mating brought them both to the point of no return before easing up just enough to drive him wild—a high-speed chase over a precipice only to slow down to the speed limit at the last second.

"Your…hands aren't…m-moving."

"I'm in ecstasy." Joshua was polite enough not to remind her of her command.

"You're in *me*," Jessie reminded him, his hands on her hips gently showed her he knew exactly where he was and who he was with bare-ass naked, outside, in broad daylight.

Sweat stung his eyes as she leaned down and bit his shoulder, hard. He knew he would leave fingerprints on her bottom. No one had ever made love to him like this. Hell, he'd never considered making love in the wide-open wilderness until he'd met Jessie.

She was his amazon, a Valkyrie. Pagan in her beauty as she loved him ruthlessly. She was as focused and intense as he had ever seen her. Wild and erotic, as sweat glistened on her skin out here in the woods where any hikers could trip over them. He didn't give a damn.

Her back arched as she took him deep into her womb.

The pleasure was agonizing.

Joshua reached down, touching his fingers to where

they joined. Her stomach muscles clenched as he unerr-
ingly found the small nub.

Eyes tightly closed, Jessie rose and fell, losing mo-
mentum as she got closer and closer to climax. Internal
muscle pulsing around him gave him fair warning.

Bracing her, his hands enormous on her pistoning
hips, Joshua helped her to a faster rhythm. Until she
clenched, curved and cried out his name...

Then she threw back her head and screamed.

7

"COULD YOU EXPLAIN to me, Felix," Joshua asked grimly, looking at his lawyer across the expanse of the other man's desk, "how the hell Vera can run up twenty thousand dollars in bills in one month and I can't even get Jessie to use one credit card?"

"Which one are you angry with?" Felix asked, keeping his eyes off Simon who sat across the room flicking through a magazine.

Joshua had arrived half an hour ago. Accustomed to his uncle's presence in his lawyer's office, Joshua got down to business immediately. That done, he leaned back in Felix's cordovan leather guest chair and stretched out his long legs.

"Neither. Both. Hell, I don't know. I don't give a damn how much Vera spends, you know that. I just wish to hell Jessie would let me do more for *her*."

"Signing over the Tahoe house should do it. Have you told her yet?" Simon asked from across the room.

"No." Joshua rotated his shoulders while squeezing the back of his neck. "I'll wait for the right moment before I give her the deed."

"December?" Felix asked, checking the thick stack of papers Joshua had just signed to make sure his signature was where it was needed.

"It's not a parting gift," Joshua said more harshly than he intended, then modified his tone. "She loves the house. I wanted to give her something…." He smoothed back his hair. "I want to make sure she's taken care of when I… She should have the house," he finished brusquely, having no intention of telling either his lawyer or his uncle how happy he and Jessie had been in the Tahoe house. It was none of their damn business.

And he sure as hell wasn't thinking about what Jessie would be doing after December 23. Giving Jessie the Tahoe house was a smart move. He would never be able to take another woman there without thinking of her. It was logical to give it to her.

"She *seems* content not to be seeing as many clients as she did before." Joshua cleared his scratchy throat. "But it will take her a while to build up her clientele after…later. The property will be a good investment for her." He paused. "Has she said anything to either of you about being bored?" he asked casually, picking up his briefcase.

"No," both men admitted in unison.

"Fine." His tone indicated he was done with the conversation. "I'm on my way to the airport. When I get back from Russia I'll give her the deed."

"Jess going with you?" Simon asked.

"No. I'm not taking her on this trip. The schedule is too grueling, and I don't think she's getting enough sleep as it is. Keep an eye on her while I'm gone, will you, Simon?"

"If I can convince her to make the time to see me," Simon said dryly from across the room. "Every moment she isn't with you is spent at your house. Gives her more time to fool around with that mausoleum you live in and fiddle around in your garden. Never seen her happier."

"Is that enough for her?" Joshua asked, recapping his pen and sticking it in his pocket.

"She enjoys being an interior designer, but I've never gotten the impression she's a career woman. Despite the way she looks, Jessie is a homebody." Felix slipped the paperwork into Falcon's personal file. "Hate to rush you, Joshua, but Simon and I have a date with a racquetball at three, and you said you had a plane to catch."

Joshua glanced at his watch. He had plenty of time to get to the airport. He rose, shaking hands with Felix and resting his hand on his uncle's back as he passed Simon's chair. Clearing his throat, he said briskly, "Bring Patti for dinner next week so you can both see the house. Jessie will have everything finished by then, no doubt." He smiled. "Anyone else would take a year to do what Jessie does in a week. She really has a damn fine talent. I'll have her call Patti to set it up." He turned to Felix. "Rustle up one of your attractive blondes and come, too." He coughed dryly before opening the door.

"Sounds like you have a cold there, son." Simon rose, slapping the magazine he'd been pretending to read on the coffee table.

"Allergies," Joshua dismissed. "I'll see you both sometime next week. Thanks for taking care of this, Felix." Joshua indicated the desk where he'd signed several dozen business contracts and his wife's bills. "Oh, by the way," Joshua turned and said casually to Felix, "where is Vera living now?"

Felix's gaze shot to Simon, then back to Joshua. "Uh…Phoenix, when last I heard. Why?"

"Get her number, will you, Felix? I'd like a word."

The moment the door closed behind him Felix turned to Joshua's uncle. "Holy hell, Simon. What was that all about?"

"God only knows," Simon said with a frown. "We've told him for years how much Vera loves to travel. He'll buy that she's on another trip. An extended trip."

"For how long?" Felix asked. "I'm a lawyer, Simon. Joshua is my client. I could be jailed for conflict of interest here. Or worse."

"Never happen." Simon waved away the possibility.

Felix's expression was serious as he said to his best friend, "If he ever finds out what the hell you and I are doing, he's going to have our asses in a sling, you know."

"By then he'll be so madly in love with her he won't be able to see straight, let alone care one way or the other." Simon shrugged on his jacket, loosening his tie.

"Then why are we doing this?" Felix demanded.

Simon scowled. "Just in case he doesn't see the treasure stuck under his nose. There're five months left. *If*— and I say *if*, mind you—Joshua is going to give Jessie her walking papers, she'll have a nice little nest egg to tide her over."

"She most certainly will." Felix grabbed his sports bag from the credenza and flicked off his desk light. "I received the copy of her portfolio from the brokerage house last week. Hell, I never expected that Senses stock to split so quickly. So far we've almost doubled her money. We're up to six million dollars for Vera."

"Close, but no cigar," Simon reminded him. "We decided on ten."

"You decided on ten." Felix hefted his bag on his shoulder. "I hope to hell you're working on how we're going to explain to Jessie why we ignored her instructions and continued taking money every month from Joshua, long after she told me to stop."

Simon opened the door for his friend. "And to think she's been slavishly depositing hefty chunks of her pay checks to pay him back. What she's scrimped and saved will be a mere drop in the bucket." He gave a quick nod of the head. "If he does leave her, I have no doubt she'll be dammed grateful to have financial security. She won't give a damn *where* it came from."

"I hope you're right about this, Simon." Felix crossed to the elevator beyond his office and pressed the down button. "The more I know Jessie, the more I realize she doesn't give a damn about material things."

"She sure as hell likes not working," Simon told him. "They *all* like not working, Felix. As soon as Jessie has that money in her hands, she won't feel as bad. You and I have had her best interests in mind ever since that farcical wedding, for God's sake. Joshua wouldn't care or even miss the money. To Jessie, it could be a lifesaver.

"I'm betting on a wedding in the very near future. Hell, he's given her the Tahoe house. You know how much he loves that place. You know I wouldn't do anything to hurt her. I love that girl as if she were my own daughter. And I know women." Simon laughed, slapping Felix on the back as they stepped into the elevator. "Hell, I had my share of lady friends before I married Patti. Trust me on this. I *really* know women."

JESSIE YANKED a navy velour robe off its hanger and pulled it on over her naked body. Its soft folds engulfed her, surrounding her with Joshua's scent. She rolled up the sleeves and tugged the belt around her waist before going downstairs to wait for him.

Too tired to bother eating, Jessie flopped down on the new sofa in the family room. She tried to read. Even the latest terrifying vampire novel couldn't keep her awake. After laying the book on her lap, she channel surfed and found an old movie. She tried to concentrate on Fred and Ginger, pulling down the soft folds of Joshua's robe to cover her bare toes.

He'd gone to Russia this time. As usual, she'd overdone it while he was gone. Sick of the sterility of his house, she'd persuaded Joshua to let her do something about it while he was away.

Conrad and Archie had been so good to give her a job when she had no experience years ago. This commission would balance things out. And the money meant nothing to Joshua, so for once she had no compunction about spending some of it. At least it was for *him*.

She had adamantly refused his offers of money and expensive gifts for months. She'd refused money, the car, a condo and a hundred other perks he'd offered. When he realized she was in deadly earnest, he'd started giving her beautiful costume jewelry. It was obviously expensive, but at least she wasn't having sleepless nights worrying about losing it. She had to admit she loved the clothes he insisted on buying for her. Things she could never have afforded herself. Things she would never have *needed*. He moved in elite circles. To him, the designer gowns and jewelry were part of her uniform. She hadn't been able to refuse, given his logic.

Little did he know that most of the clothing she had was from her college days. College and clothing he had paid for. That was why she'd worked so hard to pay back every cent he'd given her as Vera. She refused to be bought and paid for. No matter how this relationship progressed, she didn't ever want Joshua to think he'd had to pay for her services.

She couldn't stop thinking about their trip to his cabin last month. It had been a magical time. For both of them.

But it had made her reluctantly reassess what she was trying to get out of their relationship.

They had been sleeping together for months and she was still not pregnant. Each month the crushing disappointment had warred with a strange feeling of relief. The relief that the gods were giving them a little more time together.

That weekend had nudged a little place in her mind that said perhaps what she felt for him was more than the need to cold-bloodedly procreate. She'd been struggling with the decision for weeks.

She'd originally decided that having the baby alone, raising it alone, would be ideal. However, the better she got to know The Glacier the more certain she was that she would never walk away from him once she was pregnant with his child. She was positive now that Joshua would track her down to the ends of the earth if he ever found out she had stolen something so precious from him. Because, even if he didn't know it himself, Joshua would make a terrific father.

Once he forgot about his image and they were alone, he could be tender and demonstrative. The man had potential. They deserved the opportunity to explore this relationship. He made her happy. She made him laugh. Surely, there was more to what they had than just sex?

Jessie wanted to find out.

She had shed a bucket of tears before going to the drugstore. She had spent a whole day packing all the baby things and putting everything in storage.

Luckily Joshua was on one of his long trips. For days she had been alternately weepy and then optimistic. Finally she had become sick of the inactivity. The decision had been made.

The small pouch wouldn't fit into her little purse because of the divorce papers. In a moment of indecision she looked at the papers, then at the birth control packet. There was room for only one in her purse...and in her heart.

The decision was remarkably easy. She tossed the papers into the back of a drawer. The birth control fit just fine in her purse.

She'd packed a small bag and had been at Joshua's since.

Redecorating his house into a home had been exactly what the doctor ordered. The busier she was, the less time she had to think. In the last ten days she had supervised painters and wallpaper hangers, had furniture and live plants delivered and generally had a wonderful time changing the house into the home she'd always wanted. Except, of course, she'd never, even in her dreams, pictured a home quite so grandiose. And it was the first time she'd approached a job with her teeth gritted for battle and her brain conjuring up untold fairy tales.

She was worn to a nub, she thought with sleepy satisfaction, letting her head fall back on the plump pillows. The room still smelled faintly of paint. She smiled.

Not a trace of his corporate colors survived. Instead, she had filled his home with light. Beautiful fabrics and textured wall coverings, flowers and wonderful antique accent pieces had brought it all together. She'd rearranged his priceless art collection, consigning the boring pieces to the attic.

The house had been crawling with people for days, sending Joshua's security staff into fits.

Jessie rested her eyes. She wanted him home, sitting beside her, rubbing her feet as he sometimes did. Or making love to her over there on the floor by the fireplace where he'd filled the missing gaps in her education with alacrity. Telling her what a shamelessly slow learner she was, so she had to keep practicing until she got it right.

Making love with Joshua was the best experience she'd had in her life. Dashing to the bathroom first was going to take some of the spontaneity away.

It was those quiet moments with him she cherished most: Listening to music. Watching an old movie. Talking. It was amazing they had so much to talk about, considering they hardly agreed on anything. But, no matter what the subject, they were both fascinated with looking up strange facts in Joshua's extensive library. When she came up with some off-the-wall question, Joshua would laughingly look it up in one of his many books or on the Internet.

He seemed more relaxed. He laughed more. He seemed to like her touching him even when they weren't making love. And Jessie touched him whenever she felt the urge, which was often. She loved the feel of his dark hair between her fingers. She adored the scrape of his rough jaw under her mouth as she snuggled against him on the sofa. He didn't push her away. If he didn't enjoy the cuddling as much as she did, he didn't show it. He seemed perfectly content to let her tumble against him at whim like a pesky kitten.

Most of the time, if she didn't dwell on not conceiving, she was happy.

His control was phenomenal. Jessie had never seen anything like it. Conrad had been right. It was hard to tell if Joshua ever got really ticked off. She'd learned the angrier he was the quieter he got. Thank goodness he'd never been angry with her.

Their lovemaking was spectacular. Jessie could never

have imagined two people being more in tune, more compatible than she and Joshua in bed. Or on the floor. Or on a chair. They were both insatiable. He taught her to be uninhibited and inventive. Jessie blushed at some of her choice locations. She would never be able to look at the stairs again without remembering the rug burns she'd had on her butt the next day.

Jessie had practiced the wind sprint required to get to the bathroom, get prepared, and then get back to the bed. She had practiced until she was fast.

She sighed contentedly and slid down into a more comfortable position on the sofa. Even Fred and Ginger waltzing around the ballroom couldn't force her eyes to remain open.

Joshua come *home*.

JOSHUA COULD HEAR the TV as he let himself in and set his garment bag by the foot of the stairs to retrieve later. A strong smell of paint permeated the air. She'd left the front hall light on for him as she always did when he was late. A small thing, but something he always noticed the moment he walked in.

She'd placed an enormous, and rather ugly, vase on the half-circle table against the far wall. The smell of the massed fresh flowers vied with the unmistakable odor of paint and lemon furniture polish. She'd probably worked his staff mercilessly. To them Miss Jessie could do no wrong. They all adored her. A small, satisfied smile tugged at Joshua's mouth.

He loosened his tie and top button, his eyes gritty with exhaustion as he walked down the short hallway to the family room in back of the house.

"Jessie?"

He didn't remember being this tired in his life. Although his business had gone well, he'd missed Jessie more than he'd thought possible.

"Jessie?"

There was no response to his second louder call. For a moment he stood in the doorway. So much for fantasizing about her silky naked skin on satin sheets. He didn't have the energy right now anyway. He glanced at his watch. Well after midnight. She must have left the TV on and gone home.

The configuration of the room was different, the smell of fresh paint much stronger in here. His head throbbing, Joshua moved to turn off the TV before he went to bed.

The flickering test pattern illuminated Jessie asleep on the sofa, her neck at an impossibly uncomfortable angle, her feet tucked up under his robe. Her lashes cast intriguing shadows on her lightly tanned cheeks.

"Jess," he whispered with intense satisfaction. She was here. Crouching down, Joshua ran the back of his fingers across the silky skin of her cheek.

She slept as she did everything else. Totally. Nothing short of an earthquake would wake her. He took the book off her lap and marked her place.

She stirred briefly, capturing his hand under her cheek with a sigh. With a lightening of his spirits, Joshua bent and lifted Jessie to carry her upstairs.

He lay her gently on the bed, then stripped, settling under the crisp sheets beside her. The room was dark and warm, Jessie's scent tantalizing as she unconsciously snuggled against him. Before he could sleep, he wanted to feel her naked skin against him. He skimmed off the velour robe she'd appropriated and for a moment was tempted to turn on the light. She had a magnificent body and he wanted to see it. Was hungry to see it. But he could wait. Even with the brief glance he'd given the house when he walked through it, he could see she hadn't wasted a moment of the time he'd been gone. Jessie must be as exhausted as he was. She stirred restlessly as he slipped her arm out of the second sleeve, her silky hair frothing over his chest as he settled her against him.

Obviously they both needed to... Ah, hell! Jessie's open mouth found his naked shoulder and sharp little teeth took a nip before her lips trailed like liquid fire to the joint of neck and shoulder. Was she awake? Tired muscles electrified back to life as her tongue sent jolts bone deep.

He shifted to his side, his eyes adjusting to the darkness. Desire clenched in his gut. Now that she'd aroused him, she damn well better be awake! His hand made a slow and thorough inspection of one plump breast, finding the nipple pebble hard. As his body came wildly alive, he groaned aloud. He pressed her against the pillows and took her mouth. He could feel the firm curve of her breasts and hard points of her nipples now flattened against his chest. Catching a handful of springy hair in his fist, he nudged her head up so he could just make out the pale oval of her face.

"You'd better be awake, lady."

"Cyril?" Jessie whispered huskily, as her fingers climbed his shoulders.

Joshua fell on his back, taking her with him. He grinned up at her. "Cyril? You little wretch. How long have you been awake?"

"Since you started ripping off my clothes." Jessie ran her fingers through his hair, the tips lingering on his face. He needed a shave. "When did you get back?" She wriggled farther up his chest.

Joshua captured her hand and brought it to his lips, a

feeling of profound…*something* pouring through him. He had no name for what Jessie did to him. He didn't even want to think about it. Her entire satiny length was pressed the length of his body. "Half an hour ago." His answer was muffled against the pulse in her throat.

Jessie's mouth blindly searched for his. His arms went around her. They kissed slowly, savoring the moment.

"I missed you." Jessie's voice was low, husky with need.

Joshua's grip tightened as she moved with catlike grace, her smooth skin skimming over his. He heard her sigh. Shifting her, Joshua ran his hand up her side, her skin shimmering under his hand. He found her breast and tended to it with infinite care.

He'd missed her, too. He hadn't wanted to. For days, the memories of this woman had colored his thoughts. It was unprecedented. It was unacceptable. It was. He nudged her knees apart and settled in the cradle of her thighs. "Show me how much you missed me, woman." He slid into the welcoming warmth of her. They made love slowly, savoring the closeness.

Suddenly her body stiffened. "Oh, damn…I forgot to…never mind."

As her body melted into deep sleep, he reached out and turned off the alarm.

HE HADN'T HAD enough sleep. He must be getting old. Traveling had never dragged at him like this. The trips were becoming mundane. He buzzed Angela to put together a list of candidates for future travel.

Hell, he'd been almost too tired last night to love Jessie. Not that she'd been too chirpy herself. He grinned. He had left her this morning with her face buried in the pillow. He'd stroked his hand down the silky curve of her bare back, lingering on her heart-shaped butt and she hadn't moved a muscle. He'd missed too many mornings when she *wouldn't* have been fast asleep. And he wanted them, damn it. He was throwing away that alarm clock ASAP.

He picked up the phone. "Ange, get me Felix, then have Craig from advertising come up. No, I'll hold while you get through. Thanks.

"Felix? Find out where the hell Vera is off to now. I want a divorce."

JESSIE JUMPED UP off her knees as soon as the Rolls pulled up in the circular driveway in front of his house. She fought the black dots in her vision from jumping up too fast, and tugged off her soil-encrusted gardening gloves. Joshua had left before she was awake this morning. Their first morning together at the house and she'd slept right through it.

She tossed gloves aside as she pulled open the back door of the car. "You're home early," she said happily, as he swung his long legs onto the brick. "Hi, Barlow," she called over the seat. The chauffeur grinned in the rearview mirror and touched his cap, waiting for her to slam the door shut before he took off to the garages behind the house.

Jessie linked her arm in Joshua's as they walked inside. He set his briefcase down and turned to look at her; a small smile tugged at his mouth. "I have seven gardeners," he said dryly, taking out his handkerchief to wipe her dirty cheek. "Why are you digging in the dirt again?"

"I'll run up and take a quick shower," Jessie said quickly.

"I wasn't criticizing, Jess. You can do whatever you

like around—" Joshua sneezed twice. "Damn." He walked into the family room and collapsed on the sofa, pushing one of the new pillows Jessie had bought behind his head and swinging his feet up. He held out his hand. "The house looks great. You did a spectacular job, Jessie. When I have more energy you'll have to give me a tour. In the meantime, come and lie here beside me and tell me what you planted today."

"Ugh, I'm all dirty and sweaty." Jessie's nose wrinkled.

Joshua laughed hoarsely. "I love it when you're sweaty. Come here, woman. I'm too damn tired to chase you upstairs."

He did look tired. His face seemed paler than usual to Jessie as she lay down beside him and felt his arms come around her. She rested her head against his chest, listening to the steady beat of his heart.

She was afraid to interpret what it meant for Joshua to turn off the 3:00 a.m alarm and then come home early the next day. She wondered if she should read *anything* into it before deciding not to get too excited. He was more than tired—she could tell by the way his arms held her. He was more interested in holding her than in taking her upstairs to bed. She stroked his face.

His jaw was slightly rough with the stubble he hadn't shaved at his office. Jessie knew he usually shaved twice a day. His skin under her questing fingertips felt warm and dry.

"Do you feel all right?" She lifted her head from his chest to look up into his face.

His eyes were closed, but he rubbed a small circle in the small of her back where his hand held her close. "Tired," he admitted on a sigh. "Just damn tired."

He was more than tired Jessie realized as she scrutinized his pale face, scorched with two angry red patches on his high cheekbones.

Jessie carefully swung her legs off the sofa. "Come upstairs, Joshua. I think you should be in bed."

He opened his eyes, taking a moment to focus on her face. "Don't think I can get it up right now, darling," he mumbled, his lids drifting shut. "M'be later."

She laughed softly. "No sex for you, big boy." Jessie carefully slipped her arm under his back and helped him sit up. "Do you think you can get upstairs on your own or shall I call Barlow?"

"Own." Joshua leaned heavily on Jessie's arm as he stood up, almost tumbling both of them back onto the deep sofa.

Terrified he would fall, and alarmed at his pallor and disorientation, Jessie managed to get him upstairs and onto the bed. After undressing him and rolling him under the covers, she searched his phone book for the number of his doctor.

"Joshua?" Jessie sat on the edge of the bed. He had fallen into a restless doze. "I need the number of your doctor. What's his name?"

"Never get sick."

"There's always a first time," Jessie said dryly. She rested her cool hand on his hot cheek. "What's your doctor's name, Joshua?"

He coughed, turning his head feverishly on the pillow. "Jessie?"

"I'm right here."

"Jessica. Jessie. Jess," he said softly, rolling over to bury his face in the pillow.

"That's me." Jessie went into the dressing room to call her own doctor to see if she would make a house call.

He murmured her name again, shifted restlessly and hugged his pillow.

By the time the doctor arrived his temperature had climbed to 104. Jessie bathed his hot face in cool water, dribbling some of the moisture between his dry lips. He didn't want to drink, didn't want to take his cough suppressant, didn't want to do anything but sleep. He sounded like a fractious child. Her heart squeezed. Who had taken care of him when he was a child? A nanny? Had the woman loved him? Or had she just done her job?

Jessie nursed him with TLC. She managed to sponge him down without getting yelled at. First he was boiling, and then he was freezing. He hated the cold wet cloths she ran over his sweaty body. She was sweating herself by the time she'd dried him and made him take aspirin. Then she let him sleep.

Until the next time.

The next day his temperature was down and he was just plain bad tempered. Jessie carried on as if he were being his most charming best. She forced him to drink and take his medication. He couldn't resist her when she closed the drapes and lay down beside him. "Sleep," she'd say, stroking his hair, and he'd rest his head against her without a complaint. He'd be asleep in seconds.

She spent every moment with him in the bedroom, coaxing, cajoling, bullying and browbeating him until he got well. It was no hardship for her to take naps with him. He was a harsh taskmaster when he was sick. Worse when he was recovering.

After five days, he thought he was well enough to use the phone. Jessie had taken it downstairs. He was still too wobbly to try the stairs, and he fumed for hours. A short nap took care of that mood, Jessie thought with amusement watching him sleep on the eighth morning.

Whereas she came rushing out of sleep to get on with her day, Joshua woke with a soft sigh. She loved him best like this. When he was soft with sleep, vulnerable and malleable.

She leaned up on her elbow and touched his forehead. Cool, thank goodness. She'd made him stay in bed yesterday even though he could probably have been up. She'd teased him about how much control she had since he was too weak to fight back.

She slipped out of bed, careful not to wake him. Dressed in navy leggings and a thigh-length cable-stitch navy-and-white cotton sweater, she pushed up the sleeves as she made her way to the kitchen. She had the coffee on and was breaking eggs into a glass bowl when Joshua came in.

"Where's Mrs. Godfrey?" he asked, referring to the cook.

"She took her grandkids to the park."

"Hmm." He nuzzled the back of her neck.

Jessie turned to look at him. He had showered and shaved and dressed in the jeans and dark-purple shirt she'd bought him in Tahoe. "Well, don't you look handsome." She moved to arm's length, eyeing him up and down. "Great buns."

Joshua's lips quirked. "You're looking at my front, Jess."

"Trust me, I know." She grinned up at him, automatically checking his forehead with her hand. Satisfied, she turned back to the stove. "Scrambled or omelette?"

"Scrambled." He pulled the wide neckline of her sweater aside to nibble her shoulder.

She poured the egg mixture into the pan. A comb fell

out of her hair to the floor. Joshua bent to pick it up. "I don't know why you bother trying to control your hair, darling. It has a mind of its own."

She used one hand to hold her hair up as she tried to force the comb back into the thickly curling mass. Joshua smiled, his eyes getting crinkly the way she loved. "That doesn't do any good you know. It won't stay up."

"I can't do anything with it. I probably look like a wild woman."

"It looks sexy as hell."

She gave him a speaking glance. "I'm cooking breakfast here."

He looked at her innocently. "I was just making a comment."

She laughed. They hadn't made love since the night he'd come back from Russia. Considering his libido, she was surprised he hadn't taken her on the kitchen floor by now.

He still looked a little pale. She decided she could always persuade him to take a nap with her after breakfast. The meal would never get cooked though if she had to hold up her hair with her hand. Too lazy to run upstairs to look for a scrunchie, she coiled her hair off her neck and anchored it with a pencil she grabbed from the cup by the phone.

He frowned.

"What's the matter?"

Joshua shrugged. "Déjà vu."

Jessie put four slices of bread in the toaster then looked at him. "Are you sure you're feeling all right? Maybe it's too soon for you to be out of bed. Should I call Dr.—"

"Forget the doctor." He wrapped his hand around the

back of her neck, his eyes lambent as he pulled her closer. "I want to drag you upstairs and do sexy stuff to your body until you yell."

Upstairs was good.

She would make a quick detour to the bathroom before they hit the bed. She took the pan off the stove, then draped her arms around his neck and wriggled her eyebrows. "How sexy?"

"How much can you take?" He used his thumb to stroke the slick inner surface of her lower lip, his gaze scorching her face.

The toast popped up behind her. "You just got out of a sick bed." She tried to be reasonable.

"Come back to it with me." He swung her up in his arms and strode out of the kitchen, across the wide entry hall and started up the stairs.

"I don't think you should be carrying me, Rhett. You've been flat on your back for a week." She held on tighter as he picked up speed the closer he got to the bedroom.

He kicked the door shut behind him. "Didn't I tell you yesterday I wouldn't always be weak and lying flat on my back?" He settled her carefully on the freshly made bed. "Now, my pretty, what do you have to say about *that!*"

He leaned over her, the purple shirt doing wonderful things to his pale eyes. He was teasing her but his eyes were hot.

"I say, fine." Jessie started unbuttoning the cotton shirt. Her throat felt dry and her pulse had sped up. She wanted to consume him in large bites. "Hurry." She couldn't believe that throaty voice was hers.

She had no idea what happened to their clothing. Or who removed what. The moment her naked skin touched his, he went wild, carrying Jessie along on a tidal wave of sensation so intense she lost all sense of reason.

Her climax was so explosive, so prolonged she almost lost consciousness. After a while she managed to slowly open her eyes. Sunlight streamed through the open window. Blankets and sheets were mounded on the floor. Jessie could feel a pencil under her right hip. She couldn't move a muscle and she struggled to draw an even breath.

She'd forgotten the detour.

Joshua leaned over her. His face had lost its pallor. His hair was sweaty and their skin was sticking together everywhere they touched. In a moment she would be able to speak. For now all she could gather the energy to do was gaze into his eyes. They held some emotion impossible for her to read. She felt the deep breath he took through her breast and down to the juncture of her thighs.

"I'm sorry."

For a moment she was so lost in the sensual haze she didn't comprehend his words. "What?"

"I'm sorry," he said stiffly. "I lost control. Did I hurt you?" A dark frown pinched his eyebrows together.

"No!" She wrapped her arms around his neck, pulling him down. "I love what we did. I love knowing I can make you forget you're The Glacier when you're with me."

Jessie felt the brief suspension of his heartbeat under her hand. It took her a moment to realize that whatever he had felt in that shattering moment, he'd caught himself and brought his emotions back under control. Damn. She'd just have to try harder. She glanced at him under her lashes. A telltale pulse pounded in his temple. So, he wasn't as immune as he liked to appear.

"There's nothing you have ever done to hurt me. In bed or out. I promise." He lost some of the concern in his eyes. "I'm starving. Can we go down for breakfast soo—"

The phone rang and she groaned. Joshua's business calls had stopped while he'd been ill. No doubt he'd called his secretary this morning and told her he was up and about. He was definitely up—and about to be cut off. Her fingers walked deliberately down his chest.

Joshua stuffed a pillow behind his head. "What the hell do you mean you can't find...?" He glanced briefly at Jessie. "The principle party?"

She loved his crinkly chest hair, but didn't waste too much time there. He had been gone for ten days, then sick for a week. He had a lot of catching up to do. Her fingers closed around him.

She jumped when Joshua said loudly into the phone, "Then damn well hire detectives. I want her found." There was a short pause. "As death and taxes. Keep me informed Felix."

"Bad news?" She crossed her arms on his chest and tried to read the expression on his face.

"Just someone I need to contact to get some papers signed."

She made tantalizing swirls around his left nipple. "Another merger?"

"A contract dissolution. Felix will take care of it."

He looked pointedly at her hands folded on his chest. "Wasn't this hand somewhere else?"

8

JESSIE EMERGED from the dressing room in the hotel room, her arms raised as she struggled with a recalcitrant earring. The flame-red Isaac Mizrahi she wore was one of a dozen designer gowns Joshua had surprised her with for this trip to Monaco.

She'd felt like a kid in a candy store when she'd seen the gowns the hotel maid had unpacked earlier. Each gown was a brilliant, vibrant color, each more tempting than the last. The red chiffon had a short, frothy skirt, no back and a deceptively modest front—until movement revealed the throat-to-waist slit and a tantalizing glimpse of small firm, lightly tanned breasts.

"Why aren't you dressed?" she asked, seeing Joshua sprawled on the bed, his arms folded under his head. Half the bedcovers were on the enormous bed, the other half on the floor. He was gloriously naked.

Jessie met his bold look and his eyes darkened. "Don't you have jet lag?" he asked in a seductive drawl. "Perhaps you should come back to bed and take a little nap."

"Oh, no, you don't, Joshua Falcon. That's what you said three hours ago." Jessie's pulse quickened under the heat of his smoldering gaze. "We've been in Monte Carlo for four hours and already made love twice." She dropped her hand when the earring back slipped home. "I thought you brought me here to gamble."

"I did," Joshua said, rising and coming toward her like a panther, all sinewy grace and rippling muscles, arousal blatant and unashamed. "And to see you dressed like you are now. God, you look incredible." He ran the backs of his fingers inside the narrow opening of her bodice to touch bare skin; Jessie couldn't help arching her back as his hand slipped inside the opening. "You turn me on whether you're clothed or naked. I love the way your lush little breasts play hide-and-seek in this dress."

She licked her shiny red lips, watching as Joshua's eyes smoldered. "Don't get me all jazzed up," she warned, fearing it was already too late. She stood her ground as his fingers played against her sensitized skin.

"I want to see the casino," she said with a laugh, her fingers small around the thickness of his wrist, as she halfheartedly tried to restrain him. He could rip these five ounces of chiffon off her and have her on the bed in a heartbeat.

A tremor rippled across her skin. He saw it and smiled. The backs of his fingers slid from the pulse in her throat to her waist and back again. Her nipples were excruciatingly hard and blatantly outlined beneath the soft fabric of the expensive dress.

Jessie closed her eyes, waiting for Joshua to cup her breasts, to taste her nipples as he had done just before she'd called it quits and run into the lavish bathroom for a shower not forty minutes ago. She'd locked the door, hearing his mocking laughter as she shot home the bolt.

"You love being a woman, don't you?" Just the backs of his knuckles rode the edge of fabric over her midriff. Jessie arched an eyebrow, a trick she had learned from him. He seemed impervious to what he was doing to her as he continued in that soft, silky voice. "I love watching you get ready to go out." His touch moved a little higher. Jessie shivered.

"I'm always fascinated by the way you primp and fuss with your hair when you know it won't stay where you put it. And no matter what, it always looks sexy, as though I've just run my fingers through it." With two fingers, he touched the pulse at her throat, and smiled down into her eyes. Her breath hitched.

"And I'm fascinated by your concentration when you apply makeup. Every move you make is graceful, feminine. You love the textures and scents and ceremony that go with being female."

Jessie felt hypnotized by the sensual timbre of his voice and the rhythmic stroking of his fingertips. She took a step back to clear her head. "Goodness. What brought this on?"

Joshua shrugged. "I've never known anyone who enjoys being in their own skin the way you do." He reached over to pick up a toweling robe, then shrugged it on. He looked back at her with a small frown. "Given the way you were brought up, I don't know how you acquired your amazing sense of self-worth."

Embarrassed and flattered Jessie didn't quite know what to say. A lot of her self-confidence was a protective device she'd perfected growing up. "I somehow managed to teach myself. I realized, even as a child, that my mother's life wasn't mine, and I did everything in my power to make sure I knew who and what I was."

Joshua cupped her cheek. "I admire the hell out of who you are, Jessica Adams." He dropped a light, yet somehow intense, kiss on her mouth, and then strolled into the bathroom.

Jessie flopped down on the bed and stared at the closed door.

THE MAIN FLOOR of the casino was an opulent mix of gilt and mahogany, the very old with some modern concessions. It retained the same air of genteel elegance and lavish style it had when it was built in the early 1860s. Jessie was entranced. "It's not fair the locals aren't allowed in the casino." She was afraid to blink—she wanted to see everything. "They're missing a wonderful part of their heritage."

"A small price to pay, considering they don't pay any taxes in Monaco," Joshua said dryly.

"It's their heritage—" Jessie gazed around her "—not the money that matters."

"Tell that to the man trying to feed his family. Hardly anyone leaves a casino with *more* money in his pocket, Jess. They're doing the locals a favor."

"Cynic. I still don't think it's fair," she said without heat, distracted by the sights and sounds of the casino. Elegantly gowned women and handsome men wearing tuxedos strolled through the vast saloons, their voices an exotic blend of accents and pitch. Her eyes lit up as they wandered through a room with dozens of roulette tables.

"It's only the gaming rooms they're forbidden to enter, little Miss Bleeding Heart," Joshua said, amused. He toyed with the loose strands of her hair at her nape. "Everyone can come to the Grand Theater to see the ballet or opera." He lifted her hand to his lips and kissed her fingers. Her lids drifted closed and she whispered for him to stop. He tasted her knuckles and her skin flushed, but she didn't pull away.

Jessie felt the ripple in his thigh muscles as he brushed against her; she carefully moved away a few inches, brushing her palm up the back of her upswept hair feeling for those loose strands as his gaze remained fixed on her face. She had known she was playing with fire when she put on the dress, but now, as his X-ray eyes touched her naked breasts, she realized she hadn't meant to start a forest fire.

She closed her eyes briefly. If she gave in to this insatiable craving, they would be upstairs naked before she could say *strip*.

"Behave," she warned, then drew in a shaky breath.

He smiled, then tucked her arm through his. "You are a hard woman."

"Shh, I'm absorbing." The smell of wealth discreetly perfumed the air. The aroma of power and money mixed with the fragrance of the fresh flowers overflowing the priceless vases in lighted alcoves along the walls.

Jessie's gold heels sank into luxurious royal-blue-and-deep-black Axminster carpet. The murmur of refined voices wove between the dulcet notes of a small orchestra screened behind a fringe of luxurious potted palms nearly reaching the intricate gold plaster ceiling soaring above their heads.

Joshua's hand rested lightly on the small of her back as they strolled across the enormous casino, his caress absentminded. Jessie didn't think he realized how much easier it was for him to touch her in public now. The familiar contact in a crowded room meant more to Jessie than she'd ever thought possible.

"Now, why are you smiling as if you just ate a canary?" Joshua asked, leading her into the next room.

She looked up at him with sparkling eyes. "I'm happy."

He touched her face with his fingertips, as if he couldn't help himself. "This has all been here for more than a hundred years, Jess. We don't have to run."

"Someone might take my lucky seat." She slowed and looked about her as nonchalantly as she could.

"Find a table. I'll get you some chips."

She caught her lower lip in her teeth and looked up at him with a delicious mixture of terrified anticipation and unholy glee. "Not too many," she warned. "I just want to play at playing for an hour or so."

Joshua returned moments later and Jessie dropped the stack of chips into her purse, turning in a little pirouette as she perused the tables before picking the one she wanted.

"I've died and gone to heaven." She grinned, opening her small Chanel clutch and taking out a handful of black and gold chips. "Come and play with me."

Joshua leaned forward, his lips brushing her ear. "I wanted to play with you upstairs." He pulled out one of the elegant brocade chairs for her.

"Patience has its rewards," she whispered, setting her chips in neat piles on the green bias table. She could feel Joshua behind her as she concentrated on placing her bet.

Actually, she had no idea how to play roulette. She only placed bets on red or black and on the double zero. It was the adrenaline rush she relished as her chips were scraped off the table or returned to her.

With several more chips than she had started with, Jessie'd had enough. Joshua had stood behind her, his hand possessively on her shoulder and without comment for an hour.

"I'm starving." Jessie swung her legs off the high chair. Joshua laughed as he helped her scoop up her chips.

"You're so predictable." He aimed her toward the five-star restaurant with a view of the bay. "Always hungry. Come on. I'll feed you, and then you can bring me some luck."

After being seated, Jessie took a handful of chips, turning them around between her fingers. "You know, these are so pretty I think I'll just take them home and frame them so I can remember this fabulous trip."

Joshua almost choked on his wine. Jessie's eyebrows rose at his expression. "What?"

"Do you have any idea what those chips are worth, Jessie?" Joshua dabbed at the corner of his mouth with his napkin.

She shrugged. "I don't know. Five dollars?"

"Each chip is worth the equivalent of ten thousand dollars."

"What!" Jessie squeaked, her hand at her throat. "You're kidding. There must be…oh my God, Joshua. There're at least thirty-five chips here. What happened to the dollar table?"

"That's Reno. This is the big time. The sheik sitting on your right was playing with hundred-thousand-dollar chips."

"Lord." Jessie stuffed the chips into her purse and laid it carefully in front of her on the table. "If I'd known that, I would never have played."

"You were enjoying yourself. What difference does it make how much the chips are worth? It's only money."

"What if I'd lost?" Jessie felt sick to her stomach. She closed her eyes before looking back at him. He was still smiling.

"It's only money, Jess."

"Yours, Joshua. Not mine. It would have taken me forever to pay you back if I'd lost."

"You didn't." His smile disappeared and a strange look came over his features. He handed her the enormous tasseled menu. ''Decide what you want to eat and don't think about it.''

Jessie hid behind the menu, her appetite gone. She'd had no idea. She felt so stupid. In such opulent surroundings with Joshua's casual wealth, she should have guessed they wouldn't have dollar chips, for heaven's sake!

She felt like a fraud. Sitting here on the patio of one of the most famous casinos in the world, wearing a designer original. Who did she think she was?

Just Jessie Adams, daughter of a prostitute from Bakersfield.

She'd done the unthinkable. She had complacently believed she wouldn't fall in love with him. She'd thought that it was impossible. That she'd been inoculated and would be immune. As if love were something she had control over!

I love him.

She mentally tested the words, tasting them bittersweet on her tongue.

Oh, my God. How could this have happened? It had been so insidious she hadn't even noticed.

It didn't matter how much she now wanted things to be different. There *was* no happy ending. She was welfare housing: he was penthouse. He might care for her, but he'd never fall in love with a woman like her in a million years. He'd pick someone from his own social circle.

Not only was she never going to have his baby—hell, no—she had neatly compounded her loss. On December 23 she'd leave without Joshua as well.

The sparkle went out of the evening.

She asked Joshua to order for her. The entire menu was in French, and she didn't understand it anyway. He ordered their meal in his impeccable French before leaning forward and taking her hand. "What's the matter?" His voice was husky, his pale eyes intent as he scanned her face. She wondered what he was seeing there. "Jet lag getting to you at last?"

"I don't belong here, Joshua." Jessie's eyes felt scratchy, her mouth trembley. God, she hoped she wouldn't cry. Not now, not here, in front of Joshua and all these fancy people who belonged.

"You are the most beautiful woman here tonight, Jessie. Of course you belong." He picked up her hand, and Jessie realized too late she'd forgotten to put on the red nail polish she'd brought with her. Her nails were short and unpolished. She curled her fingers in his hand. Even her hands didn't belong. Her throat closed up. She was going to cry, damn it.

"Jessie, look at me."

She raised her eyes and looked at him through a shimmering veil of tears.

"What's this all about?" he asked gently, his thumb rubbing circles on her palm. She bit her lip helplessly. "The chips are no big deal—"

"I'm sorry." Her voice was muffled by the napkin she had pressed to her mouth. "I don't know what's wrong with me." She peered at him over the damask. "It must be jet lag." She glanced up just as the waiter brought their first course. "Saved by the food." She injected a cheerful note into her voice.

Determined not to spoil an otherwise marvelous evening, Jessie got a firm grip on her emotions and picked up her fork.

Jess was sure the Boeuf Alexandra she had just eaten must have been delicious. She liked artichokes, and the truffles were interesting, but she could barely taste them.

Damn it. She didn't want to be dwelling on the end when she still had weeks and weeks left to enjoy with him.

For a split second she reconsidered her decision to use birth control. It was darn inconvenient and maybe…no. She'd made that decision and wouldn't retract it.

She straightened her spine and tucked her arm through Joshua's as they left the restaurant. "Where are we going now?"

"You sure you don't want to play roulette a little more?"

Jessie gave a mock shiver. "Way too rich for my blood. In fact, here." She handed him her small shell-shaped clutch. "Stick this in your pocket so I don't have to worry about it. I'll watch you play…whatever it was."

"Chemin de fer. See those tables over there set on the raised dais?" Joshua led Jessie across the chandelier-lit room. He talked to a gentleman standing guard at the entrance. The man gave Joshua a deferential bow and ushered them into the exclusive area. Chemin de fer was a complicated high-stakes card game, Joshua explained quietly to Jessie, much like baccarat. As he took his seat, Jessie refrained from asking what these chips were worth. She didn't want to know.

All the other seats were taken by spectators. This time it was Jessie who stood behind him.

She enjoyed the action. Even if she hadn't a clue what the players were doing or how the betting worked, she was engrossed in watching. At one point she slipped off her high-heel sandals. The carpet felt luxuriously soft under her stockinged feet.

A waiter brought her a drink which she left beside Joshua's on the table. Dinner settled uncomfortably in her stomach. She was thirsty but wanted water, not alcohol. She looked around for a waiter.

A wave of dizziness caused her knees to buckle. Saliva flooded her mouth. She swallowed convulsively as prickles of hot and cold washed over her skin. Her sandals slipped from her lax fingers to drop with a thud to the floor. Blindly she felt for the back of Joshua's velvet-covered seat. "I n-need to sit dow—" The lights dimmed, and then went out completely.

"Jessie?" She heard alarm in Joshua's voice, which came from far, far away... Something cool and damp moved gently over her face. "Open your eyes, sweet love."

Not Joshua. He had never called her love in his life and he'd never sounded that panicky. Jessie drifted.

"Jessie, open your eyes. Now." How typically Joshua to order her conscious.

His lips. Joshua's lips. He kissed her hand. His fingers felt safe and hard around hers. Jessie's eyelashes fluttered as she managed to drag her eyes open. Joshua was kneeling beside her where she lay on a sofa, his eyes narrowed on her face. "What the hell happened?" he demanded as soon as her eyes opened.

His mouth was white bracketed, his hair disheveled as though he'd run his fingers through the dark strands. There was even a pleat of worry between his aristocratic brows. His grip on her hand tightened as she stared up at him blankly. She winced and he relaxed his hold. Just a little.

Her stomach rolled once, twice and then seemed to settle. So much for the five-star dinner that cost as much as the national debt of a small country.

"Jessie?"

"What?"

"What happened, damn it?" He turned to a shadowy form behind him. "She must have a concussion. She doesn't seem to—"

"I just fainted, Joshua." Rolling her head so she could look directly at him, she managed a weak smile. "I don't have brain damage—I'm fine." She struggled to sit up, grateful when Joshua supported her with his arm. They were in an office. Two men stood discreetly across the room.

"I don't think the rich food on top of all the excitement did my stomach any good. I'm sorry if I embarrassed you."

"You didn't," Joshua said shortly, scanning her face. "God, you're as white as a sheet."

"That's 'cause you just wiped my makeup off." Jessie rested her head against his arm. She was feeling much better now and enjoyed Joshua's worried look. "Please tell me my dress stayed in place, and I fell like a lady."

"There were so many men vying to pick you up we almost forgot why you were lying on the floor," Joshua said dryly as he smoothed back her hair from her face. Her skin felt clammy. His hands felt cool and dry.

"Before I embarrass myself anymore, can we go back to our room?"

"I'll have the good doctor come up to check on you."

"I don't need a—"

Joshua gave the doctor instructions in rapid French before picking Jessie up. She felt as light as a feather, and as pale as a sheet. Her brown eyes were enormous in her pale face. He'd picked up the plastic combs she used to hold her hair up and stuffed them in his pocket.

"Make sure my bottom isn't showing." Jessie closed her eyes as he carried her through the casino to the elevator. Joshua hid his smile, making sure the short dress was tucked neatly against her legs with his arm.

"You're quite decent," he said gruffly, maneuvering her into the empty elevator.

"I feel ridiculous." Jessie's voice was muffled against his pleated shirtfront.

"Everyone thought you fainted very elegantly," Joshua teased as he managed to open the door to the suite and get her inside.

"I know you're not telling me the truth—that I fell flat on my nose in front of a million well-dressed gazillionaires and their diamond-studded wives. I bet everyone saw my underwear." Her lower lip trembled. When she looked up at him there were tears in her eyes. "I'm sorry I embarrassed you."

He used his thumb to wipe away the steady stream trickling down her cheeks. "It's only a big deal to you, Jessie. Nobody noticed, I promise. Seconds before you wilted, the prince and his entourage walked in. Everyone was looking at him, not you."

"It's going to get worse," she suddenly said, her face draining of every vestige of color. "Don't slow down until we reach the bathroom."

Joshua set her down just in time before she was violently sick. He held her head as spasms wrenched her slender body. When he was sure she was done, he supported her as she washed her face and brushed her teeth, then he carried her back to bed.

"Don't." She moaned as he wiped her face with a cool damp cloth. He had never been more relieved than when the doctor knocked on the door some minutes later.

When the man had left, advising rest and simple foods

for a few days, Joshua helped a very wilted Jessie undress and crawl back under the covers.

She looked up at him with those big brown eyes as he sat on the bed beside her, careful not to jiggle the mattress.

"Can I get you anything?"

"No, thanks. I feel like an idiot. Why don't you go back to the casino? I'll see you later."

"I'm staying right here, with you." Sliding his arm around her shoulders, he gently pulled her close to his side. "Close your eyes and try to sleep."

JESSIE WOKE HIM the next morning, bright-eyed and ready to start the day. She lay across his chest. He groaned. "You're sick. Go back to sleep."

"Nope." She leaned harder, nudging him with warm sleek skin. "I feel fabulous, and you promised we'd go for a cruise today."

"I'll attest to the 'feel fabulous' part." He slid his hand down her back to her bottom.

"Oh, no you don't." Jessie rolled over, then kicked off the blankets. She was like a jack-in-the box as she shot out of bed.

Naked and glowing, she paused at the bathroom door. "Come on, Joshua, get dressed, please?" She fluttered her eyelashes, managing to sidestep him as he backed her against the Louis Quatorze credenza. "I'm taking a *quick* shower, then I want to go somewhere lovely for breakfast."

After her "lovely" breakfast, Joshua found the yacht and crew he'd hired the day before.

Dressed in brief white shorts that showed off her gorgeous legs and a cropped top that made his mouth water, Jessie sprawled in a deck chair beside him. Her ponytail,

caught up in a hot-pink scarf that matched the stripes in
her top was, as usual, quite crooked. She looked tanned,
healthy and sexy as hell.

The crew discreetly kept their eyes on their business
as they sailed lazily up the coast.

Joshua had stripped down to his black shorts earlier
and settled back against the soft cushions with a sigh of
pure pleasure. The hot Mediterranean sun baked his skin
as the smell of the ocean and Jessie's subtle fragrance
lulled him into a light doze. He opened his eyes when
he felt soft lips on his cheek some time later.

"You're sleeping away this beautiful day," Jessie
complained, running her warm hands up his bare chest.
He saw his own sleepy face reflected in her sunglasses.
Gulls glided above them in a painfully blue sky and the
white sails snapped in a breeze he couldn't feel.

"There's a nice big stateroom downstairs," he suggested, lazily running his hand around her back under
the short top. She wore no bra. Her skin was hot, smooth
and slightly sweaty.

She arched her back at his touch. "With a nice big
bed, I suppose?"

"Probably."

"How about lunch first?" She wriggled her eyebrows.

Trust Jessie. Laughing, he took her hand and allowed
her to lead him below deck.

Chilled lobster and a dozen mouthwatering salads vied
with fresh fruit and several dessert dishes, the fare spread
out artistically on a long, linen-draped buffet table. The
crew discreetly returned to their duties after closing the
door.

He watched as Jessie helped herself to a bit of everything. Her plate was piled high by the time she brought

it to the small table at the large window overlooking the bow.

"You're going to be sick again if you eat all that," he warned as she bit into a chunk of lobster. She had acquired more of a tan and her skin glowed with health and vitality.

It was hard to believe she was the same woman he'd helped into bed last night. He'd never experienced anything like the terror he had felt seeing Jessie on the floor of the casino. While she'd slept the night away in his arms, he had been wide-awake and waiting to see if he'd need to call the doctor.

"No, I won't." Jessie dribbled mayonnaise on the succulent white flesh before picking up another chunk with her fingers.

She was so damned stubborn. Joshua pushed her bangs out of her eyes then settled back to watch her eat.

There was not a morsel of food left on her plate when she finished. After rinsing her fingers in the finger bowl beside her plate she yawned. "I'm not taking a nap," she warned as if she could read his mind. She dried her hands on the napkin he handed her. Hers was probably on the floor.

He looked at her coolly. "Who said anything about a nap?"

"You have that let's-take-a-nap look about you." She wore not a scrap of makeup and she looked so beautiful she took his breath away.

"I didn't get a wink of sleep last night, Jess. Take pity."

"You just want to do nasty things to my body."

"That, too."

IT WAS A darn good thing they'd taken a nap after they had made love after lunch. Joshua figured he had another long night ahead of him. Because by dusk when they got back to the hotel, Jessie was as sick as a dog again.

She came out of the bathroom, her face pasty. "Don't you dare say 'I told you so.'"

"Crawl into bed, Jess. I've called the doctor." God, he hated this. He watched her, worried out of his mind, as she limply climbed under the covers and closed her eyes.

Joshua paced while the doctor examined her.

"It's not fair. I didn't understand a word either of you said," Jessie complained after the doctor had presented his bill and left.

"He still thinks it's some kind of food poisoning." Some of her color had come back, but she still looked washed out and limp.

"Thank you for being so good to me, Joshua," she said with a simplicity that made him certain that very few people in her life had been good to her. The thought infuriated him. He felt overwhelmed by a damned heart-wrenching emotion he'd never experienced before he'd met Jessie.

He traced the dark circles under her eyes. Was the doctor right? Could a touch of food poisoning and jet lag make her this sick? More than likely, she had caught that damn bug from him last month.

"I did this to you," he said, feeling guiltier than he could ever remember feeling. He felt helpless in the face of her illness. There wasn't anything he could do.

"You don't make me sick." She gave him one of her special smiles, one that pierced his heart, as she reached up to touch his face.

"I probably gave you my cold." Joshua smoothed a

thumb across one silky eyebrow and her eyes fluttered. "Close your eyes and rest."

"I just want to go home. I'm too embarrassed to throw up in that fancy bathroom again," she said in a woeful voice, which almost made him smile. "I want to be sick in my own toilet and sleep in my own bed."

"Then home it is," he said gruffly, as she looked up at him with the absolute trust of a puppy. "Close your eyes and rest while I make the arrangements."

PERVERSELY, as soon as the plane took off she felt fine. "What are you doing?" she asked from the sofa where she had been made to lie down and take a nap.

"Paperwork. Why are you awake?"

"I'm lonely."

"I'm only four feet away from you, Jess." She tried to look pitiful. He smiled and held out his hand. "Want to sit in my lap?" he asked softly. She felt her heart smile.

"I have to go to the bathroom first." She threw off the light blanket and picked up her purse.

"Are you okay?"

"I'll be back before you've noticed I'm gone."

Jessie made quick work of the birth control. She came out, snapped the door closed behind her, tossed her purse in the general direction of the sofa and padded over to his seat while he watched her with those pale eyes of his. His hair was smoothed back neatly, and he was wearing his yellow Tahoe shirt and jeans. She removed the papers from his lap and placed them carefully on the table beside his wide leather chair.

The engines hummed as she straddled his lap. He leaned back and settled her against his chest, her bottom nestled against him. She put one arm around his neck and the other around his waist, resting her head against his chest. She loved the way his arms enfolded her with gentle strength. "Make love to me," she demanded softly, her hand running lightly down his midriff to the snap of his jeans.

"I don't think that's such a goo—"

She smiled up at him, then her lips came down on his, cutting off words and thought. She rubbed erotically against his instant erection as her mouth clung and seduced. He nibbled gently but Jessie was having none of that. She brought both hands up to hold his head in place as she aggressively deepened the kiss.

He widened his mouth, giving her only moments to be the aggressor before he took over.

"What if Joe comes in—?" she asked suddenly.

"He won't. Don't look away, Jessie. You started this. Finish it."

"Is that a dare?" She ran her fingernail lightly down his now open shirt, and he shuddered. He smelled of soap and the brandy he'd been sipping.

Static electricity spun her hair into wild ripples and curls around her shoulders and down her back. She probably looked like a wild woman. "Make love with me. Now."

The top button of his jeans came undone at her touch, and she slipped her hand inside. There, she encountered crisp hair and hard flesh. He dragged his mouth across hers in a brief searing kiss and then held her wrist firmly away from him.

"There's nothing I want more right now than to make love to you, but let's make it last." Joshua drew her hand up his chest and kissed her palm, and she curled her fingers against his cheek. It felt rough—he needed a shave. Her skin tingled as the tip of his sharp teeth skimmed over the pad of her thumb.

He reached over and picked up the phone beside him on the wall. As he instructed the flight crew, he slowly pulled her T-shirt over her head. His breath felt warm on her bare skin. He put the phone gently back in the cradle. Lifting her with both hands on her hips, he set her on her feet. Methodically, he removed her jeans and underwear in one clever move. Jessie kicked them aside, her hands going to his jeans.

"Let me do it, darling." He rose quickly to shuck off his jeans and shirt, then sat and pulled her onto his lap.

"Here?" Jessie looked over her shoulder. The door between cabin and cockpit was only a few dozen yards away.

"They can't hear us." His mouth found the sensitive spot beneath her ear.

Jessie wrapped her arms around his shoulders as he guided her hips down. The leather chair felt cold on the outside of her calves, his thighs hot. Her back arched as he filled her liquid heat. His hands held her still. "Don't move," he whispered against her mouth then nibbled at her lower lip.

"Oh, God." Jessie closed her eyes. The sensation of him filling her was exquisite. She felt the roughness of his hand move up her side, lingering on the indent of her waist before climbing to her breast. He caught her nipple between his fingers, manipulating the hard bud until she moaned. Instinctively, insistently, she wanted to press down.

His left hand held her hips still. "This is torture," she complained, panting now, body on fire. She blindly found his mouth, sliding her tongue inside only to shudder deliciously at the dark, familiar flavor of him.

She used her own hands to tease and torment him. His nipples were just as hard as hers, his skin just as slick, as he drew out the agony for both of them.

Jessie tasted the salty skin on his shoulder, nipping him with her teeth until she felt him leap inside her. She trembled and pressed down, her body desperate to start the rhythm that would bring them both release.

His hand firmly on her hip frustrated and aroused her. She used her hands to drive him wild, feeling his low growl of excitement in her own bones and tissue. Blood rushed in fiery trails through her body and electrified her skin.

Joshua shifted his hips slightly, lifting her enough to lave her breasts with the hot, dark promise of his mouth. She clung to his shoulders, digging her short nails into his skin, wild with wanting, frantic for release.

I love you. I love you. I love you, Jessie wanted to cry out loud. She bit her lip instead, her mind spinning, her reason going. She pressed down against the punishing grip of his hand on her hips.

He muffled her shout against his chest as he plunged inside her with enough force to convulse her body, the sensation so piercingly exquisite, tears squeezed between her tightly closed lids. Every muscle, every nerve in her body participated. She arched her back, grinding in counterpoint as she felt the sweet waves of release building.

Joshua's face was sheened with sweat, his eyes glazed and unfocused. Jessie could feel her internal muscles pulling him deeper. She watched through her own sweat and tears as his jaw grew rigid and the tendons in his neck stood out in relief.

The climax they shared seemed to go on forever. Their

bodies locked in mortal combat until they collapsed, satiated.

Jessie leaned weakly against him, her arms leaden, her body limp. Sweat cooled on her burning skin. Small tremors shook her as sharp aftershocks clenched muscles and nerve endings already pushed beyond endurance.

One moment she was awake. The next she wasn't. Her hand lay curled against his chest, and her breathing was deep and still uneven. Joshua watched her with a bittersweet twist in his gut. He ran a light finger down her bare arm, her skin feeling like satin. She didn't move. He'd still been inside her when she'd fallen asleep as easily as turning off a light switch. She hadn't even twitched as he'd carried her to the bedroom in the back of the plane.

In that fleeting moment, she was more precious to him than his most priceless sculpture, his most exquisite work of art. Her loveliness had increased as he'd known her—not just the animated face she showed to the world, but the soft, intensely private face she wore when no one was looking.

It was becoming almost impossible to keep any emotional distance from her. Jessie could always make him smile. And each time, he felt an unfamiliar softening inside him. He wasn't sure he liked it, but didn't know how to prevent the odd sensation.

He wanted to gather her against his body, hard, and never let her go. She was a priceless treasure, and he'd been complacent in his possession of her, until he'd seen her so pale and weak.

Only then had he instantly and painfully realized that, unlike a painting or sculpture, Jessie *could* be taken from him. By something even he couldn't fight, couldn't negotiate and couldn't buy.

9

ALTHOUGH JESSIE HAD lost some of her tan, she glowed
with good health tonight. The lighting illuminated her
face as she leaned forward in her seat, absorbed by the
action onstage. Joshua smiled as her lips moved silently
with the music. Alone with her in the small secluded
box overlooking the stage, he couldn't resist running his
hand lightly up her back, letting his fingers rest under
the thick fall of her hair. She wore a tangerine-colored
dress with straps that crossed her smooth back. Her long
coral-and-jet earrings made a soft tinkling sound against
the back of his hand.

Jessie turned, giving him the special smile that
touched his heart. His fingers tightened slightly and her
smile widened. "*Phantom* is absolutely wonderful," she
whispered, her breath soft against his face as she leaned
over. In the flickering light Jessie's eyes sparkled.
"Thank you so much for bringing me t—"

She was just too damn hard to resist. He kissed her.
Not the way he needed to. That would have them thrown
out of the theater. Joshua simply ran his tongue back
and forth over her lower lip, tasting the liquid sunshine
of her smile. The arm of the plush seat dug into his ribs.

The theater and music disappeared. She moaned as he
pushed aside the hem of her dress and slid his hand up
her thigh.

The audience applauded and the house lights came up.

Jessie giggled as they abruptly parted. Joshua leaned back in his seat, and pushed his hair back with both hands in a frustrated attempt at control. He felt his own lips twitch in response to her amusement.

"You're going to get us arrested one of these days." Frustration made his voice low.

Jessie's big brown eyes widened mockingly, dancing with naughty highlights. "Who me?" She pulled her skirt down over her knees. "It's not my fault you can't keep your hands to yourself."

"Yes, it is." Joshua untangled an earring from her hair. "What the hell am I going to do with you, Jess? When I'm around you I behave like a randy schoolboy." And when he wasn't around her he thought like one.

Jessie fleetingly traced his mouth with her fingertips, bringing him sharply back into focus. "And I behave like a randy schoolgirl. So what?" She rose out of her seat, her slender body sensuous and graceful as she reached down to take his hand. "It's hot in here. Come on. Let's go downstairs for something cold to drink during intermission."

By the time they traversed the crowds and descended the stairs to the lobby, Jessie looked pale under her makeup. Joshua thought she'd been feeling better since they'd returned from Monte Carlo. She'd refused to see a doctor. He didn't like worrying about her. He wasn't used to worrying about anyone.

"I'm taking you home."

Jessie looked up at him sharply. "Why?"

"You look like you're about to pass out."

"I'm not. It's just warm in here." She licked her lips. "I'm loving the play. I'm fine, truly, Joshua. Let's stand outside for a little bit and get some fresh air. Okay?"

"It's freezing out there. Wait here. I'll get your coat."
He glanced over her head. "Damn, this is all I need."

"What? Who?" Jessie glanced around. "Oh, Paul and
Stacie."

Joshua watched as his cousin and wife came toward
him. Paul was a decent enough guy, if one didn't expect
him to work for a living. As tall as Joshua, with equally
dark hair, they had often been mistaken for brothers. But
while Joshua worked seven days a week, twelve hours
a day, Paul seemed to think the world owed him a living.
His cousin had never resented Joshua having the controlling interest in Falcon's. He was more than happy to
cash his dividend checks and continue his carefree lifestyle. Joshua hadn't seen either of them in almost a year.
He could have gone another year without seeing his
cousin's wife.

Petite and blond, Stacie hadn't changed her Grace
Kelly hairstyle in ten years. She always wore discreetly
elegant, understated clothes and maintained a superior
aloof air that had, years ago, driven him mad. She looked
dull and far too controlled to Joshua now as she smiled
up at him with collagen-enhanced lips.

"Paul. Stacie." Joshua's hand tightened at Jessie's
waist as she listed against him. He gave her a worried
glance before glancing back at the other couple.

He could look at Stacie dispassionately, her cool
blond beauty seemed soulless against Jessie's vibrancy.
He couldn't believe he'd ever asked this woman to
marry him.

Stacie's contact-lens-blue eyes flickered from Joshua
to Jessie and then, dismissing the other woman, back to
Joshua. He noticed she and Paul stood several feet apart.

"You've met Jessica Adams?" He asked though he

didn't give a damn. The room was hot. Out of the corner of his eye, he saw a faint sheen on Jessie's face.

Diamonds sparkled in Stacie's ears as she shot an amused glance up at Jessie. "Oh, yes, darling, we've met your calendar girl." She laughed. He used to think that trilling laughter sexy. Now all he wanted to do was put his hands around her diamond-encircled throat and squeeze. Hard.

Stacie stroked his arm. Her nails were fashionably long and a deep wine color. Joshua shook her off. He felt as though a spider had crawled along his sleeve.

"No need to be angry, darling. It is an indisputable fact you only keep your mistresses for a year."

"We were just on our way outside for a breath of fresh air." He ignored Stacie. "Nice seeing you, Paul. Come to a board meeting sometime." Holding on to Jessie he moved through the crowd to the doors leading to the street.

"Oh, Lord, it *is* hot in here." Stacie fanned her perfectly made-up face with her program as she followed them. Her perfume, while ridiculously expensive, was as repulsive to Joshua now as fly spray. The foyer was packed, body to body. There was no moving quickly, no matter how much he wanted to. Her voice rose as she said over her shoulder, "Get me a drink, Paulie. I'll meet you outside."

As people gave way, Joshua kept a careful arm about Jessie's waist. Her face was paler now and damp strands of dark hair clung to the moisture at her temples.

"Do you need to sit down again?" He felt her slender body tremble against his arm and saw her swallow convulsively. "Bathroom?" He was already steering her in that direction as Jessie nodded mutely.

It seemed as if she were inside for hours. Joshua held

up the wall. Ignoring the few people lingering about the lobby, Joshua finally pushed open the door to the ladies' room.

"Oh my God, Joshua! You can't come in here!" Jessie looked up from where she leaned against the vanity counter, a damp tissue at her throat. Her color was back, and she had fixed her hair and applied lipstick.

"You've been in here for hours." The carpet felt plush underfoot as he walked toward her, his gaze fixed on her face. The room smelled of woman. Combined perfumes and powders, silks and furs, the lighting flatteringly muted.

Jessie met him halfway, slipping her hand into his. "Thank you for coming to find me." Her eyes danced. "Is the coast clear out there? Can we go and see the last act?"

"You don't want to go home to bed?" Joshua pushed open the door, ignoring the stares as he ushered Jessie across the lobby and upstairs.

"Nah. I feel great. I was just a little wonky for a minute."

Joshua settled in his seat beside her just as the opening bar of music began. He took her hand, placing it against his knee. He inhaled deeply her scent of fresh peach and Joy. "I'm sorry she took those shots at you."

"They didn't bother me," Jessie assured him. "I feel sorry for her. Anyone that mean must be very unhappy."

Joshua closed his eyes as the music swelled in time with his heart. Only Jessie could feel sorry for a woman like Stacie. Bringing their clasped hands to his chest, Joshua leaned back to enjoy the rest of the play, Jessie's hand against his heart.

His biggest concern right now was Jessie's health. These weak spells were happening with alarming regularity. He didn't like Jessie being sick. Tomorrow he would insist she see a specialist.

On the way home, she dozed contentedly beside him in the car. But when he was about to take his freeway exit, she'd asked sleepily to be taken to her cottage instead. He could tell that, although she was no longer pale, she was distracted.

He insisted on going upstairs with her, because he wanted to make sure she was really fine. They made love with slow, delicious languor and fell asleep in each other's arms.

Joshua was rudely jerked awake by Jessie's alarm clock. She mumbled in her sleep as he dressed and let himself out.

It was icy cold and pitch-dark, as he climbed into the car and stuck the key in the ignition. Damn. The engine turned over, loud in the absolute silence. He rested his hands on the top of the steering wheel and stared back at the dark windows of her cottage, imagining Jessie snuggled deep amid her blankets, sleeping securely the whole night through in her own bed.

He felt…cheap.

He glanced at the clock on the dash then started to laugh.

It was 3:00 a.m.

THEY FLEW TO Tahoe for a few days. The weather was cold and sharply crisp. While Jessie cooked a roast, Joshua sat in the kitchen. She smiled as he meticulously folded linen napkins and stuffed them into the little copper napkin rings she'd brought with her.

Jessie opened the oven to baste the meat. The house was already filled with the mouthwatering scents of the meal.

Joshua, finished with the table, poured two glasses of wine. He set hers on the counter where she'd been cutting the lattice for an apple pie. "I'm starving," he complained, tying a towel around her waist. Jessie couldn't see the point: she was already covered practically from head to toe with flour.

"Take the roast out so it can rest, then we can eat." She waited until he'd set the heavy pan on the counter before saying casually, "How do you feel about Thanksgiving?"

His eyebrows rose. "Thanksgiving?"

"Yes. The holiday that comes in November?"

He smiled indulgently. "I don't care, one way or the other. Why?"

"I love Thanksgiving. Can we come up here for it?"

"Sure. I don't see why not."

She'd never cooked a turkey in her life. Jessie mentally started planning. She wanted the holiday to be perfect. There would be turkey, pies.... This Thanksgiving had to be Joshua's best. She wanted to give him good holiday memories to store up.

The roast leg of lamb turned out perfectly, moist and tender, the potatoes fluffy and the carrots glazed to perfection.

Joshua laughed. "You are the only woman I know who sounds as if she's having sex when she's eating."

She loved seeing him so completely relaxed. He was wearing the jeans she'd bought him last time and a fisherman knit sweater that did very nice things to his shoulders. "I love holidays." She felt warm and dreamy and so content she could melt.

After being told to take her wine into the living room, she lounged in front of the fire while Joshua cleaned up the kitchen. He came and sat on the other end of the sofa, pulling her feet into his lap. He massaged her toes through her thick, wool socks.

"When I was a kid," she said, watching the fire spark and leap in the stone fireplace, "I had a scrapbook. I'd look for food pictures and holiday pictures and paste them into my special book. I loved the pictures of families the best. You know the ones? Happy moms and kids eating Campbell's soup in a big country kitchen."

He stopped kneading. "What happened to the book?"

She felt herself blush. "I still have it. Silly, huh?"

"No." His voice sounded rough, and she turned her head to look at him. "It's damn sad. Why have you never married and had the family you so obviously want, Jessie?"

Tell him, she thought. Oh God, this was the perfect opportunity to tell him. The words gathered and dispersed in her mind. All the food coupled with wine and the warmth of the fire had dulled her brain. The moment passed.

"I fell in love with the wrong knight."

"How old were you?"

"Twenty-one."

"Did he break your heart forever?" he asked roughly, setting her feet aside so he could throw more logs into the already roaring fire. She watched the sweater stretch over his broad shoulders and the way the jeans lovingly cupped his behind.

"At the time I thought so." *I had no idea how much worse it could get.*

"I never thought such a thing as love really existed." He picked up her feet, pulling off her socks. He tossed them on the floor. His hands, big and warm closed over her bare toes. "It hardly seems worth the risk of a broken heart."

"What you get from love is greater than the risk of never loving at all." She would have this year to remember for the rest of her life.

"If you get to know someone too well, you can see all their faults and failings." He stared into the orange flames, his jaw set. Outside, the darkness pressed against the windows, cocooning them in a suddenly very small world.

"Or you can learn to care?" she said softly.

He shrugged, looking uncomfortable. "I despise anyone weak."

"Perhaps they were just human?" Who was he talking about? Stacie? His mother?

A muscle jumped in his jaw. "My father saw me as weak."

"You *were* weak, Joshua," Jessie said softly. "You were a child."

"The thought of being that weak again terrifies me." He said it like a grim confession. Jessie's heart ached for him.

"Love makes people strong, Joshua. The love of a mother for a child, or a man for a woman. We all need someone to care about us. We all try to attain that special place where we feel loved and safe."

"People are exactly where they want to be." His eyes appeared particularly pale as he turned to her. "The choices we all make lead us to where we are at any given time. If a person doesn't like where they are then they should make different choices, shouldn't they, Jessie?"

"I suppose so," she answered drowsily. She'd certainly made a series of bad choices. His logic seemed rather convoluted, but then she was almost asleep.

A log popped. Joshua's fingers kneaded her instep. Jessie floated in a warm haze.

"Let's have a party when we get back," Joshua said out of the blue.

"Mmm, okay."

"I want a big party, Jessie. We'll invite everyone we know. You can boss around the caterers and staff to your heart's content." Jessie felt a small smile curve her mouth.

"Like parties suddenly?" she asked around a yawn. She thought he hated parties.

"This one will be spectacular."

"Joshua," she said, on the precipice of sleep. "*Why* are you having a party?

OCTOBER

"GOOD TIMING. I just woke up from a nap. Oh goodie, chocolate." Jessie reached for a cookie off the Spode plate. Archie and Conrad had arrived unannounced at the cottage bearing chocolate chip cookies. She'd led them into her small kitchen overlooking the vegetable garden.

Jessie absently coiled her hair in a knot and secured it off her neck with a pencil while the two men exchanged a glance over her head.

"What did the doctor say?" Conrad demanded.

"How are arrangements going for the party tomorrow?" Archie asked at the same time. He handed Jessie a paper towel, shooting Conrad a narrow look.

"Great." She poured them coffee and herself a glass of water. "I love bossing people around. I've found I have a real knack for it." She sat down and took another bite of her cookie. "In fact, I'm going over there in a couple of hours to check on things and have dinner with

Joshua. It's so sweet of him to have a party to show off the house.''

"Yeah," Conrad said dryly. "Sweet."

"Well, it *is*."

"He's proud of the job you did," Archie pointed out. "Your work has been getting better and better, Jess. He wants to showcase your talent."

"What a nice thing to say." She licked chocolate off her thumb as the two men lapsed into a rather loud silence. Jessie sighed. "I have good news and I have... other news."

"What's the good news?" Conrad crossed his feet before snagging a cookie he didn't really want.

"The good news is...I'm glad you think my talents are improving 'cause I'll be coming back to work full-time...soon." It was pretty weak, but, after all, this was just the dress rehearsal. Right now she felt as if she were in the hot seat as two sets of eyes bored into the center of her forehead.

"Well?" Archie prodded when she didn't say anything for a few moments.

"The other news is...I'm pregnant." Jessie looked from one to the other. "And don't either of you say I told you so," she warned as they exchanged glances.

"I thought you were using birth control now."

Jessie pulled a wry face. "*Most* of the time in the last few months, yes."

"It's supposed to be used *every* time," Conrad pointed out unnecessarily,

"Sometimes there was no *time*."

"Oh, please *don't!*" Conrad rolled his eyes.

"Oh, well, another little thing gone awry with life," Archie said drolly, patting her hand. She gave him a smile.

"You don't consider that bad news?" Conrad dropped his feet to the floor, leaned his elbows on the table and scowled.

"Nope." Jessie bit into another cookie.

"Then why have you been biting your nails?"

"Tonight I'm going to tell Joshua everything—"

"Everything?" Archie's eyebrows rose.

"Everything." Jessie rose to stand by the window. The garden looked sad and gloomy in the half-light. Most of the trees were bare and there weren't many flowers. She had to try to remember that after winter, came spring. No matter what. "Oh, God. What a mess. I'm ecstatic about the baby. Thrilled. Over the moon. But I'm terrified of Joshua's reaction."

"Isn't that a little like the thief that's sorry *after* he's caught?" Conrad asked soberly.

"I wasn't *caught.*" Jessie chewed her thumbnail. "I really thought I could pull this off, but you guys were right." She leaned back against the windowsill, braced by her arms. She wore her fluffy pink robe but her feet were bare, and cold, on the vinyl floor. She shivered.

"I should have been up front from the beginning. I thought I'd get pregnant faster. I never planned on *this.*" She swallowed the lump in her throat with difficulty before she managed to tell them both what they knew already. "All I've done is fall more deeply in love with Joshua." She sighed. "This is going to cut what little time we had left short. Finding out he's about to become a father won't send him dancing through the streets in celebration."

She pushed away from the window, crossed back to sit at the table and pulled her feet up beneath her. She wrapped her arms around her knees.

"The game was fine when it was just the two of us.

But I'm not going to play games with our baby. I can't lie by omission anymore. Besides—'' she rested her chin on her knees ''—how can I expect Joshua to make a rational decision about us when he doesn't know all the facts?''

"He'll be furious," Archie warned.

"I know," Jessie said calmly. "But I still have to tell him."

JOSHUA WALKED into the dining room and surveyed it with a critical eye. The table was elegantly draped with a pale-pink damask tablecloth, the delicate cream-and-blush colored roses had been part of Jessie's order from South America for the party tomorrow night. China and silver gleamed. Stemware sparkled.

He swallowed the dryness in his throat as he checked his pocket for perhaps the twentieth time in the past half hour. God, he was as nervous as a schoolboy. He smiled self-consciously as he walked back down the hall into his den and poured himself a stiff drink.

Jessie was magic. His talisman against the cold loneliness he'd let fill his life. Jessie was warmth and laughter. She made him believe he really mattered to her. She made him believe she knew a part of him no one else had ever seen. She was soft and loving, and so open and honest with her feelings; it was like looking into a crystal-clear mountain pool.

Joshua sank into his favorite chair. In the gathering darkness he could see part of the curving driveway from the mullioned windows in his den. He'd be able to see Jessie's little red car as she approached the house.

Jessie with her sparkling brown eyes and throaty laugh. Jessie with her electric hair. Jessie with her long, slender dancer's body. She had that sensuous way of moving that always made him want her.

If what he had with Jessie was just good sex, it would have been easy to dismiss. He'd had good sex before. But with Jessie even the sex was different. As much as he'd tried to deny it, Jessie was right. It was lovemaking. It was glorious, blow-the-top-of-your-head-off great. But there was more. There was her humor, her intelligence, her honesty and integrity. With Jessie he had learned to relax, smell the flowers. And finally, in a small measure, Joshua had to admit he'd learned to trust.

He suddenly wished he *had* married half a dozen times, because with Jessie he wanted everything to be perfect. If he'd tried a real marriage before, he'd have the bugs worked out by now.

He rolled up the sleeves of his blue-and-white striped dress shirt then rolled them down again. Was he too dressed up? Was he too stuffy? Should he wear the jeans she'd bought him? Christ, this was ridiculous—he'd already changed twice. He laughed out loud, ridiculously happy.

Jessie would be home soon. They would have a drink, go through to dinner, and after the staff served dessert, he would take the little box out of his pocket. Joshua closed his eyes, leaning back in the big leather chair as he imagined the look on Jessie's face when she saw the ring. She'd get that sexy little twinkle in her glorious eyes, probably jump up and fling herself at him…. Joshua lost himself in pleasant daydreams.

He hadn't heard her car but he heard the front door open. Heard Jessie's high heels on the marble, the wood, the carpet.

He opened his eyes. God, she looked glorious in a royal-blue wool dress and high-heeled black suede boots. She tossed the dark coat she carried onto a chair by the door.

Her hair was curled wildly from the wind, her cheeks flushed, her eyes bright. Without a word she crossed the room and settled herself on his lap, curling her arms about his neck, the sweet curve of her butt nestled against him. She smelled of fresh peaches as she raised her mouth to his.

"Is that a gun in your pocket or are you just happy to see me?" she said in a Mae West drawl.

Joshua laughed, burying his hands in her hair. It was still a little damp and smelled of peach shampoo. He crushed her mouth with a bruising kiss, plumbing the depths as she relaxed against his chest. Her fingers curled around his open collar, holding on for dear life.

"God, Jess," he managed to moan before she lowered her head again.

"We have to talk," Jessie said against his throat. She sounded reluctant. He ran his hand down the soft wool covering her back.

They were going to have a lifetime to talk. "After dinner. How do I get into this thing?" Her skin was warm as he slowly lowered the zipper down her back, detouring to unclasp her bra on the way down.

After Joshua had peeled away the dress, Jessie stood so it could fall unnoticed to the floor. She looked seductive in tiny bikini briefs and black boots. He slid his hands up her thighs to her hips, drawing her close for another kiss.

She yelped when he swung her up in his arms. With one swipe, he cleared his big burl desk, laying her down on the cool leather surface.

"This feels very naughty." Her voice was husky, her

eyes alive, the lights in them dancing. The heels of her boots tapped on the face of the desk.

"You're overdressed." He pulled the small damp strip of satin down her smooth legs. Jessie sprawled bonelessly, her breath uneven.

He dropped the fragrant scrap to the carpet, running his hands up the flexing muscles of her long legs. And he laughed hoarsely when she said in a lazy drawl, "Glad you got rid of that. No wonder I was so hot."

She watched him through heavy-lidded eyes as he stripped off the shirt he'd so carefully put on. Her eyes grew lambent, her knees flexed, as he kicked off his shoes and dragged socks and slacks off in two swift jerks.

He'd wanted it to last. He'd wanted to linger over each delectable soft inch. Showing her how much he wanted her. Loving her until she was too weak to refuse him anything. But the moment he plunged into her tight, slick warmth, the moment he felt the rough suede of her boot-clad legs wrap about his flanks, he was lost.

Their climax was immediate and turbulent, leaving him stretched across her body, his face pressed against her damp neck.

"It *was* a gun in your pocket," Jessie said with a faint laugh.

He gently lifted the drift of hair off her face and used the backs of his fingers to explore the texture of her sex-warmed cheek.

With his other hand he tilted her face up before dipping his head toward her. She gave him a drowsy, sexy look at the touch of his lips on her forehead.

He stroked down her side, enjoying the way her skin shimmered under his hand. He continued to pet her and she groaned, rising up to bury her face against his shoulder. Their bodies were slick with sweat.

"I'll give you twenty years to stop that." Jessie looked like a wanton, pagan princess with her hair spread in a dark cloud, her arms curved seductively above her head. Joshua stood between her thighs, his arms braced against the desk.

"You're insatiable."

Eyes that were almost all pupil stared back at him. Sleepy, sensuous and sated. "That's a problem?" she asked lazily as her foot slid up the back of his thigh, and she ran her hands up the muscles flexing in his arms.

"Not to me, it isn't." Her feet met and crossed in the small of his back; he could feel her sharp high heels drawing him closer. He braced his arms firmly for a moment, looking at her with fresh new eyes, his heart playing an unfamiliar beat.

"You drive me wild, Jessie Adams. When I'm with you I want you. When we're apart I think about you constantly. You worry me. You make me laugh. You make me believe in dreams."

Her crossed ankles proved stronger than his will as she drew him against the open heat of her. Joshua lowered his chest, feeling the pillowy softness of her breasts flatten under him. He whispered against her swollen mouth, "I want to wrap you in a cloud and put you on top of the highest mountain to keep you safe." His gaze never wavered as he lifted her hand to his lips. "I'm excited by you, Jessie, and yet strangely calmed by your presence. You're unpredictable and your crazy hobbies give me heart palpitations. You have the strangest, strongest set of principles of anyone I know, and I'm learning to trust you more than I have ever trusted another human being in my life."

Her face drained of color, deathly pale. He felt the flutter of her fingers as she tried to withdraw her hand from his. "What is it, love?" Jessie bit her lip and worry immediately slammed into his chest.

She closed her eyes for the longest moment then licked her lips before she looked up at him. "I went to the doctor today." Her voice shook. She bit her bottom lip and took a deep, shuddering breath, her eyes dark and huge.

A cold chill of dread raced up his spine. He lifted himself away from her, sex the last thing on his mind now. For a moment he felt as though every particle of his body had frozen. A fear he'd never known drew a black ominous cloud over his vision. It made his heart jerk and his hands sweat.

He blinked, too terrified to look at her and yet too terrified not to. He thrust his fingers through his hair in frustration and swore under his breath. "You went to the doctor today.... Oh, Christ, Jessie." Joshua squeezed his eyes shut, a fist squeezing his heart. He forced open his eyes. Her lips were bloodless, her eyes dark with pain. Oh, God, it was bad, really bad, for Jessie to be this upset.

"What the hell did he say? Whatever it is we can deal with it together. Christ, I have more money than God. We'll get the best specialists on the planet. We'll—"

The phone rang just as Jessie said his name in a terrified, tremulous voice and struggled to sit up.

"Tell me, for Christ's sake," he demanded, ignoring the insistent ringing of the phone inches from Jessie's head. It wasn't like Jessie to be reticent in telling him anything he wanted to know. Her wonderfully expressive brown eyes wouldn't meet his. The phone's insistent ringing was annoying the shit out of him.

"Tell me," he ground out, his back teeth grinding painfully.

"I—I—" Jessie's teeth bit into her lower lip. "Answer the phone first."

"The hell with it. What did the doctor s—"

Jessie grabbed the phone off the hook and handed it to him.

"Yes!" Joshua snatched the instrument to his ear, his eyes fixed on Jessie's averted face. What the hell would he do if Jessie died? What the hell would—

"*What* did you say?" he demanded as he registered what Felix had just said on the other end of the phone. "Vera wants five million dollars?"

If possible Jessie went even whiter. Hell, this evening wasn't going exactly as he'd planned. He'd thought to propose first, explain his sham marriage later. The shit would hit the fan now. Jessie had the strangest expression on her face as she slid off his desk.

"Fine. Give it to her!" Joshua snapped at Felix, impatient to get off the phone. Jessie had pulled on her dress. She looked sick as she frantically searched for her underwear. Joshua found the scrap of satin stuffed between the papers on the floor and handed it to her. She crammed it into her purse and grabbed her coat by the door. "Just pay her off. It's worth it." Joshua slammed the phone down. Jessie stood poised, ready for flight out the door.

"Now, what aren't you telling me? What the hell did the doctor say?"

SHE WORE A sunflower-yellow wool dress which covered her from her throat to midcalf. Suede high-heeled boots in a deep cinnamon matched the turtleneck under the dress. In her ears she wore huge painted sunflowers. She looked vibrantly alive and breathtakingly lovely.

And furiously angry.

"And I couldn't have talked right then if my life had depended on it," Jessica told Felix angrily. She stood before his desk, having driven to his San Francisco office to be there at precisely nine the next morning. "I was so darn mad, I ran. God only knows what Joshua thought." She drew an angry breath. "I know you're *his* lawyer, Felix, but I thought you and I had a business arrangement. So would you please explain to me why 'Vera' wants five—" she almost choked on the amount "—five million dollars?"

The intercom buzzed announcing Simon Falcon. Jessie rolled her eyes. "Did you call him in a panic while I cooled my heels in your waiting room? Damn it, Felix. How could you do this to me?"

Simon closed the door behind him, resting his hand on Jessie's shoulder. "Sit down, honey. This is not what you think."

Jessie shook off his hand and flopped furiously into the soft leather chair opposite Felix's desk. She glared first at Joshua's lawyer, then at his uncle. "What are you two up to? I told you years ago to stop taking Joshua's money." Jessie clenched her fist on her knee. "Damn it, I've almost saved enough to repay what I *have* taken for the past seven years. No wonder he's got such a poor opinion of women. And now you two have made it even worse. God. I can't take much more of this," she said thickly, dashing impatiently at the persistent tears.

"Just hang in there, honey." Simon looked at her worriedly, as he leaned over to pat her hand. "Joshua'll never miss the money. He's a generous man. He has plenty to spare. We just wanted to make sure you'd be financially solvent by year's end." He looked helplessly at his accomplice. "If he didn't fall in love with you. And we—"

"Well," Jessie snapped, "he won't *now,* for God sake! I don't need Joshua to bankroll me, Simon. I have a job. I can support myself," Jessie said through her teeth. "And in the new year I'll go back to it." She jumped up and started to pace, the yellow dress swishing around her legs.

Both men looked alarmed as tears ran unchecked down her face. She continued to dash them away with her fingertips. "Damn it, damn it, damn it. He already thinks every woman he meets is a conniving opportunist. Now he thinks Vera wants five million dollars for a divorce! Are you two nuts? How could you d-do this to him?"

"Honey." Simon glanced from Felix to Jessie, his face creased with worry. "In a month Joshua…" He searched for the right words. Jessie let the tears fall. She was so tired. So tired of being tired. Crying in front of these two men was the least of her problems.

"A lovely women like you should be worshipped, my dear," Simon said uncomfortably. "Joshua's a fool to let you out of his sight. But you knew this was going to happen."

Jessie drew in a deep, shaky breath. She felt raw to the bone. "I don't want to be worshipped. I wanted to be lo-loved." Her breath bubbled. She hated this. Hated it. "In four weeks, Joshua and I would have broken up." Jessie swiped at her cheeks with the hankie Felix handed her. She got makeup all over it. She scrunched it in a damp ball in her fist. "I don't want his money. I *won't* take his money. Let 'Vera' give him his divorce. But if you two try to take one more cent from Joshua, I'll—I'll do something nasty.''

Simon and Felix rose. ''Honey, we just did it so when it was over you'd have something.''

''I'll *have* something, Simon. Trust me. Something far more lasting and important than money.''

10

IT HAD BEEN a hell of a morning and it was barely ten. Joshua had told Angela to hold all his calls as he tried Jessie's number for the umpteenth time.

He was frantic.

Where the hell was she? He'd tried calling a dozen times last night. He'd sat in his car in her driveway waiting for her to come home until the sky had lightened over the trees. He'd been too agitated to wait inside. Still no sign of Jessie. He'd talked to Archie, to Conrad, to Simon and, finally, to the hospitals. No one knew where the hell she was.

Unease and worry had turned into dread. She'd sped out of the house so fast last night, she hadn't answered his questions. And as much as Joshua loathed admitting it, the unfamiliar ball of lead in the pit of his stomach was fear. He was tormented with it.

He pressed a finger to his temple, warning himself to rationalize this. He had known she wanted to tell him something last night. Something important. Something she'd found hard to share. What the hell could it be? The suppositions were becoming more and more alarming. In the last hours he had come up with every worst-case scenario possible. And every way he could think of to correct it, rectify it, and make it better. Unless it was terminal.

If it was terminal he couldn't do a damn thing. Even *he* couldn't fix that.

He closed his eyes. He ignored the ringing phone. He ignored the faint hum of voices in the outer office. His concentration was complete and total. His focus unwavering. He wanted to pray but for a moment, had no idea *how*. He figured God knew his track record and wouldn't care. Words tumbled frantically through his mind. He begged, bargained and made promises, his eyes squeezed so tightly shut, they watered.

He reached for the phone again. He'd have Felix send out one of his P.I.'s. He drummed a tattoo on the highly polished surface of his desk as he waited, feeling demented, the ice in his soul making him burn. Christ, for all he knew Jessie could be lying dead somewhere—

Hell, he wouldn't think like that. Joshua looked up impatiently as his office door opened. "I told you I didn't want to be disturbed, Angela, unless it's—" The lead ball in the pit of his stomach dissolved like mist. He slammed down the receiver.

Fear dissipated into something he understood even less. Anger then relief, then something else too fragile to name.

"Where the hell have you been?" he demanded, as Jessie crossed to sit in the visitor's seat opposite his desk. The brave red of her wool suit leached every vestige of color from her face. Her hair was pulled back with a cream-colored clip that matched her high-heeled shoes and blouse. She crossed her lovely legs with a whisper of nylon and pulled her skirt down.

Her face seemed finer boned and drawn this morning. Dark shadows haunted her eyes. She looked fragile, as though she'd been crying.

Joshua's throat tightened. "God, I'm sorry." He

cleared his throat. "I'm not angry at you. When I couldn't find you I... Jesus, Jessie..."

"I'm sorry you were worried." She sounded as subdued as he felt frantic. His blood pressure rose two more notches. "I..." She licked glossy red lips and swallowed before she looked up at him. "I needed a little more time."

Worry made his voice harsh. "Where were you last night?"

"I stayed at a hotel in San Jose."

"Why, for God's sake?" Joshua resisted scrubbing his face, instead clenching his hands together on the surface of the desk. His palms were damp. "Don't hold it in, Jessie, whatever it is. Just say it." He resisted the need to hold her. He had never been more afraid in his life. If he touched her now, he was terrified he'd inadvertently break her in half when she told him the bad news. The bones in his hands protested the excruciating pressure being exerted.

Wide brown eyes looked at him steadily. She drew a breath. "I'm pregnant, Joshua."

For a split second the relief that Jessie wasn't going to die was so profound he couldn't speak. His fingers felt arthritic as he slowly released their death grip.

Then he stared at her. Actually *heard* what she said. Pregnant.

He had been thinking the best doctors and specialists in a sanitarium in Switzerland. *She* had been thinking child support.

Rage consumed him.

For a moment he went deaf and blind with it. "You're pregnant." Frigid anger relit the fuse low in his belly. "You're pregnant?"

He stood, his fists braced on the desk. "Whose is it?"

Jessie flinched imperceptibly. "Yours, of course."

"Not in this lifetime, lady." Jessie's eyes went dark. A thundering pulse pounded his temple. Contempt tightened his voice. "I had a vasectomy years ago."

She sucked in her breath. "Impossible."

Joshua delivered the next thrust as the fire in his gut blazed, his voice dangerously even. "Right after the third of my mistresses claimed I was the father of her child. It didn't work for them, and it sure as hell won't work for you. I shoot blanks."

The heat in her cheeks returned full force as she catapulted from the chair to lean over his desk, her eyes blazing. "You son of a— Why didn't you tell me you'd had a vasectomy? How *dare* you keep something like that from—"

"How dare *I?*" he asked lethally and she collapsed back into the chair sputtering with impotent anger. If looks could kill, he'd be in the morgue.

Her sudden flair of fiery temper was no match for his own icy rage. "Nice of you to look me in the eye as you stabbed me in the back, Jessie." He looked at her with utter contempt. "At least the others controlled their greed until their contract was up. That's why you wouldn't commit by signing the contract, you wanted out the second you found some kind of hold on me. You couldn't wait, could you? You should have done your research before coming up with this far-fetched scenario."

He picked a hair off the shoulder of his charcoal Armani suit. He stared at the curling filament for a moment before dropping it to the floor. He had worn this suit to the theater with her. He would burn the damn thing the moment he got home.

"That's not true," Jessie said steadily, a pulse pounding hard at her throat. "I didn't plan this pregnancy." She glanced away, biting her lower lip before glaring at him defiantly. "Well, okay, maybe at first I did. But then I cha—"

For a moment his emotions blackened his vision. "You planned this from the beginning, did you?"

"Yes. No," she floundered, cheeks scarlet, eyes glittering.

"Well, which was it? Yes or no?"

"I changed my mind." Her voice was unnaturally calm. "I knew I couldn't do it without discussing it with you first—"

"Right." He was old enough to know better. "A 'happy' accident?" She flinched. "You were right," he said cruelly, flatly, his eyes unwavering on her face. "You *are* just like your mother." Emotions started ripping through his control. "Wasn't she a money-grabbing whore, too, Jessie?"

"Oh, God. Don't do this, Joshua." Her voice quavered and he saw her swallow dryly before she managed to say raggedly, "Please." Her eyes went dark, as if a careless hand had snuffed out that vibrant bright inner light of hers. His careless hand.

But he wasn't done yet. Not by a long shot.

"Oh, I beg your pardon. You refused to take my money, didn't you?" His voice sharpened, turned to jagged ice as he demanded venomously, "What do you think those earrings you're wearing are worth, Jessie?"

She put an unsteady hand to a diamond-and-ruby hoop. "I don't kn—"

"Try in the neighborhood of fifty thousand."

Her eyes widened and her hand dropped as though burned. "You told me it was *costume* jewelry."

"The 'bigger the better,' isn't that what you told me?"

"Yes, but I mea—"

"Can't tell a diamond from a piece of glass, Jessie?" he asked mockingly. "You'll have to take a quick gemology class before you get your claws into your next victim."

She took off the earrings and laid them carefully on his desk, her eyes blank and dark.

The chair creaked under his weight as he sat down. "Oh, that trembling lip is almost effective. But you forget. I've screwed the best actresses money can buy. Your performance in bed almost makes this fiasco tolerable." He gave her a cold humorless smile. "Almost."

"Giving me your virginity was worth the jewelry. I consider it a fair trade. What you lacked in experience in bed you made up for in enthusiasm." A chill vibrated through him. "That act would have earned you a small bonus." He paused. "If you hadn't let some other man benefit from what I taught you," he finished savagely as she sucked in air and seemed to brace herself for another blow.

An uncomfortably tight band restricted his breathing and perspiration stuck his shirt to his back. "All the protestation about the gifts I gave you was a blind for the big payoff, right, Jessie?"

"No." Her damn lying eyes stayed steadily on his face. "I told you, I only wanted you."

"Well, you *had* me." His anger almost obscured his vision. "Is there anything else?" he demanded when she sat before him motionless.

"Yes, actually, there is." She touched her purse. "But now is obviously n-not the time to—to—" She waved away her words with a shaking hand. She rose, all elegant grace and proud fluid lines. "I haven't slept with anyone but you, Joshua. When you calm down you'll realize that."

"I'm perfectly calm." His back teeth ground together. "I'll give you thirty seconds to explain how you think this could possibly have happened."

She moved to the back of the chair, putting it between herself and his anger. "I don't think this is the right time to discuss this."

"It's the perfect time," he pushed. "What should we put it down to? Immaculate conception?"

"We made love morning, noon and night. You'd better sue your doctor. Your vasectomy didn't work."

"You said you were on the pill."

"No, I said I'd take care of birth control...." She looked at him and paused before saying, "You're right, yes. I admit getting pregnant was initially my objective. My *only* objective. Not because I wanted to trap you, but because—because I wanted a baby. Then I fell in love with you and I *did* use birth control, except that a lot of times I didn't have time and I—oh, damn it." Large brown eyes filled as she admitted lying through her beautifully straight white teeth.

He watched the performance unmoved. A band of pink painted her cheekbones. "I eventually *did* use birth control, but I didn't realize I was already pregnant." Jessie rubbed her forehead. "I hadn't conceived in all those months...I don't know...perhaps this baby is meant to be born."

Joshua laughed.

She sagged, catching herself with a hand to the back of a chair as her knees seemed to give way. He watched her struggle with her tears. Pride tilted her chin. She had appeared so innocent, so absolutely unconcerned and unimpressed by his wealth. He looked at her, really looked at her and his chest hurt with the purity of her face, the absolute resignation in those liquid brown eyes.

A pulse throbbed at the base of her throat. Joshua had to drag his gaze away from her smooth skin. He knew from personal experience that looks could be deceiving. She was out to get him, just as the others had been. Oh, she wanted money, and lots of it apparently, but she'd come closer to getting far more than that.

Goddamn her soul. She had almost had his heart.

He closed his eyes against the sweet curves of her body, against ever feeling the electricity of her hair against his skin, of ever hearing her small breathy moans of passion. He looked at her for the last time and his voice was as cold as his soul. "I'll call Felix. He'll arrange the usual settlement. You can contact him this afternoon."

Her jaw jerked up. "Can't we talk about this rationally?" Her voice was rough and raw. She looked as though she were trying to push the tears back into her eyes as she pressed her fingers to her cheekbones. She never had a damn tissue when she needed one. The tears came faster. "I love you."

"You love my lifestyle."

She squeezed her eyes shut, blocking him out. Tears leaked between spiky lashes. He hardened his heart as a sob escaped her. "Oh, no," he growled. "Don't go all pale and piteous on me now. I like you much better when you're spitting like a little cat." His gut burned with the betrayal he felt. This was as close as he'd ever been to striking a woman. He didn't want her looking white-faced and soft. He wanted her to come out of her corner fighting. She had already delivered the fatal body blow, but *he* wanted to finish it, put her on the mat and start counting.

It wasn't like Jessie to just stand there. Why the hell wasn't she defending herself more vigorously?

Because she had planned this all along. Everything had been a lie. Every goddamned word. Every action had been to set him up for this. The big payoff. Her agenda hadn't changed one iota from the first moment they'd met.

He cursed her for having wounded brown eyes and skin so soft and sweet the taste of her stayed on his tongue. He cursed her for trying to pull off a paternity suit. He would have given Jessie his last cent and rushed out to earn more if she'd asked. He cursed her for bringing him so low that he had to grind his teeth and lock his knees to prevent himself from falling to the floor and begging her to stay anyway.

Pain and humiliation swamped him in a tidal wave, so deep, so dark, he thought he might never recover.

"Tell Felix not to bother. I didn't sleep with you for your bank balance or the size of your wallet. All I ever wanted was..."

He raised an inquiring brow, daring her.

"I love our baby," she said and looked right at him. "I don't need or want your damn money." She swallowed with difficulty before saying with awful calm, "I didn't mean to fall in love with you. It snuck up on me and caught me by surprise. I hoped you would eventually fall in love with me. I thought...hoped..." She choked back another sob. "I wanted nothing from you—"

Fury ripped through him. "Except that million-dollar baby," he mocked, not caring as her face crumpled, and she started to shake. He didn't give a damn. "Take a damn DNA test. If it's mine, I'll claim it. But I don't think that'll be an issue.''

"No."

"No?"

"I won't take a test. I know who the father is." Jessie dashed a hand across her wet cheek. "And no, you damn well will *not* take my baby. I paid for her in blood. She's *mine*."

He didn't realize he'd rounded his desk until he found his hands clamped on Jessie's slender shoulders. He could see his temper had stunned her. Well, hell, he wasn't done yet. As she stoically stared up at him, a comb fell from her hair. Strands were stuck to the tears on her cheeks.

"Tonight was supposed to be our engagement party. I was going to marry you. I was going to care for you and cherish you for the rest of our miserable lives." He laughed harshly, letting her go. She staggered, caught herself and rubbed her upper arms, shivering violently.

"A little more patience and you could have had it all, Jessie."

"Joshua, please…"

He strode to the closed door ready to snap it open and push her through if she stayed a moment longer. He heard her draw in a long shaky breath behind his back. Damn her. Damn her to hell.

He punched a hole in the wall with his fist. The sound loud and violent in the unnaturally quiet of his office. A mirror fell, shattering into a million broken shards on the thick carpet.

"Well, hell," he said sarcastically. "Another seven years bad luck." A cruel fist tightened around his heart. His hand throbbed and pain radiated up his arm. He jerked open the door. "Get the hell out. I never want to see your face again."

Her eyes went blank before she closed them. "If you ever change your mind—" When she opened them again, they were filled with regrets.

"Don't hold your breath."

She picked up her purse and straightened, looking from the hole in the wall to his hand, then back to his face. Pale, but resolved, she walked to the door and paused.

"Do I have to call security?" he asked coldly.

She didn't turn, but her fingers whitened on the edge of the thick oak door. Her shoulders stiffened and her chin came up. "Goodbye, Joshua."

"AND I SOBBED," Jessie said disgustedly, dry-eyed and furious. She paced Archie and Conrad's family room. "I cried!" She threw up her hands in disgust and kicked off her shoes.

"You're pregnant with his child and the son of a bitch broke your heart," Archie commiserated. "Of course, you cried."

"He lost his temper." Jessie wrapped her arms around her waist and glared at the far wall. "He was so angry." Tears welled. "So hurt." Jessie pressed her fingertips into her eye sockets. "Damn it, my hormones have gone haywire. Why did I have to cry?"

"Because the closed-minded jerk hurt you!" Conrad perched on the arm of the sofa.

Jessie spun around. "He is *not* a jerk." She grabbed the box of tissues Archie held out as she walked by him. "Well, okay, he can be a jerk." She wiped her nose. "My crying only made him feel worse."

"*Him* feel worse?" both men asked in unison.

Jessie blew her nose. "All the poor man wanted was a nice uncomplicated affair. I wasn't supposed to fall in love with the man."

"Excuse me for a moment as I try to instill a touch of reality into the conversation here. Didn't he contribute to your pregnancy?" Conrad asked, eyebrows raised.

"He claims to have had a vasectomy." The tears dried like a puddle in the desert sun. "I could just strangle him for not telling me that." She was furious all over again.

"Shit, Jess. You are Pollyanna." Conrad snatched a handful of tissues from the box in her hand. Dabbing the trail of mascara running down her cheeks, he said firmly, "Call my father. Get every dime that bastard has. Arch and I will be surrogate fathers."

Jessie gave him a distracted smile. "You two will make excellent daddies, but don't blame Joshua for being angry. I shattered his last few remaining illusions. If this had happened in January as planned, we wouldn't be having this conversation. It's not his fault we wanted different things. He never once in all these months pretended to be anything he was not. Or promised me anything he didn't deliver. I was the one telling all the whoppers. He was starting to trust me." She chewed on a fingernail. "He was so hurt, he claimed he had wanted to marry me!"

"You're *already* married," Archie reminded her.

"Oh, for heaven's sake! *He* doesn't know that!" Those darn tears spilled again. Jessie scrubbed at her face. "I'm the one who betrayed that trust. I'm the one who's been living a lie. If the pregnancy made him angry what's he going to do when he finds out the rest of it?"

"You better skip the country," Archie said, half joking.

Jessie tried to smile. It was an impossible task. "How come when you get your heart ripped out you can still feel it breaking inside?"

She wondered at her own naiveté to think that she could spend twelve minutes with Joshua, let alone twelve months, without having her foolish heart broken into little pieces. She should have divorced him years ago. She shouldn't have carried the divorce papers around with her for years. She should have signed and filed them.

Instead, she had only memories and a handful of papers to prove she had ever known and loved him at all. And a tiny baby who would never know her father. Jessie felt the sting of tears again.

Her throat tightened. She had come to know him so well. How could she hope to salvage his pride after what she had done to him?

She should have come right out and told him who she was. She should have done a lot of things, Jessie thought morosely. What she should *not* have done was fall in love with him.

She had listened to him in his office. And although the words had been cruel, she had seen beneath his anger to the hurt tearing him apart.

Or she thought she had. She couldn't forget that she'd misdiagnosed his feelings before.

She'd looked at the strong lines of his face, so dear and so heartbreakingly familiar. Her eyes blurred as she struggled to store up memories like photographs. It took no effort to remember every line beside his pale eyes, nor the way those eyes had cut through her like an icy laser beam.

Now it was over. Irretrievable. Somewhere, in a small rational part of her heart, Jessie had known it would come to this. Movies and romances had happy endings. This was real life. A woman like her could never in a trillion years bring a man like Joshua Falcon to his knees.

She settled her hand over the small roundness of her tummy. He had inadvertently given her something more precious than Tiffany diamonds or real estate, something she'd wanted more than anything else.

"Be careful what you wish for," her mother used to say wistfully watching the door close behind another man. Jessie's breath wedged in her throat as it tightened.

"What are you going to do, love?" Archie asked.

For a moment she couldn't speak. She was chilled soul deep. The weight of tears pressing down on her chest was almost unbearable.

"As Scarlett said, 'Tomorrow is another day.'" Jessie managed a wobbly smile before grabbing another handful of tissues out of the box. "But first, I need to cry for a while."

It wasn't only what they *had* that she'd miss. It was what they *could* have had.

11

IT WAS mid-December. A time of year Joshua already loathed. He felt as though he'd spent the past weeks living in a vacuum. Everywhere he looked, Christmas glowed and shimmered. Every store window blazed with red and green.

He closed his eyes and could see her. Those big brown eyes sparkling, that sweet, succulent mouth just waiting... In his mind, he could hear Jessie's throaty laughter. He could smell fresh peaches. Aw, hell.

All he could think of was Jessie. Jessie mischievously wearing a crown of holly. Jessie laughing up at him before welcoming him home. Jessie, Jessie, Jessie.

Jessie loved holidays. Christmas was her favorite. The story about her dream book had almost broken his damn heart when she'd told it. All those carefully cutout pictures from newspapers and magazines. All those unfulfilled dreams and wishes.

If any of that had been true. He'd convinced himself that even *that* had been part and parcel of her lies. She'd wanted that damn baby. She hadn't had a change of heart. She'd planned and executed her attack with the finesse of a general. Her weapons were state-of-the-art, old as Eve, and had almost worked. God, she had been furious when he'd told her he'd had the vasectomy. Furious!

He didn't want to think about Jessie. The fact that this

time of year would forever remind him of her pissed him off even more.

He depressed the button to open the gates to the estate, dreading the dark and empty house. He was glad he'd invited Simon over for drinks before they went out to dinner tonight.

He'd hardly seen Simon since he'd met Jessie. He liked his uncle's company, even when he knew the older man was doing something to manipulate him. Well, tonight he'd tell Simon in no uncertain terms that Jessie was definitely a conversation topic that was off-limits. They'd have a few drinks, get a meal and life would get back to normal.

He'd given most of the servants the month off. He was sick of the dark, accusing looks from his staff. They had adored her. To them, *he* was the villain of the piece. He should tell them about the miracle conception.

Since Jessie had left him, he was getting used to coming home to a dark house. He'd become accustomed to Jessie waiting inside for him. She'd have had every light in the place on in welcome. He didn't even want to think about her warm smile or her comforting arms. The house she had briefly made into a home was now a house again, a place he dreaded entering.

Well, he'd been fine without her before, and he'd be fine again. He didn't need her.

His fingers tightened convulsively around the leather steering wheel. Traitorous little witch. He'd narrowly missed making a complete fool of himself. The tabloid press had already made mincemeat of her. A calendar girl who couldn't even cut the full twelve months. Speculation ran rampant. Joshua ignored it as he always did. It was the job of his public relations team to control what was in the press, only bringing to his attention anything needing his immediate input.

In this instance Joshua turned a blind eye, instructing the PR people to do nothing to stop the innuendo and speculation. He didn't give a damn what happened to her. Jessie had made her bed. Now she would have to lie in it. He didn't even care who she lay in it with.

He wanted to believe she had been nothing but a brief interlude. Quickly forgotten. But the reality was she'd sure as hell changed his life. Never again would he have a mistress for a set period. God, he already felt like a hermit. Sex was the last thing on his mind.

She'd even ruined *that* for him.

He planned to spend the holidays in London this year, and had no intention of telling his friends and business associates there that he was even in the country. Part of him regretted giving her the house in Tahoe. She wouldn't even let him dislike the holidays in his usual location.

It started to rain. A fine depressing mist coated the bare branches of the trees, bowing down the shrubs in the long beds as Joshua pulled the Jag up to the front door. He should change his plans and go somewhere sunny instead, he decided, sprinting up the curved front steps and unlocking the door. Somewhere hot and clean.

Somewhere he'd never been with Jessie.

The first thing that struck him as the front door closed behind him was the smell. He closed his eyes, inhaling deeply.

Obviously he'd gone over the edge. The house was completely empty, yet he smelled a strong scent of pine and cinnamon and the pleasant aroma of apple wood burning.

Joshua tossed his overcoat over the table in the entry

hall and strode down the hallway to his den. And came to a dead stop, his eyes narrowing.

The Christmas tree took up the entire corner by the windows. Brilliant with small white lights, glittering with gold and green and shiny red, the smell permeated the room. In the enormous fireplace, a fire blazed, sending up sparks of blue and orange, which reflected off the packages piled haphazardly beneath the tree. A plate of home-made cookies sat beside the crystal decanters on the drinks trolley.

Jessie.

Joshua's heart took up a frantic rhythm. He drew in a breath as if he were dying.

Jessie was home.

He flexed his still sore right hand. Fool. If she were here he'd kick her out in about two seconds. He didn't need her, and he sure as hell didn't want Christmas, this year more than any other. Damn her.

"Jessie!" He spun away from the room, storming like a demented fool through the empty, quiet house, shouting her name. Everywhere he looked were signs that Jessie had come.

And gone.

Crazed, he threw open doors to unused rooms, banging through closets. His bedroom carried a trace of her scent, but no Jessie. Her side of the closet still held her clothes. Every damn dress he had given her. He slammed the door shut to block out the scent of peaches and Joy and loneliness.

He was enraged at her intrusion. Just when he'd gotten over her. Damn her. How dare she just walk into his house and destroy what little peace of mind he'd found?

The image of his Jessie, big with another man's child pressed against his synapses. Would that picture *ever* go away? Or would it be replayed with one of Jessie holding the other man's child to her breast?

Joshua went back downstairs. His jaw ached and he realized how hard he was gritting his teeth. She had done this to torment him. He wouldn't allow it. Slipping back into his controlled and more manageable persona, Joshua poured a stiff brandy. Trying to show his appreciation for the 1884 Bas Armee, he ignored the tantalizing scent of fresh-baked cookies.

He took the drink with him, staring down at the presents beneath the tree. A green felt cloth, sprinkled with what looked like gold dust, lay like a blanket over something long and curved. Pinned to it was a note.

Joshua crouched down; his fingers trembled slightly as he slipped the note off the fabric.

"Suspend disbelief," she'd written. "Pretend you are seven years old and you've just come downstairs Christmas morning." Joshua closed his burning eyes for a moment. "I can't be part of your future. I've only been a small part of your present. I wanted to give you back something of your past." She hadn't signed the note.

"Damn it, Jessie." He took a deep gulp of Armagnac.

He carefully removed the cloth then sucked in a breath. It was a train. Perfect in every detail. The Lionel engine, black and shiny, was followed by the coal tender. Behind it, freight cars and flatcars carried smaller presents.

The train disappeared behind the sudden mist in his eyes. Joshua sank to his knees, blinking rapidly. Joshua flicked up the on switch. The train started with a whistle and a moment later a puff of smoke rose from the stack. A reluctant smile tugged at his mouth. It hurt, deep inside him.

She had arranged the track around the room, under

the desk, around the chairs and tables. Joshua watched it for almost half an hour, clearing his mind. He had no idea why she'd done it. He didn't want to be charmed.

He stood to refill his glass, absently taking the plate of cookies back to his vantage spot on the floor. Biting into a cookie, he closed his eyes, listening to the clack-clack of tiny wheels on small tracks. He would have given his soul to own this train at seven.

Jessie had remembered.

Jessie who had never received a present until she turned twenty-one. Jessie who'd never owned a toy until she was an adult. Jessie who had never asked him for a damned thing.

A small package slipped from a car as it passed his knee. With trepidation Joshua opened it. Inside was a red Duncan yo-yo. The next package was marbles. The next a Swiss Army Knife. Blue.

Each gift represented something he'd wanted as a child. He opened a gaily wrapped package from under the tree and found the flannel shirt she had promised him in Tahoe. The next box contained a brown bomber jacket.

He tugged off his suit jacket and slipped his arms into the sleeves, smelling leather and a faint, faint trace of Jessie. He slipped his hand into the pocket to pull out the long white silk scarf. She'd heard every secret his heart had revealed and made them come true. She hadn't forgotten anything.

He sat back as the brandy warmed his insides and the fire caressed his skin. He picked up a throw pillow off the couch. It still carried her scent. "Damn you," he seethed, crushing the pillow to his chest. As always the scent of her aroused him. He groaned deep in his chest.

"Damn you to hell," he said. After all, she had sent him there.

He viewed the dozens of precious gifts and mounds of wrapping paper that lay around him, as his train made another circuit of the room. He'd wanted all these things as a child. And *Jessie* had given them to him. Twenty-seven years later.

As the train continued its route about the room Joshua reached for the last gift beneath the tree. It was a narrow, flat box wrapped in gold paper with an iridescent red ribbon. This gift had been buried beneath all the others, almost behind the tree trunk.

Joshua sipped at his drink. He wanted to believe everything that had happened in his office had been a bad dream. That Jessie had never betrayed him. That Jessie was going to walk in any moment, her liquid eyes loving him, laughing that throaty laugh of hers.

The presents were so typical of her, so unexpectedly right. She knew him so damned well—which was why she had been able to sneak under his defenses and render him senseless.

No. Make that *stupid*.

He turned the last package over in his hand. His fingers twitched against the bow. He frowned as he looked down to see his thumb caressing the silky gold paper. He felt ridiculously reluctant to open this last gift of Jessie's. As if by not knowing what it was, he could keep her here in the room with him for just a few more minutes.

Why the hell did almost everything that woman did have to charm him so? His gaze lingered on the piles of shiny paper tossed about the room. Had she meant for him to do more than "suspend disbelief" for the minutes it had taken to open her presents? Had Jessie imagined he was fool enough to believe that bullshit about both the birth control and his vasectomy not working?

The bitterness of gall filled him. He, a man who never vacillated, never had a moment of indecision or ambivalence, was suddenly filled with the most serious of doubts.

More than anything he wanted to believe Jessie's ridiculous story. He shifted from anger to agony in the blink of an eye. It hurt to breathe. He felt as though he were slowly dying without her. Joshua dashed another three fingers of brandy into his glass and tossed it down his throat.

Gasping for air, he waited a moment for the moisture from the alcohol-induced tears to leave his eyes before he glanced at the Rolex on his wrist. The last thing he needed right now was company. Did he have time to call off the evening he'd planned with Simon? Not unless he caught his uncle on the car phone, and what the hell would he use as an excuse?

I came home and Jessie had been here. If I close my eyes I can smell her. She left me every present I'd ever wanted in my life. The box in his right hand cut into his palm. *And she took away something I never knew I wanted…until I met her.*

He shifted in an attempt to ease the uncomfortable tightness in his chest and leaned against the edge of his desk. He was no romantic fool. The arrangement with Jessie was no different than he'd had with numerous other women. Jessie's premature departure was nothing more than a mild inconvenience.

"Yeah, right!" Joshua said out loud as the engine whistled and emitted small puffs of smoke. He closed his eyes. The box in his hand crumpled along the edge as his fingers tightened.

The wind picked up outside, clicking small branches annoyingly against the windows. While he had been sitting on the floor playing like a child, darkness had touched the sky and darkened the room. He hadn't bothered with lights. From beneath the chair across the room he could see the narrow beam of the headlight on his train. That small beam, the amber glow of the dying fire, and the little white lights twinkling on Jessie's tree provided enough light.

Joshua put the empty snifter on the desk, then went over to the fire to open the last gift before Simon arrived.

The paper crackled before revealing its delicious secret. The thought made him smile. Just as Jessie had intended, no doubt.

He took the Swiss Army knife Jessie had given him out of his pocket, stroked the smooth plastic with his thumb, then opened the blade and cut the tape.

Sitting on his haunches before the fire, Joshua carefully removed a sheet of paper from inside the box. The paper smelled of Jessie and it took him a moment to open the single fold.

"Joshua," she wrote. "Please forgive me for what I have done to you. Simon and Felix only kept their silence because I begged them not to tell you."

The paper rustled in his hand. What the hell did Felix and Simon have to do with this?

"I never meant to lie to you, but I wanted a baby so badly. I must admit I would have done almost anything in my power to achieve my goal. I erroneously believed I would conceive immediately. I never for a moment thought that I would fall in love. I think even after I changed my mind about getting pregnant, I subconsciously knew I could never make you love me. There were so many times we were in such a hurry I forgot all about protection."

Yeah. Right!

"I wish I could have been there to love and protect you when you were a child, but since I wasn't, I hope the presents will mean something to you.

"I understand, with your deep mistrust of women, why you didn't believe me about our baby. I know you have been lied to about this before. But the fact remains—we did make this baby together."

Sure, Jessie.

"I know you never want to see me again. I am so sorry for causing you pain."

There were wet splotches blurring the writing. Tears of course.

"If you change your mind...we'll be waiting. If not, then I hope eventually you will be able to forgive me and find a love of your own.

"I will love you forever and a day.

"Your Jessie."

He was tempted to toss the box and its contents into the fire. He'd had enough. She had managed to reduce him to idiot status with the gifts as it was. The band tightened around his chest, just where his heart should have been.

Damn it, Jessie.

The box contained several items. Joshua rose and turned on the desk light so he could see everything more clearly. He couldn't take much more. He wanted to dispense with this last gift before his uncle came in.

It was hard for him to breathe as he opened the next folded piece of paper. Joshua frowned, rotating his shoulder. What the hell...? It was a credit slip from Tiffany's in San Francisco. What had Jessie done? Returned all the jewelry he'd given her? It didn't make sense. Stapled to the back of it was a similar receipt, informing him that the rest of the jewelry was at his lawyer's office for safekeeping.

He held on to it for a few moments before setting it on the desk. He was suddenly dying for another drink, but his feet couldn't have moved across the room right then if he'd tried. Intrigued, he flipped open the next document. What the…?

A cashier's check…for over six million dollars? Where on earth had Jessie got this sort of money? And why was she giving it to him?

He removed a trifolded legal document from Jessie's Pandora's box. It looked well-worn, folded many times as if it had been opened and read many times. Light reflected off a shiny square stapled to the top right-hand corner. His eyes scanned down to the signature at the bottom of the page. He stared for a confused moment at the petition for dissolution of marriage.

He frowned, absently tilting the shiny square to the light. It was a Polaroid picture. A picture of a gangly young girl with wiry orange hair and huge brown eyes, filled with anticipation.

The pain came so suddenly it knocked him to his knees. It ballooned in his chest making Joshua grimace and squeeze his eyes shut as he staggered back against the desk. The red wave washed over him leaving him shaken and breathless. Sweat slicked his skin.

Jessie had managed to do what she'd planned all along. Not content with *ripping* out his heart, she had managed to induce a heart *attack* instead.

Headlights swung up the drive. Too far away. Too late.

Joshua snagged the phone, cradling his left arm against his chest. He managed to hit speed dial.

"Hi, this is Jessie. I can't come to the phone right now…"

A firebomb exploded in his chest. Like flame it shot down his arm.

The receiver dropped from his nerveless fingers. It clattered onto the moving engine and then fell to the carpet with a dull thud. Dimly he heard the whistle of the train as its wheels spun uselessly. Then his pulse thundered in his ears blocking out everything else.

The phone. Had to…911…call…pain…Oh, God. This was it…had to…had…

Black snow swirled, his vision dimmed and he felt himself falling into a dark hole.

"J-Jessieee."

"YOU'RE DAMNED LUCKY," Simon said from his seat beside Joshua's hospital bed.

"I'm fine. It was only a severe anxiety attack." Joshua grimaced, feeling ridiculous.

"It *could* have been a heart attack. The doctor said it was a warning to slow down."

"Yeah. It certainly had that effect." Joshua moved restlessly beneath the covers, his long legs uncomfortable in the too short bed. "Thanks for getting there in time to help, Simon."

"You scared the hell out of me when I found you. Thank God, I remembered I had a key. When I saw you lying there you were so still, and your lips were turning blue. Hell, boy, I almost had a heart attack seeing you like that." Simon got up to pace. Joshua envied him his mobility. They had stuck all sorts of monitoring tubes into him.

Simon ran a hand through his white hair. "You do what they tell you, you hear? They said twenty-four hours' observation and you'd better comply. I have every intention of going before you do, so don't screw up my plans. Understand?"

Joshua shifted restlessly under the covers before reaching over and removing something from the bedside drawer.

"Explain this to me while I wait," he demanded, his jaw tensing. The machine beside the bed beeped.

"What's th—? Oh. Jessie's divorce papers."

Joshua closed his eyes, forcing himself to calm down. The monitor beside the bed emitted several high-pitched, nurse-alerting beeps. She bustled into the room, tsk-tsking, and warned him to take it easy. She took his pulse, straightened sheets and generally annoyed Joshua further. Simon gave him a warning look.

The moment the woman left Joshua said coldly, "Simon? An explanation."

"She said she was going to give you the darn thing. Well, there you have it. Jessie's divorcing you."

"Hard to do since we were never married," he said, needing to hear Simon confirm what he suspected.

"Jessie is Vera, son."

The monitor emitted a series of beeps. "It's true then."

Simon nodded slowly.

Joshua sat up against the metal headboard ignoring the tape tugging painfully at his skin from his movement. "Are you telling me that you knew all along that Jessie was Vera? All these years when you casually mentioned the new decorator Conrad and Archie were training, you knew who she was?" He winced as he pulled the needle from the back of his hand.

"Got her the job, myself." Simon stared, fascinated, as Joshua ripped another tape and needle combo off his skin. "Do you know what you're doing?"

"Obviously not." Joshua grimaced as a bead of blood welled on his hand. He looked up at his uncle. "Jesus, Simon. Whose side were you on?"

"You married that poor child and walked out on her without even taking the time to learn her name. She became part of the family that day—someone had to help her. Felix and I took her under our wing. It was the least we could do."

Joshua swore. He tossed aside the blankets, swung his feet to the cold floor and stood up.

"Where do you think you're going?" Simon asked, alarmed.

"There's something I have to do. Then I'm coming back to finish off you and Felix." Joshua slammed drawers. "But first I have to find my clothes."

"She always was a grasping little bitch," Simon said mildly, watching his nephew with penetrating blue eyes. Another drawer slammed.

"Don't call her a bitch," Joshua warned through clenched teeth. "Aha." He found his shoes, then his socks. Why the hell couldn't they keep everything together?

"Grasping."

"Jessie never asked me for a thing, Simon."

"Selfish, then. All women are."

Joshua opened the wardrobe and removed the rest of his clothing. "Jessie is the most generous, kindhearted woman I've ever met." For a moment his hands were filled with brown leather and the mingling scents of Jessie and unfulfilled needs. He tossed the jacket on the rumpled bed.

"Incapable of loving a man, though."

"Bull." Joshua pulled on underwear and stood to fasten his pants. "Jessie is filled with love."

"All she wanted was expensive presents. That's what they all want."

"Jessie didn't want presents."

"Wanted the notoriety of being with Joshua Falcon in public. Liked the Lear, I bet."

"No." Joshua slipped on his shirt. "She didn't care much for the Lear. She said she preferred the commercial flights because the people were so damn interesting." He buckled his belt and looked on the bed for his socks.

"Well, hell," Simon pushed. "A mistress should know her place. She should have taken pride in the fact she belonged to you, darn her." Simon glanced at Joshua from beneath heavy lids.

"A woman doesn't belong to a man like a dog, Simon."

"No? Well, I don't see why she was humiliated when the gutter press labeled her your 'Calendar Girl.' Hell, she knew it was only for twelve months."

"Ten." Joshua plopped down to pull on socks and shoes.

"Couldn't go the distance, could she? She didn't even have to put in a full year to reap the benefits."

Joshua searched his pockets. "There were no benefits, Simon. Jessie gave it all back. Hell, the only way I could give her jewelry was to tell her it was fake."

Simon hooted. "And you believed that, son? Hell, a woman can spot a cubic zirconium at forty paces. A clever ploy, no doubt. Women can be very conniving. We men have to watch ourselves. God forbid we give them an inch."

"Give it up, Simon. I know what you're trying to do."

Simon sighed before rising. He gave Joshua a hard look. "Jessie's the best thing to happen to you in your life." Simon turned his back to stare out the window. He watched Joshua in the reflection before he turned around again. "Don't let what your father did with his marriages mark *your* life. You could change that pattern, Joshua.

"Jessie is a fine woman. She has spunk and backbone and as much integrity as you do—and more love in her than a man could use up in three lifetimes. How could any man be so damn stupid as to let her slip through his fingers?"

"Well, hell," Joshua said caustically, feeling the sting of his uncle's displeasure added to his own guilt. "Excuse me for being human!"

"We'll discuss your alleged species later, in the meantime what are you going to do about Jessie?"

"What the hell am I supposed to do? She hit me with a one-two punch to the groin."

"Are you sure it wasn't your heart?"

"I doubt she thinks I have one." Joshua slipped the folded piece of paper off the bedside table into the pocket of his jacket. "Didn't I have my wallet when they brought me in?"

"In the nightstand," Simon said absently. "You haven't lost a thing. Jessie gave up everything for you. She gave up a job she'd trained for and loved. She gave up most of her friends. She remained at your beck and call even when you didn't—beck or call, that is." Simon heaved a weary sigh as he rose from his chair. "Tell me, Joshua, have you ever considered what being your mistress does to a woman like Jessie?"

Joshua eyed Simon, who looked as old as he felt at the moment, but said nothing.

"As men, have we ever considered what it must be like when everyone knows the woman we're with is only temporary? Not good enough to have them stick around. Patti pounded into my head how a woman feels. I tell you, son. It stinks. They're forever scorned and pitied. The trash magazines tear their guts out for public consumption. And we turn around and start hunting for the next woman before they even know we're done with them, oblivious to the carnage we leave behind."

"I've never treated Jessie that way."

"Asked yourself why?"

Joshua gave the older man a penetrating look. "I've thought about it." His tone was grim. "In the past weeks, I've thought of little else."

"Well then?"

Joshua stared at his uncle. "You want this for her very badly, don't you?"

"I want this very badly for *both* of you, son. But mostly for you because, I have to tell you, I believe Jessie could limp along with her life without you. But I don't believe you're going to manage much of a life without *her*."

"She's pregnant."

"Congratulations."

"The child isn't mine."

"Don't be absurd. Of course it is."

"I had a vasectomy years ago."

Simon shook his head. "It wouldn't be the first time nature won over a surgeon's knife. If you have doubts, check it out. Hell, you're already here. When you're finished, ask your doctor for a refund."

Joshua sank down on the side of the bed. "Jesus, you

crafty bastard, haven't I gone through enough humiliation for one day?''

Simon smiled. ''Guess not.''

JESSIE SAT in her car looking at the diner. This is where it had all begun. The beginning of the end. Rain sluiced down her windshield, blurring the lights. The whop-whop-whop of the wipers was starting to get on her nerves.

A sharp white spear of lightning illuminated the sky: thunder rumbled overhead. Perfect, just perfect. The cold desolation squeezed around her heart, and she choked on the lump in her throat.

Her eyes were dry, but still burning from the last bout of tears, as she got out of her car. Bareheaded, she made a mad dash for the door. The familiar smell of grease and pine cleaner assailed her on the way to a back booth. She removed her damp raincoat and glanced around. Half a dozen customers, most of them truckers, occupied the adjacent booths.

A young family sat at the counter. Mother, father and two cute toddlers. Jessie stroked her hand down her tummy and gave the little girl a smile. The child played peekaboo over the back of her chair until her mother reprimanded her, making her turn around to eat.

Jessie enjoyed the momentary distraction. A gum-chewing waitress rounded the counter and asked if she wanted coffee. She ordered food she wasn't hungry for, then stared morosely at the scratched beige Formica tabletop.

For the past few weeks she'd stayed in a hotel in San Jose. She hadn't wanted anyone to know where she was until she'd figured out what she was going to do, and where she was going to go.

Joshua Falcon's reach was long and deadly. The rational part of her mind told her to move to another galaxy far, far away. Unfortunately, she wasn't that smart. She had other plans.

Her heart did a one-two thump. Anger would have been wonderfully cathartic, but she had no right to it. Other than the way it had been delivered, everything Joshua had said in his office had been true. From his point of view.

She didn't have a leg to stand on. Her pain, however, despite knowing she'd asked for it, was very real. She'd always prided herself on taking responsibility for her own actions. She was one-hundred percent responsible for her own broken heart. Joshua had never lied to *her*.

The waitress set down the special. Jessie poured a blob of ketchup on the plate beside the fries. She *had* wanted this baby. She wasn't sorry about any of it. She waved a fry in the red blob before biting it in half.

She'd taken a chance on love. And lost.

Until the next round.

If she was mad at anyone, it was herself. For believing she could change a man so set in his ways. The Glacier. Rock hard and implacable. Slow to melt. So accustomed to a woman's betrayal, Jessie ached for him.

She sipped the industrial-strength coffee as she glanced around. So much had changed in her life since she'd last been here. It was strange to see everything had remained the same at the diner. The same dusty plastic plants hung from the yellowed ceiling. The same rips marred the same vinyl seats. The same cheap tacky Christmas decorations sprouted haphazardly about the place.

Jessie sighed. At least there were some constants in life.

She glanced at her watch then looked out the rain-sprinkled window. She squinted against the bright flash of lightning that illuminated the almost empty lot. She waited for the thunder but the whop-whop-whop outside sounded more like her aged windshield wipers.

She ate two more fries, eyed the greasy battered fish, then picked up the fork and swam the cod through a ketchup sea.

It was very late, well after ten. Jessie wondered what time Joshua had arrived home tonight or if he was even in the country. What had his reaction been to the tree and gifts? God, she hoped it softened him a little, made what she'd done a little easier to take. With Joshua it was impossible to guess how he'd react.

She'd give him twenty-four hours to digest everything, then she'd use whatever it took to make him see he loved her, too.

Wherever he was, he'd better be alone. Jessie straightened. It was early for mistress number...whatever, but Joshua had been angry enough to ignore his own calendar.

Jessie rested her cheek on her hand and closed her eyes as pain swamped her. She couldn't bear thinking of him with another woman. She'd promised herself she would never read another paper or watch tabloid TV ever again. She couldn't stand the thought of Joshua *kissing* another woman.

Beneath her fingers she felt the warmth of her cup as it was refilled. "Thanks." Jessie wondered what the waitress thought of her sitting here mumbling to herself and opened her eyes.

Unless waitress attire had drastically changed since she'd worked here, someone else had poured her coffee. Jessie's heart leaped to her throat. Wishing, and not daring to hope, she kept her eyes on the pair of size twelve Haas shoes beside the table. She heard the creak of leather.

"Jessie."

The familiar voice sent a shock wave through her. She slowly lifted her gaze. He looked exhausted, but gloriously handsome. His dark hair was disheveled. He wore jeans and the brown bomber jacket over his red Tahoe shirt. He handed the coffeepot he'd commandeered back to the waitress and stuffed his hands into his pockets.

"Have you stopped having evening sickness?"

She swallowed hard, gripping her coffee mug with both hands because she wanted to touch him so badly. "Yes. I feel wonderful now."

Joshua sank into the seat opposite, his eyes fixed on her face.

"How did you find me?" She couldn't tell by his somber expression what he was thinking.

"I leaned on Conrad and Archie. They told me you were on your way up to the cabin. Then I hopped the helicopter. I had a feeling you'd stop here."

Jessie looked out at the parking lot. Amazingly, a black, silver and burgundy Falcon helicopter was parked next to her car.

"I wanted to go to the cabin one more time." Jessie's eyes stung. Not now, damn it. "I was going to mail the deed back to you next week."

He took her hand, his eyes grave. "I wanted you to have it." Joshua's fingers tightened around hers. "Damn it, Jessie." His voice was tight. "This isn't what I came up here to discuss." He ran his splayed fingers through his hair. It stood up in shark fins. Jessie stared.

"If you came for more apologies, you have them." She tried to pull her hand away, but he used both hands to hold her in place. She gave him a pointed look. "But I won't apologize into infinity."

"I don't want apologies."

"I can't handle... What do you want, Joshua?"

"I want you to marry me."

Jessie squeezed her eyes shut. When she opened them the look she gave him was cool. "I don't blame you for wanting to hurt me because of the lies I told you. But please," she started to rise and he held her firmly in place, his hands warm around hers, "please, don't taunt me."

Jessie bit the inside of her lip to keep it from trembling. Her eyes filled with the annoying tears that still plagued her. She stared out the window, willing her eyes to dry.

"Mommy? How come that man's kneeling down by the lady?" The sweet piping voice of the child at the counter brought the noise in the diner to an abrupt silence.

"Turn around, honey. It's rude to stare."

Jessie turned as the child was forced to look away by her mother.

"Marry me. For real. Forever, Jessie." Joshua's voice was so low she had to strain to hear him.

Hope leaped in her heart. She opened her eyes slowly. Joshua was on one knee, head bowed, beside her. "Oh God, Joshua." Jessie's sob caught in her throat. "Please, don't." She couldn't bear to see him so humbled.

He looked straight into her eyes. His were sheened and his jaw clenched. "Be my wife, Jessie." His voice had an almost imperceptible break in it. "Please."

She reached out and touched his face. His skin felt chilled.

His hand covered hers. "Say yes."

"Get up, please."

"Say yes first."

"We have to talk," Jessie said desperately, not allowing hope to bloom. "There are so many things we haven't sai—"

He rose and put two fingers across her mouth. "Shhh. We have a lifetime to say all the things we want to say." He sank into the seat opposite, his eyes fixed on her face.

She tasted blood as she chewed the inside of her lip. Life was hard enough on a child. She would never subject the baby to a father who didn't love it wholeheartedly.

"It's Thursday," he said, his lips twitching slightly as Jessie looked at him blankly. "Remember? You told me once you only married strangers on Thursdays." He picked up her hand, toying with her fingers. Jessie felt the electricity of his touch down to her toes.

"That was a lifetime ago," Jessie whispered, stunned he'd remembered. "So much has happened in between—"

"Yes. I finally grew up." He sounded impatient with himself. "I should have held on to you then, Jessie. We could have had those seven years *together* if I hadn't been such an insensitive ass."

"You were my knight in shining armor," Jessie told him quietly, her fingers gripping his. His gaze was so serious as he scanned her face.

"A pretty damn tarnished knight." His lips twisted. "I allowed what my mother and Stacie had done to me to color my emotions. And, like a fool, I almost lost the best thing to happen in my life." He tilted her chin with his finger. "Can you ever forgive my transgressions, Jess?"

"You know I have." A hot wash of tears bathed her

cheeks. Her stomach churned as she fought the impulse to throw herself into his arms.

"Ah, Jessie." He leaned forward and dabbed the tears spilling down her cheeks with her napkin. "I went home late yesterday afternoon," he said, turning the napkin to a dry corner. His pale eyes remained fixed on her. "I was dreading going into that damn cold, dark house one more time. Ready, in fact to put it on the market. You were everywhere, Jess. Everywhere and in everything. Everywhere I looked, everything I heard, everything I tasted and smelled.

"And I realized I could sell all my houses, the yachts, the planes, it wouldn't make a damn bit of difference. Because no matter where I was, no matter what I did, you would always be there with me. In my heart."

She stared at him wide-eyed, her heart in some kind of weird time warp. Too terrified to believe what he was saying. And just as terrified not to.

"I opened each of the presents you gave me and I wondered who had taught you to be so loving. Who had shown you how heart-achingly wonderful a loving touch could be. Not your mother. Not a man."

He dropped the soggy napkin and reached in his pocket, then withdrew his handkerchief and resumed blotting her tears. "I realized, almost too late, that what you were giving me was what you had always craved for yourself. Tenderness, caring, trust and unconditional love."

She wanted to say something, anything. But her heart seemed to have stopped beating. The world, her world, had paused on its axis.

Again Joshua reached into his jacket pocket. He pulled out an envelope, then laid a small blue box on the table between them.

"I love you, Jessie Adams. I might be a slow learner, but when I've learned the lesson, I assure you, I never forget. I can't imagine my life without you. Please, re-marry me and put me out of this misery."

Jessie stared down at the box with blurred vision.

He nudged it closer.

"What about the baby?" She took his hankie from him and wiped her cheeks. He gave her that smile she loved, the one that crinkled the corners of his eyes, and pushed an envelope across the table.

"And I love our baby."

"You don't believe she is your baby," she reminded him, forgetting how to breathe.

"It's…a she? She is my baby, Jessie. If she's part of you, then it's part of me." He smiled. "Do you know what a good father does for his children?"

Jessie could think of a thousand things. She shook her head.

"The best thing a father can do for his children is to love their mother."

Jessie's chest ached.

She dabbed her eyes with the hankie again. "I'll be glad when my hormones get back to normal," she said waspishly. "I hate all this crying in front of you."

He smiled. "You can do anything you like in front of me, Jess."

"What's in the envelope?"

"Open it and see." He took a sip of her coffee. "Only you would be more interested in the envelope than the jewelry box."

She gave him a look before she opened the small vel-vet box. "This is definitely real." The diamond was not ostentatious, just exquisitely beautiful, surrounded by baguettes, in a simple gold setting. She pushed it across the table and stuck out her left hand. "Put it on quickly," she demanded.

Joshua laughed. Coming around to her side of the table he eased her against the window. She closed her eyes as his fingers threaded through her hair. She tilted her mouth. Then he kissed her. Softly and leisurely and with every fiber of love he could muster. She felt giddy when he let her up for air.

The few patrons of the restaurant applauded and Joshua made a big production of sliding the ring on her finger. His gaze devoured her face before lowering to rest on her tummy.

"God, Jess," he said breathlessly, one hand reverently touching her through her thick sweater. When he finally looked up, his eyes had filled with tears.

"I love you, Joshua Falcon."

"I know you do, Jessie. And I plan to spend the rest of my life cherishing you. There'll never be a day you won't know how much I love you in return."

"Are you sure?"

"Absolutely, unequivocally, and positively." He pushed her bangs out of her eyes. "Are you going to open this?" he asked, his arm around her. He nudged the envelope closer.

"Is it important?"

"No. Just a small test I had."

"What kind of test?"

"Sperm count."

She looked at the sealed opening.

"And you haven't opened it?"

"The results make no difference to me, I told you that."

"And you'll marry me again and love the baby no matter what that piece of paper says?"

"Without a moment's hesitation," he assured her.

Jessie handed the envelope back to him. "You open it."

"It makes no—"

"Open it."

She watched as he slit the envelope open with his Swiss Army knife, unfolded the single sheet and scanned the test results.

"Well?" She raised an eyebrow.

"It says—" Joshua swallowed roughly and looked at Jessie with his heart in his eyes. "It says you are marrying an idiot who adores you, and that we'll live happily ever after, and have at least two more children."

Jessie felt the smile blossoming from her heart. "I love a happy ending, don't you?"

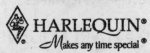

HARLEQUIN® Duets™

Ready to take on the world—and some unsuspecting men—these red-hot royals are looking for love and fun in *all* the right places!

Don't miss four new stories by two of Duets hottest authors!

RED-HOT ROYALS

Once Upon a Tiara
Henry Ever After

by Carrie Alexander
September 2002

A Royal Mess
Her Knight
To Remember

by Jill Shalvis
October 2002

Available at your favorite retail outlet.

HARLEQUIN®
Makes any time special ®

More fabulous reading from
the Queen of Sizzle!

LORI
FOSTER

with

*Forever
and Always*

Back by popular demand are the scintillating stories of
Gabe and Jordan Buckhorn. They're gorgeous, sexy
and single...at least for now!

Available wherever books are sold—September 2002.

And look for Lori's **brand-new** single title,
CASEY in early 2003

If you enjoyed what you just read,
then we've got an offer you can't resist!

Take 2 bestselling
love stories FREE!
Plus get a FREE surprise gift!

Clip this page and mail it to Harlequin Reader Service®

IN U.S.A.
3010 Walden Ave.
P.O. Box 1867
Buffalo, N.Y. 14240-1867

IN CANADA
P.O. Box 609
Fort Erie, Ontario
L2A 5X3

YES! Please send me 2 free Blaze™ novels and my free surprise gift. After receiving them, if I don't wish to receive anymore, I can return the shipping statement marked cancel. If I don't cancel, I will receive 4 brand-new novels each month, before they're available in stores! In the U.S.A., bill me at the bargain price of $3.80 plus 25¢ shipping and handling per book and applicable sales tax, if any*. In Canada, bill me at the bargain price of $4.21 plus 25¢ shipping and handling per book and applicable taxes**. That's the complete price and a savings of at least 10% off the cover prices—what a great deal! I understand that accepting the 2 free books and gift places me under no obligation ever to buy any books. I can always return a shipment and cancel at any time. Even if I never buy another book from Harlequin, the 2 free books and gift are mine to keep forever.

150 HDN DNWD
350 HDN DNWE

Name	(PLEASE PRINT)	
Address	Apt.#	
City	State/Prov.	Zip/Postal Code

* Terms and prices subject to change without notice. Sales tax applicable in N.Y.
** Canadian residents will be charged applicable provincial taxes and GST.
   All orders subject to approval. Offer limited to one per household and not valid to
   current Blaze™ subscribers.
® are registered trademarks of Harlequin Enterprises Limited.

BLZ02-R

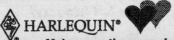

HARLEQUIN® *Blaze*™

The Masterson brothers—Zane and Grey.
Both gorgeous, both oh-so-sexy.
Identical?

Natural-born lady-killers Zane and Grey Masterson are
notorious among the female population of New Orleans
for their "love 'em and leave 'em smiling" attitudes.
But what happens when they decide to switch places—
and each brother finds himself in an intimate struggle
with the one woman he can't resist...?

Find out in...

***DOUBLE THE PLEASURE** by Julie Elizabeth Leto*
&
***DOUBLE THE THRILL** by Susan Kearney*

*Both books available in August 2002,
wherever Harlequin books are sold.*

**When these two guys meet their match,
the results are just two sexy!**

HARLEQUIN®
Makes any time special®